"A villain is just a victim whose story hasn't been told."
-Chris Colfer

COLD LITTLE HEARTS

USA TODAY BESTSELLING AUTHOR
OLIVIA WILDENSTEIN

PART 1
BEFORE

ONE

Brook

A girl who stitches quilts.

This is the first thing I learn about Ivy Redd. After skimming through her *Masterpiecers* application, I toss it aside because quilt making is not really art. I admire people who stitch stuff. My grandmother was one of them. Up until the day she died, she met with her quilting club each week. They'd cut and sew squares of gaudy-patterned fabric with fervor, as though their lives would fall apart if they paused.

Dominic, the president and founder of the Masterpiecers School, picks up the application and thumbs through it.

"Don't bother. It's quilts," I say, grabbing the next file.

He studies the picture stapled to the last page. "You are too rash in judging this girl. She has something. What do you think, Josephine?"

He hands it over to the vice-president of the school.

"*Pas mal.* But we only have one more slot. And I found the perfect *candidat.*"

"Really?" Dominic leans back against the silk upholstery of his wooden chair. One of the school's graduates, Christos Natter, carved it. One side is curved and smooth, while the other looks windblown, stretching irregularly toward Dominic's bulky chestnut bookcase. "Who struck your fancy?"

Josephine flings a file onto the eighteenth-century French desk. It lands next to the industrial steel lamp.

Dominic glances at it. "No."

"*Pourquoi pas?*"

He flaps his hand in the air. "He's a former soldier, not an artist."

She folds one leg over the other and rests her hands on her bony white knee. "That is not a reason, Dom. He is skilled. Look at that rope he wove while he was on tour."

"Come on, Jo. It's a rope," Dom says.

"And this"—she nods toward Ivy Redd's file—"is a quilt. Why does quilt trump rope?"

"Because!" The way he looks away from Josephine says there's more to his staunch refusal than the medium of the pieces.

"You both have a special person, who you did not pick on merit," she says. "I am certain Chase is a talented boy, Brook, and Maria—actually, I am not certain Maria has anything to offer besides her body, Dom—but I accepted. Now consent to my choice."

Dominic reddens at the mention of his ex-girlfriend, a former beauty queen and ham-fisted artist whose claim to fame are crude renditions of overly made-up pageant contestants. I heard he impregnated her, and the only way to get rid of the baby was accepting her onto the show.

Josephine rises, and her tailored pearl-gray dress slips right into place over her skeletal body. "I will alert Mr. Kevin Martin that he has been selected. Oh, wait. That is why we have Brook now, *n'est-ce pas?* To do all the menial jobs."

I glare at her, although she's right. That is why I'm here. "I'll notify the contestants this afternoon."

She gives me a crooked smile before stepping out of Dominic's office.

"She hates me," I tell Dom some time after she shuts the door.

"She hates everyone."

"Except her fiancé."

"I doubt she even likes him."

As I straighten out the files of applicants who didn't make the cut, Dominic tut-tuts.

"What?"

"The girl who sews quilts; keep her application aside. We'll be needing it."

I slip it out of the pile and put it on top. "Why?"

"Because." He shifts his eyes toward his cell phone. Dominic is certain we are being listened to. "She's a sound runner-up." As he talks, he grabs a piece of paper embossed with his name and scribbles something.

I scratch the stubble on my cheek as I read it. When my jaw unhinges, Dominic picks up his message and shreds it into a dozen tiny pieces that he drops into his leather bin. They flutter down like confetti, settling in the dusky emptiness. I doubt anyone will collect them and glue them back together, but just in case, I crouch down, swipe some into my palm, and stick them inside my blazer pocket.

I have as much to lose as Dominic. No, that's a lie. I have more to lose because it's my name that's being used, not his. Mine.

"It's a beautiful day, isn't it?" he says, all cheery again. "I love spring. Don't you?"

I'm tongue-tied.

"I'm heading out for lunch. I'll see you tonight," he says.

"Tonight?"

"Didn't your father tell you? We're having dinner all together at his house. To celebrate the sale. It went well, didn't it?"

I make a jerky head movement that's supposed to be a nod.

"Did it pay the bills?"

"Not all of them."

He pats my shoulder. "I'm sure they'll get paid soon. I have an idea." His fingers clamp down around my shoulder like a metal claw. I'm starting not to like his ideas. "I'll tell you later." He squeezes once, then lets go and walks out, whistling a tune that sounds like something from *Les Misérables*.

Clutching the pile of applications against me, I stop by my office, which is more of a glass cubicle than an office. I don't even have screens or blinds. As I heave the folders onto my desk, I notice one of the secretaries fanning a leaflet out in front of a young boy. It throws me back in time. Four years to be exact. I stood at his exact spot, overwhelmingly excited at the prospect of starting at the Masterpiecers. Four years ago, when everything was still so peachy. When my family was still rich. When my little brother didn't despise me for having usurped "his life." The school has strict laws forbidding siblings from attending. Supposedly, it's to discourage family feuds. Didn't discourage Chase from hating my guts.

Movement behind the secretary catches my attention. Josephine stands next to her triangular-shaped desk, where a lone potted orchid holds court over an ultra-flat computer screen and a pencil cup made of cerulean blue clay. It looks as though a kindergartener crafted it, when in fact, it was an alumni from this school.

Josephine sees me staring. There's something unsettling about the way she gazes back, eyes sort of slanted. My shirt collar suddenly feels tight, so I pop the top button open. She smiles that glacial smile of hers, then gazes down at my jacket pocket. I stick my hand inside protectively before reassuring myself that Josephine Raynoir does not have X-ray vision. I rub the pieces between the pads of my fingers, feeling the raised edges in the vellum where Dominic inked his command: *Find out who Kevin Martin really is.*

Josephine flicks a switch and her glass walls blur. I am left with the shadow of her body moving about like the giant stick insect I won at a fair when I was twelve. I kept it in a terrarium, which I couldn't be bothered to clean. Our housekeeper, Carmelina, was too frightened of the bug to touch the thing, so the sides became filthier and filthier until my mother got so sick of it, she seized the glass case and dumped it on the curb for some other little boy, or some garbage collector, to find.

I eye my trashcan, but decide against putting anything inside. It's lunchtime, and even though I'm not hungry, I walk out of Delancey Hall, a two-story building with glossy green ivy scuttling over the brick walls. It was named after Dominic's favorite adviser, Robert Delancey. A few years back, when I was starting on college applications, *The New York Times* dedicated its entire art section to the man. It was titled *The Monocled Star-Maker*. My father read it out loud to us over breakfast.

"Art is Chase's dream, Dad. Not mine," I remember telling him, mostly to get him off my case.

Chase looked up from his big bowl of cornflakes, milk dribbling down his chin. He was fourteen then. His upper lip had finally grown some fuzz.

"*I* wasn't given a choice," Dad said.

"Well I'd like a choice," my seventeen-year-old self demanded.

"And you'll get one," Mom chimed in, clicking into the dining room for breakfast. She dropped a kiss on my forehead, and then tried to peck Chase's, but he ducked away from her. "Right, Henry? We always said we would let the kids choose."

In the end, after two years spent at Duke University, I asked to transfer into the art school to my father's delight. It was the same year Chase sent in his college applications. His top choice was the Masterpiecers, but I beat him to it, something he never forgave me for. Just like he never forgave me for consoling his ex after their messy breakup.

As I walk toward Riverside Drive, I grab the slivers of paper from my pocket and dump them inside the nearest trashcan. Then I slip my phone out and open a search window in which I type Kevin Martin's name. There are several pages of results. I add the words 'retired sergeant.'

There is only one result: *Kevin Martin, Private Investigator*.

Dominic was right. Josephine is investigating him.

JOSH

It's strange keeping a secret from your best friend. In my case, from my two best friends. The girls who, in spite of being two years younger than me, and somewhat cool—especially Ivy—ate their lunches with the fat kid every day.

Yes, once upon a time, I was that kid whose belly plopped out of elastic-waisted pants and whose cheeks earned him the nickname of Hamster. Ivy would smack anyone who dared call me by my furry moniker, while Aster reassured me I was the handsomest boy she'd ever laid eyes on. Said she'd had a crush on me since the age of five when we met in the McDonald's jungle gym, where I rescued her from the ball pool.

I drop on the couch, draping one arm around the back cushion. "What time are they broadcasting the selection?" I ask Ivy, who's sewing something red. Her fingers move so fast, tucking the needle in, gliding it out, in, out, it's hypnotic.

"At nine. Hopefully, Aster will be home by then."

"They work her too hard at that pizzeria."

"It's good for her."

"Is it?"

"It gives her purpose."

"The ad agency gives her purpose," I say.

"Yes, but it's an internship. She doesn't make any money."

"She would've been better off working at Mom's bakery."

"Possibly. But she would have seen it as charity, and you know as well as I do, that she hates charity." Ivy sets the red thing down next to her. "Joshy, if I get picked—"

"*When* you get picked."

Ivy wrinkles her nose. For as long as I've known her, she's made that face when she's nervous. "*If* I get picked, will you stay with her while I'm gone? I know it's a lot to ask, what with you guys being broken up and everything, but I don't like the idea of leaving her on her own."

"Why are you even asking, Ives?"

"Because you have a new girlfriend now."

Heat crawls up the sides of my face. It prickles, like when I slap on aftershave after nicking my skin. "How do you know about Heidi?" I half-whisper, gaze darting toward the door.

"Don't worry. I haven't told Aster," she says, tucking a strand of blonde hair behind her ear. It's flat and shiny, unlike her sister's springy corkscrews. "Is it serious?"

"I don't know."

"Promise me you won't tell Asty until it is?"

I nod, ogling the threadbare carpet because Ivy has a way of looking at you that's really unsettling. Maybe it's because her eyes are so light. *Nah.* Aster has light blue eyes too. That's not it. "How did *you* find out?"

"I saw a picture of you two on her Facebook feed, and guessed."

I lift my gaze back up to hers. "Crap. What if Aster saw the same picture?"

"She's not friends with Heidi." Ivy leans forward and pokes my chest. "You can't keep secrets from me for long, Joshy."

Actually, I can.

And I have.

Twice now.

I never told the twins I met their father two years ago. He's a man they're better off not knowing.

Like I haven't told them the FBI put my chief on a huge case a couple days ago, and I'm part of the task force.

I so wish I could tell someone about my latest assignment. Anyone. But especially Aster and Ivy. They're like my sisters. Well, Ivy is; not Aster. Aster is something else to me, something pure and painful and complicated.

Our relationship was bittersweet and intense. We loved deeply, but not well...because she wasn't well. Her mental health pierced the fragile bubble that had formed around us. I still remember the exact moment it happened. It was the morning the gynecologist phoned Ivy to tell her that her twin left her office upset, convinced she had just endured a miscarriage although she hadn't. It took us hours to locate Aster.

She was covered in snow on a bench, in the middle of Highland Park, clutching her empty abdomen. Cradling her in my arms, I carried her home. She believed her jeans were soaked in blood when in fact it was a mixture of snow and urine. I ran her a warm bath, sponged away the imaginary blood, and let her fall asleep in my arms one last time.

"Joshy?" Ivy says, flapping her hand in front of my face. "I lost you there."

I fire up a smile to raze my brain of that chilling, snowy morning. "What are you making?"

Ivy bites her lip. "A bag."

"That's cool."

"It's Mom's last quilt. Maybe I shouldn't turn it into a bag."

"At least it's practical now."

She smirks. "I can't believe how dense you still are about art."

"Dense? Really?" I chuckle. "It must be so hard to be an artist around all of us *dense* Kokomoans."

"You're not *all* dense," she says, still smiling that brazen, brilliant smile of hers.

"Just me?"

She winks.

I fling the remote control at her, making sure it arches up in the air and falls a foot away.

"Using force to retaliate, Joshy? How very masculine of you."

I laugh. She laughs. It's always been like that between us. Easy.

"Turn the damn TV on so I don't have to listen to you assault me verbally anymore," I tell her.

"*Assault you verbally?* Learn those big words in cop school, Officer Cooper?"

"I know you underestimate me because I have all this awesome muscle"—I flex my arm and my bicep bulges—"and you're into nerdy, little artists."

She snorts. "I'm not into anyone."

"Luke's still pining for you."

Ivy went out with him briefly when she was thirteen. Five years later, they attended prom together. But that was it.

"Luke's a bit boring," she says.

"Because he doesn't know who Monette is?"

"Monet, not Monette. And no. There was just no chemistry between us. I tried *twice*."

"You want a medal?"

"No." She purses her lips as she says the word, which makes me grin.

I stretch my arm out to grab the remote control and surf the channels, while Ivy resumes transforming the quilt. We sit in comfortable silence until Aster arrives, right in time for the announcement.

Ivy tenses, fingers curling like claws, and her skin, which is usually this gold-copper shade, even in the winter, has turned as pasty as the balls of fondant my mother kneads at the bakery. Heidi's dying to work there instead of at the Dairy Queen where she picks up a few hours here and there, but I don't know how I feel about introducing her to Mom. I mean, Mom knows her, but not as my girlfriend.

Aster surprises me with a hug, which makes me forget all about Heidi and my mother.

"Did I miss it?" she asks, plopping a bowl of popcorn on the coffee table and taking a seat between us on the lumpy, L-shaped couch.

"No," Ivy says. She sounds croaky, like someone who's coughed a lot. She grabs a fistful of popcorn and tosses it inside her mouth.

I shoot my gaze to her face, and sure enough, she's wrinkling her nose. "Relax. They cannot *not* pick you."

Aster squeezes Ivy's hand. "You're the best."

"I'm not the best, and yes, they could *not* pick me. They probably didn't pick me. I make quilts."

"Works of art," Aster chimes in.

Ivy yanks her hand out of her twin's and reaches for more popcorn.

"The most beautiful works of art," Aster continues.

Ivy sighs. "Please stop."

Aster's lips wobble, so I circle an arm around her shoulder. Her rough curls tickle my jaw.

Dominic Bacci's face materializes on the television. He smiles. The dude's always smiling. And he's always tanned. He's so rich he probably spends his life vacationing on yachts. He's sitting across from a heavily made-up anchorwoman with feathery blonde hair like Faye Dunaway's. Dad's a big fan of hers. Or was. Can't recall if she's dead.

"You've made us wait a whole year, Dominic! Do you have any idea how excited we all are? And I'm speaking for the seven million viewers watching us tonight," she says, her voice reflecting the enthusiasm animating her plastic features.

"These contests take meticulous planning. We pour our hearts, and our sponsors' money"—he winks at the camera—"into these competitions. You should see what we came up with this year."

"For those of you unfamiliar with the show," the anchorwoman says, "the third *Masterpiecers'* contest will begin on August 21st. The top contestant will win not only admission but a full tuition scholarship to the exclusive Masterpiecers art school, as well as a hundred-thousand dollar check." She smiles, lips as plump as whoopee cushions. "So, Dominic, who are the talented eight who made it onto this year's show?"

Dominic, still grinning, extricates something from the inside pocket of his velvet blazer. "Let's see." He gazes down at the paper. "Number one." He raises his eyes to the screen, which has been split to display the contestants' images alongside his face. "Miss Lincoln Vega."

A picture of a pretty blonde girl brightens the black square.

"Number two...Mr. Herrick Hawk."

The picture of the blonde transforms into a picture of a guy with poufy black hair and a neck scarf.

"Number three, Miss Maria Axela."

A super smiley, Hispanic-looking woman replaces the scarf dude. She has on red lipstick.

"Number four—" Dominic takes a dramatic pause. It's probably to give viewers a chance to quit hyperventilating. "Jared J."

Another toothy person fills the split screen. This time, it's a guy with a grown-out buzz cut, kind of like mine.

Aster sits up straighter. She chances a glance at her sister, who's hovering on the edge of her seat, no longer munching on popcorn.

"Number five, Maxine Specter."

Maxine's hot, even though she has a proper buzz cut.

"Number six..." Dominic's grin widens. "Chase Jackson."

Unfortunately, the hot chick is replaced by this somber-faced dude who looks like he's just gotten dumped.

"That's Brook Jackson's little brother," Ivy says, sounding spellbound.

"Who's Brook Jackson?" I venture.

"One of the judges. He graduated from the school two months ago," she explains, eyes stuck to the picture of the brother.

"I wonder how *he* made it onto the show," I mumble.

Obviously, it's not a question, but Aster answers anyway. "It's because he's the judge's brother."

I wince.

"Number seven, Mr. Nathan Stein," Dominic says.

A picture of an old dude with greasy hair pops onto the screen.

"The last spot will be yours. I can feel it," Aster tells Ivy.

Ivy bounces her legs so fast it makes the couch vibrate.

"And finally..." Dominic pauses theatrically again. "Number eight..." Another long stretch of overwrought silence. "Mr. Kevin Martin."

Ivy leaps off the couch just as Aster reaches out for her.

"They're stupid," Aster says, following her sister into the kitchen.

Ivy bangs things around before trotting back out with a spoon and a tub of pistachio ice cream. I'm torn between trying to comfort her and pumping my fist in the air. If Ivy had made it onto the show, she would've left Kokomo...and probably forever.

Brook

The doorbell of Dominic's townhouse chimes, ricocheting against the marble floor and the Plexiglas frames encasing the dyed sand creations of a Masterpiecers' graduate.

His housekeeper scuttles to open the door while I pace his octagonal living room with the stiff, purposely mismatched furniture and the loud turquoise rug.

"What's the emergency?" Josephine asks, breezing past the housekeeper into the living room. Her cheeks are flushed, and not from make-up.

"Sit down, Jo," Dominic says, gesturing to a peacock-green loveseat.

Josephine sits, straight as a board. *"Que se passe-t-il?"*

"Pictures surfaced. Pictures of Kevin Martin. They're going to be aired on the evening news edition," Dominic says, making sure his voice sounds dismal.

She cocks an eyebrow. "What sort of pictures?"

"You tell her, Brook."

I freeze.

"Brook?" Dom says, peering at me.

"Kevin was photographed at a white supremacist rally," I blurt out.

"You don't say." Josephine doesn't sound convinced. "Can I see?"

Dominic's jaw pulses. "It's not pretty."

"I am not faint of heart. *Montrez-moi.*"

So I prop my cell phone in front of her face. She grabs it and flicks her fingers against the screen to blow up the shot.

"Where did you get these?" she asks.

"They were sent to me by an anonymous source."

"Belonging to a religious group is not against school regulations."

"A religious group?" I say incredulously. "This is not a religious group, Josephine."

"Miss Raynoir." Her upper lip twitches. "I am not your *copine*, Brook." She shoves the phone into my hands. "So you have disqualified him, I suppose?"

"Of course. We can't encourage racism. Our school stands for tolerance and morality," Dom says.

"Morality? Is that what the school stands for?"

"What are you implying, Jo?"

"*Rien.* I misspoke." She rises and her silky, oyster-colored pants billow around her legs, tenting over her protruding hipbones. "So who is the lucky runner-up?"

"The girl who makes quilts," Dominic says.

She tilts her head. For a second, she doesn't say anything, and then she nods. "She is a sound choice."

I'm surprised by her approval.

She seizes her Hermès bag and walks toward the door. She

stops midway and turns. "Have you asked Mr. Martin about the pictures? Maybe he can explain himself."

"We've informed him," Dominic says.

Or rather I've informed him. I called him up last night and told him we'd found unsettling evidence that compromised his selection. When he asked what it was, I told him to turn on his TV tonight. Fun phone call.

The front door slams shut, making the plastic frames shudder. Warm street air gusts inside the house. I must stare at the armored front door for a long time, because Dominic has walked over to me, holding out a cup of tea from a platter that wasn't in the room when Josephine was still there.

I take the tea from him, but don't drink it.

"Let's go over the contest ideas," he suggests.

Applying pressure to the spot between my shoulder blades, he guides me into his adjacent study, and presses me into one of the four big leather and velvet chairs. The thick, wine-colored drapes are closed, which makes the small room feel tighter and darker. The only sources of light in the room, besides the faint trickle of afternoon sun around the curtain edges, come from the shelf lighting of his bookcase and from the elephant-tusk desk lamp built into the copper coffee table.

"Did I mention the *Times* is doing a big spread on the competition next week?"

He pulls a file from the bookcase and places it on the table, then scratches his pencil against the top. *A package will arrive for Dean.*

I blink up at him. I received my Duke University friend's last package, an articulated pewter statue full of rolls of cash, barely ten days ago. Scheduling deliveries so close together isn't smart.

Dom tips his head toward the file. "And I booked Patrick Veingarten for the group photograph. He has some magnificent ideas."

All you need to do is sign for it, he writes.

Beads of sweat slide down my neck. *All I need to do?* It will be my name on the package again. Not his. Not Dean's.

"How fun is it that Chase is coming to compete?" Dom asks.

I choke on my saliva and cough. Is he threatening me or reminding me of his generosity?

While he resumes his monologue about the upcoming photoshoot, he scribbles some more. My attention is glued to the lead tip of his pencil. *You'll get a commission for this one as well.*

If only my family hadn't needed the money...didn't still need it. My pulse pounds against my eardrums, harder than it used to during workouts with my personal trainer. I can't afford a personal trainer anymore; not that I'd want to take orders from yet another person. I jiggle my leg. Dominic claps his hand against my kneecap to steady it, then he turns to the next page.

"Patrick's ideas are genius. He wants to use frames and..." His voice vanishes in the fog of my brain as I take in the head-shot of a girl with long blonde curls and an uneasy smile. Her face isn't unfamiliar to me, but I can't quite place it.

"Who's that?"

Dominic places his index finger against his lips. "Sistina."

It's not Sistina. Sistina was in my graduating class.

As he says, "I've commissioned her to build structures remi-niscent of French Renaissance frames," he writes, *Package is coming from Indiana. Like Ivy Redd.*

I rack my brain. Ivy Redd? Ivy Re— The girl who stitches quilts!

He flips to the next page.

It's the picture of the quilt she'd attached to her application. The one that looks like a Klimt. The one I dismissed. Dom taps his finger against it, then draws little circles inside.

"You understand?"

"Yes." Her quilt will be the package.

"Good." He lowers the pencil tip to the paper again. *Troy will mail it.* He must sense my nervousness, because he adds, *Your share will be 10%. Of 4 million dollars. That should help your family.*

I grab his pencil and write. *And Chase will win?*

"That's not up to me," he says, disturbing the slick silence that has settled over the small, airless room.

He snatches the pencil from my stiff fingers and removes the words he wrote, blowing the eraser crumbs onto my lap. "I have a feeling this year's show is going to be stupendous," he says, fostering a smile that takes over his entire face.

He looks like the Joker in Batman. I was terrified of the Joker as a kid. Still am, although I've never shared this with anyone. Only Chase knows. He found out one night when I woke Carmelina up to change my bed sheets because I had a nightmare about the Joker. I was eight. Chase was five. He'd heard me cry through our shared wall. I didn't think anyone kept memories from that early, but my little brother isn't anyone. He's wired differently. He listens and stores information like a human pressure cooker. That's why I forbade my father from breathing a word to him about our colossal debts. I was afraid that if Chase blew, we'd make *Page Six* of the *Post*.

FOUR

JOSH

In the middle of a briefing, my chief gets called out of the assembly room. I'm supposed to pick up Heidi in twenty minutes for a movie date. As I wait for him to return, I text her that I'll be late. The dot dot dots light up, so I know she's typing back, but nothing appears. The dots blink again. And then they stop again. No answer. Is she mad?

I don't have time to ponder this as the chief is back, jaw flushed.

"What happened?" asks Fred, my hefty, thirty-seven-year-old partner.

"The tip we got was a bust. There was no meeting between Mann and the Discolis," Guarda says. He pinches the tip of his handlebar mustache and rolls it between his fingers. He always plays with his mustache when he's stressed out. "The Feds want us to stand down. They think Mann is getting spooked."

Behind the chief, on the screen always displaying the news

channel on mute, I catch the words *Breaking News* and *Master-piecers*. I push away from the long desk and approach the monitor. A black-and-white picture of a heated rally appears. I frown as I attempt to understand its connection to the art school. A sentence scrolls along the banner at the bottom of the image, right underneath the reporter's lively face.

Contestant number 8, Kevin Martin gets eliminated for ties to the racist group.

This is huge news. So huge that the chief is standing beside me, silent for once. I'm about to turn away when a new picture flashes on the screen. It's a headshot of Ivy. I step in closer.

"Isn't that your girlfriend?" Fred asks. He's halfway through a bag of Werther's Originals. How he can fill his body with that much fat and sugar is beyond me.

"No. It's her twin." I should have added that Aster isn't my girlfriend anymore.

"How can you tell?"

"She doesn't have a beauty mark over her lip."

"And here I thought Dominic Bacci had no values," the chief says.

I gape at him. "You follow the competition?"

"My wife does. She's obsessed with him." His eyes dart around the room. "They were probably forced to pull him off the show. Imagine all the viewers they would've lost if they hadn't."

"I hope he loses more than just his spot on this reality TV show," Fred adds.

We watch the TV a while longer.

"Are we still going to investigate Troy Mann, Chief?"

"How long have we known each other, Fred?"

"Going on ten years now."

"Have I ever closed an unresolved case?"

"No, Chief."

"There's your answer."

"Can't we get in trouble?" I ask.

Guarda smirks. "You're so young, Cooper, so idealistic." His expression grows serious. "If you want to work for some halfwit who plays by the rules, then I'm not your man. If you want to learn the ropes from someone who cares about justice, then you've come to the right place."

Fred twists his lips as though he were trying to dislodge a piece of sticky caramel.

"Before Jackie died, she asked me to train you, to give you a spot on my team. But I won't uphold my promise if I don't feel like your heart and mind are invested. So what'll it be?" the chief asks.

The mention of Jackie makes my eyes sting as though the chief squirted pepper spray into them.

Jackie was the cop who made me want to become a cop. I met her the same day I met the twins in the McDonald's jungle gym. She was the responding officer. I still remember how she'd knelt down beside the twins and me, and showed us her badge, then told us the story of a man she'd just arrested for stealing a gumball machine. To this day, I'm not sure if her story was made-up or real.

And now I'll never know.

Stupid liver cancer took her from us a year ago.

"I'm not letting a crook from my hometown get away with multiple counts of fraud," I finally say. There is no way I'm letting Jackie down.

Both my partner and my boss nod. "Good boy. We'll meet back here tomorrow at fourteen hundred hours," he says, leaving before us.

Guarda is ex-military. He diffused a bomb once, saving his entire regiment. It won him a big medal, which he keeps displayed on his work desk in place of his nameplate.

"Could I lose my badge?" I ask Fred when it's just the two of us.

"You might. Or you might get an honorific award."

"I don't care about awards."

"Doing the right thing always pays off. And getting a prick off the streets is the right thing."

"Look who's idealistic now?"

"It's not idealism, Coop, it's integrity." He checks his wristwatch that's so tight it looks embedded into his pudgy wrist. "I gotta hurry. The wife hates it when I'm late for dinner." On our way to the locker room, he asks, "What you up to tonight? Victory drinks with the new contestant?"

"I have a date."

"With her sister?"

"With another girl. Aster and I aren't together anymore." I glance down at my phone. Heidi finally answered me.

I must look disappointed because Fred asks, "Got stood up?"

"She's going to hang out with her mom. Her parents are divorcing."

"Must be tough on the kid."

"She's doing a summer semester at Ivy Tech to stay out of the house."

"What she studying?" he asks, banging his locker shut.

"Culinary Arts. She wants to be a chef." I grab my windbreaker and put it on.

"Seriously? I thought programming was the 'in thing' these days. All I hear around the dinner table is Facebook this and Twitter that. Apparently someone's even coming out with flying cars soon. If that's true, I hope the precinct will replace ours."

As Fred goes on about futuristic automobiles, I zone out. I have to pick up flowers for Ivy. To congratulate her. She needs to know I'm proud of her since her mom is no longer there to tell her. Not that her mother ever expressed much pride in her daughters.

I drop Fred by his car and then get into mine. All the nice florists are closed at this hour, so I drive over to Kroger on the corner of South Washington and pluck a bouquet of red roses from the gray plastic buckets that line the shop window.

I dump it back into the water. I can't give Ivy red roses. Red roses are romantic. I eye the white ones. What does white mean? I look it up on my phone. *Traditional wedding flowers.* Hell no. I check what baby pink represents. When I read some stuff about poetic romance, I grab a bouquet of multicolored tulips.

On my way over to the twins' apartment, I drive by the pizzeria where Aster works. I watch her ring up a customer. She's smiling. She must have heard the news of Ivy's acceptance. It's good to see her happy. After the past year, Aster deserves a break. Plus her grin reassures me she's taking her meds. When she's off them, she doesn't smile much.

As I glide away from the curb and drive in the direction of Ivy's apartment, I glance at the tulips. I should've bought a bouquet for Aster. I count the flowers when I stop at a traffic light. *Twelve.* I can make two bouquets. I start unwrapping the plastic when the light turns green. While driving, I reassemble the flowers. The car swerves, and I jam my foot against the brake. Pulse hammering, I pull up by the curb to rearrange my flowers.

Six and six.

Both bouquets look puny. I squash all the flowers together again.

Today's Ivy's day. Aster won't be jealous.

One of the tulip heads lolls from its tubular stalk. Another falls off. The bouquet looks scruffy, as though I picked the flowers from someone's backyard. Groaning, I toss the whole thing out the window. Ivy's not a flower person anyway.

Brook

In the basement of Delancey Hall, there is an amphitheater complete with a drop-down screen that spans the length of the enormous stage. It took two years to dig up the equivalent of four floors to accommodate the hundred rows of seats that curve around the stage in a semi-circle. It's in this theater that Dominic will project the features of the eight contestants. He's invited the entire student body, and from the sight of the packed auditorium, it seems like they all cut their vacation short to attend.

As Josephine and Dominic come on stage, everyone stands.

"Hello, my masterpiecers!" Dominic's brown eyes crinkle with the delight of being on stage. "I am so touched that you—all of you—have returned early from your holidays to watch the marvelous feature we have put together for you. Soon, you will be greeting a new, freshman masterpiecer. Am I wrong in assuming some of you have bets going as to who will win?"

Laughter warbles all around.

"To a great show, great talent, and a great forthcoming year! I cannot wait for the end of the summer to discover what you all have in store for me."

Everyone applauds as Dominic passes the microphone over to Josephine. She steps away from Dominic, holding the mic with two hands as though afraid he might snatch it back. She utters lots of niceties in a tone that doesn't sound especially kind. I asked Dominic once why he'd selected her as his VP. "What would happen if kids raised kids?" he'd said. "Josephine's the responsible one, Brook. The parent. Because she's here, I'm allowed to remain a little reckless."

Recently, Josephine was proving to be too responsible in Dominic's eyes. Before she'd even hired a PI to sniff around Dom, he was already looking for a replacement, or so he'd told me the night of our school's graduation ceremony back in May, the night Dominic offered me the job of personal assistant, the night he asked me to run the first "errand."

A round of applause fills the amphitheater, not as loud as that proffered to Dominic. He takes Josephine's arm and escorts her off the stage. White feathers line the bottom of her floor-length dress, creating the impression that she's walking on a cloud.

The lights dim and the colossal curved screen brightens with the first feature on Lincoln Vega, an attractive girl who spent most of her childhood sleeping on a street in Alphabet City, begging for money.

She shows the interviewer the subway station in which she reproduced Picasso's *Demoiselles d'Avignon* in chalk. And then she explains how her passion for chalk art began. "The city streets were my canvas. The city streets were my everything."

With no shame, she speaks of her drug-addicted parents and recounts her childhood on the asphalt, stealing day-old Wonder bread from the convenience store and digging through trash-cans for leftover treasures. She survived poverty. This is what I silently repeat to myself as I watch the rest of her feature. If she survived it, I can too.

If it comes to that.

Which it won't.

I shift in my seat as the second feature begins. A close-up of Herrick Hawk fills the screen. It's so close that most of the pompadour he sports doesn't make it into the frame. Grinning, he fingers the blue paisley scarf knotted around his clean-shaven throat and walks the camera crew through his outra-geously ornate house, making them zoom in on the trompe-l'oeil details of his Michelangelo fresco. Standing in front of a wall decorated with exotic blue mountains, his parents are stiff and broad-eyed. They take a step back when Herrick introduces them to the camera, but still offer shy smiles.

I lean in toward Dominic and whisper, "They make me think of that *American Gothic* couple, you know the farmer and his wife."

Dominic smiles and whispers back, "Yes, but silk-screened into an Italian Renaissance painting."

I chuckle.

Josephine gives me a pointed stare that reminds me of my seventy-year old professor back at Duke, Miss Hendrix. She was so frigid and unpleasant that Dean started a bet about whether she was a virgin or not. It had reached such astonishing proportions that by the end of freshman year, the wager pool was in the tens of thousands of dollars.

Feature number three has started. Nathan Stein. This one makes me uncomfortable, for he speaks of the art the Nazis stole from his family during the Second World War, art he is still trying to locate, but that hasn't surfaced. I glance over at Dominic, who doesn't look uneasy like me, but who also isn't smiling anymore. Nathan shoots the camera a painful smile.

When the next feature begins, I lean in toward the screen so I don't miss a single beat. It's Chase's feature. Dominic promised it was fine, but until I see it, I will not be appeased. My brother speaks of his passion for collecting art. When the interviewer asks him about his talent as an auctioneer, Chase dismisses the compliment. It's not false humility, although it comes across that way. Even though Chase thinks the worst of me, I think the best of him. He's my little brother, the tiny baby my mother made just for me. I'm hoping this competition will heal the bond of brotherhood severed over a school and a misinterpreted night with a girl.

When my brother vanishes off the screen, a woman with a buzz cut and long feather earrings replaces him. Maxine Specter. Although Dominic doesn't know her, he knows her parents. They're avid art collectors, which she exhibits by walking us through their Hamptons home that makes my parents' former beach house look like a surfer shack.

The next feature is on a guy who's already sort of famous. Jared J. is a graffiti artist who's made a name for himself with cans of spray-paint and public walls. His application was a unanimous favorite for both Josephine and Dominic. Although they love growing new artists, having someone with a social following looks good for the show.

Dominic's former beauty queen, Maria Axela, is next. Her portraits of pageant friends are kitsch. It's painful to watch her speak with such pride of her art. She's like those contestants on singing competitions who think they possess a golden voice, but who sound like farrowing pigs.

Contestant number eight's face materializes on screen. I blink as my gaze meets clear blue eyes. Ivy stares into the camera lens with such disconcerting intensity that I find myself sitting up straighter. I've spoken to her like I spoke to the others, so I know her voice, yet it sounds nothing like the voice I remember. Can overwhelming guilt distort the senses?

SIX

JOSH

I first heard Troy Mann's name three months ago. He grew up on the wrong side of Kokomo with an alcoholic father on welfare and a too-soft mother who ended up running out on them. His one saving attribute was his brain. By junior year of high school, one of his teachers managed to convince the dean that he was too advanced for the school. He was offered a scholarship into a private establishment, before scoring a full ride to Duke University.

Troy chose drug trafficking as an extra-curricular activity. Stupid choice for a smart boy. Not only did he get jail time, but he lost his scholarship and was kicked out of Duke during his junior year. My mother would have slapped me silly if I'd gone and ruined my chances, but Troy didn't have a mom, and his dad just didn't care.

A snitch for the FBI informed them of other sorts of trafficking. Troy must have realized he was being monitored because he stopped all illegal activity. He moved back in with his father and started working for a construction company as a legit metal welder. And then Troy's life changed again. He met a girl called Stephanie and settled down. Apparently she got pregnant, but it didn't work out, or so Heidi told me—Stephanie is one of my girlfriend's thirty-two cousins.

I tap out the Maroon 5 song playing on my phone against the steering wheel. If I hadn't made trooper, I would have moved to Nashville and become a drummer. Instead of pounding drums, though, I pound pavement in search of criminals, which has made both my parents super proud. My mother tells everyone in her book club what a good son I am, and how eligible I am. That part, I wished she'd quiet down about. When she heard I was dating Aster, she cautiously reminded me it would be a complex relationship because of her "affliction." She'd asked me why not Ivy, to which I'd responded: "Just because they're twins, it doesn't make them interchangeable."

A bird chirps on a nearby red maple. It's such a nice day, yet I'm stuck in a car with no air conditioning. I've been staking out Troy's newest construction site for the past week, and like every day, nothing happens. He goes in at eight, has a sandwich with the guys around noon, leaves at five, and drives straight home to Stephanie. I'm waiting for him to make some mistake to link him to the Discolis, the big Indiana mob family he's apparently running errands for again.

I check the clock on the dashboard: 4:57 p.m. On cue, Troy Mann emerges from the building's foundations with his black messenger bag slung across his shoulders. I wait until he's inside his metallic blue Cadillac Eldorado before revving up my car. I count to five slowly and follow him. He goes left—like every day this week. And then he goes right—like every day this week.

My cell phone lights up with a call from the chief. I pick up and put him on speakerphone.

"Just got news that Troy received a call from New York yesterday."

I wait for my chief to elaborate because getting a call from another state isn't illegal.

"The Feds tracked it to a burner cell. Something's about to go down. Any activity in the work place?"

"Nope." I spin my wheel right at the intersection. He's four cars ahead of me. "And it looks like it's going to be another quiet evening. He's driving home."

"Phone back once he gets there."

I hang up and tap my fingers against the wheel until the light switches to green. I'm so absorbed by my finger drumming that I nearly miss the slight left Troy makes at the junction. Hoping my tires don't squeal, I spin the wheel.

"That's not the way home," I mumble out loud. "Where are you going?"

We must drive for a good twenty minutes off course. Finally, the Cadillac turns into the parking lot of a motel off Route 9. I pull up against the curb some fifty feet away. I can still see him from my vantage point, but not well. I hop over the crooked fence and move into the shadows of the thick palm trees planted next to a kidney-shaped pool.

Troy's head swivels back and forth as he enters the motel, like a spectator at a tennis match. I crouch down lower. When he's out of sight, I straighten up but don't come closer. Five minutes later, he's back out. I duck again. He climbs inside his car and swerves out of the lot in my direction. I scramble around the tree trunks and fling myself onto one of the lounge chairs. It creaks and the backrest, which must have been poorly hooked into the base, slams down. Reeling from the impact, I pull my hands behind my neck and try to act like I'm tanning.

The Cadillac doesn't slow, and soon it glides around a street corner. I drag myself off the lounge chair and phone Guarda. "Hey, Chief, I think you're right."

"What happened?"

"He took a detour. Stopped by a motel. I'm going to go check it out."

"Good, Coop."

After he disconnects, I walk past the flashing orange sign advertising vacant rooms. A scrawny middle-aged man sits behind the desk. He looks up from the television he's watching.

"Can I help you?" he asks.

I tap the badge hooked onto my belt. The clerk's eyes roam over it before returning to my face.

"Is there a problem, Officer?"

"The guy who just came in, chin-length black hair, denim shirt."

"Yeah?"

"What did he want?"

"He wanted a room."

"A room?"

He nods.

"Just any room?" Sweat trickles down my neck and soaks into the collar of my navy shirt. It must be close to a hundred degrees inside.

"He asked for 2B."

"What's in 2B?"

"Same thing that's in all the other rooms around here. A bed, a TV, a—"

"No, I mean who's inside 2B?"

"He is," the scarecrow clerk says.

"I saw him drive off."

"Then I guess no one's in there."

"Do you have an extra key?" I ask.

His blond eyebrows mash together on his forehead. "Yeah. But I gotta go inside with you."

"Fine. Take me."

He comes around the reception desk. He's even skinnier

standing than he is sitting. At least if he tries anything funny, I can take him out with my right hook. Actually, I could probably flick my fingers to knock him out.

As we walk to room 2B, I scan the quiet lot. Once he unlocks the door, I kick it open and flick the lights on. Nothing seems out of place. I'm not sure what I was expecting. Duffel bags of cash on the bed? Bricks of white powder?

"Was this room rented out recently?" I ask the clerk.

He shrugs. "Not that I know. I'd have to check the books."

I step inside the room. Careful not to disrupt anything, I look under the bed, behind the TV, in the nightstand drawers, and walk through the bathroom. I even peer into the toilet tank. Nothing. The room is clean.

Annoyed, I trek back out. The clerk locks up and walks me back to the front desk. He takes out a large appointment book and runs his long finger over the 2B column.

"No one's used it since late June."

I sigh. "Well, if he comes back, or if anyone else asks for 2B, phone me," I say, sliding my card across the desk.

"Yes, Officer—" He reads the card, "Joshua Cooper."

Don't know why he feels the need to say my full name.

"Are you Moses's son?"

"Yeah. You know my dad?"

"We went to high school together! He tutored me. Did he become a teacher in the end?"

"Yeah."

"Well, good for him. Good for him. Say Dennis says hi, okay?"

"I will."

"And I'll call you if that man returns."

"Or if anyone else asks for 2B."

"Aye-aye." He salutes me, then smiles. He's missing a couple teeth.

Once I'm back in the car, I call the chief and tell him what I found, or rather, didn't find. On autopilot, I drive home, park, and take the elevator to the third floor. The heat in the hallway makes me fear the heat inside my apartment. My AC is broken, so sure enough, it's stifling. I turn on my desk fan, then stick my face close to it and shut my eyes.

When two hands slink around my waist, I spin around and trap the person's wrists. Breathing hard, I loosen my grip and frown. "What are you doing here?"

"I wanted to see you," Aster says.

"How did you get in?"

She blinks, and her blue eyes look shiny, almost glittery, like bouncy balls from 25-cent dispenser machines. "With the emergency key."

"Is this an emergency?"

"No." She looks down. "It's not."

I sigh, hook an arm around her shoulders, and pull her against me. But then I think of my sweaty shirt and push her away. "Didn't mean for it to come out like that, Asty. I've just had a long day. What do you need?"

"I—I—" She bites her lip. "I just wanted to see you." She tries to hug me but I press her away again.

"I need a shower."

"Okay. I'll wait."

I take a quick, cold shower, after which I don't bother drying off, considering the heat. I tie my towel around my waist and walk back out.

"What do you think you're doing?" I snap.

Aster jumps away from my desk.

I cross the room and shut Troy Mann's file. "You're not supposed to see this!"

"I'm sorry. It was just there."

"I could get in real trouble for this. Forget you saw him, okay?" I say, stuffing it inside a drawer.

She nods, then moves closer to me and lifts her hands,

settling them against my pecs. "I miss you," she whispers, pushing up on her toes.

When I realize what she's planning, I jerk backward. "We can't. I can't."

"Why not?"

"I just—We're not together anymore."

She curls her fingers over the top of my towel.

"Aster, I said no."

"One last time, Josh. Please. Just one last time. And then I'll leave."

I grab both her hands in one of mine. "What's gotten into you?"

A sob catches in her throat. "I feel so empty, Josh."

"I have some leftover lemon cake from the bakery."

"Not that sort of empty." She touches her abdomen. "In here." She touches her heart. "And in here. I feel empty."

I don't say, "You were always empty," but I think it really hard hoping she'll get my silent message.

"I need you," she whispers.

"Are you taking your meds?"

Her eyes widen in shock.

"Aster?"

"Yes." She grits her teeth. "I'm taking them."

"I don't mean to upset you. I just care."

"If you cared...if you cared you wouldn't treat me like a baby. You'd treat me like a woman. You'd love me. You'd give me a—"

"Don't even say it." I've lowered my voice to sound soothing instead of harsh. "You're nineteen and I'm twenty-one. This is not the right time for a baby."

"Will it ever be the right time?"

"Babies are a lot of work."

"But they bring so much joy."

"Can we find other ways of bringing you joy? You always

liked flowers. Maybe we can go to Home Depot to pick up some new plants. I'm sure the buttonbush would like some company."

"Mom hates the buttonbush."

"Hated," I whisper gently. "She's not here anymore. Besides, this is for you. Not for your mother."

Her eyes shimmer. "I love you, Josh. I loved you since the day you rescued me from the ball pool."

"I didn't really rescue you," I say, flushing.

"All the other kids kept jumping on top of me. You pulled me out. That's called rescuing." She cradles my jaw with her hands. "You love me too, don't you?"

"I do, just"—I look away—"not like that anymore."

I think all she hears is the last part of my sentence because she bounces away from me and sprints out of the apartment. I don't run after her, because running after her would mean something—something I don't have the heart or the energy to rekindle.

Brook

After an endless day of helping set everything up in the Metropolitan Museum, I feel like I deserve a drink. Or two. I drive over to Humi, the newest fusion restaurant on the Manhattan dining scene.

Sure enough, the restaurant is packed and the noise level is deafening. I came here to avoid thinking, and that's exactly what I intend to do once I sit in front of the backlit bar and order a martini. By the second one, I start to unwind.

When a blonde girl tips some of her drink on my jacket sleeve, I don't even care. She pats it dry with some paper napkins, even though I tell her it's fine.

"I'm so so sorry," she keeps repeating.

I place my hand over hers and glance up at her face. Her eyes are unnaturally large, enormous really, straight out of a Margaret Keane painting. "It's okay."

The girl tries to engage me in a conversation, but talking feels like an effort and I don't want to make an effort. I just want to drink, perhaps even get drunk. After two more martinis and two spicy tuna rolls, I get the check. The restaurant is more crowded now, and moving toward the exit reminds me of kayaking in a blustery sea.

I did that once with Troy and Dean in Florida right before a storm hit. I thought we would never make it back to shore. Troy tied the three kayaks together so that no man was left behind, then all three of us plunged our oars over and over, arms pumping fiercely, shoulders burning with exertion, eyes stinging with salt. Drenched in rain and sweat, we'd made it back to the beach, feeling like victors after a grueling fight.

As I hail a taxi, a silver Ferrari zips up to the curb. Before the tinted window rolls down, I let out a sigh.

"Brooky," Dean exclaims. From the way his eyes glow in the obscurity of his car, I can tell he's high. I used to find it exhilarating to hang out with a guy who didn't have a care in the world. I don't anymore. "Get in."

"I'm going home. I seriously need to unwind, Dean."

"Just get in."

Sighing, I drag the passenger side door open and climb in. "What do you want?"

"Good to see you too, brother."

"How did you even find me?"

"Lucky guess."

I tilt my head to the side. "I'm not buying that."

"Okay, fine. I know the hostess. And she knows you. She's obsessed with Dom's little show, and she called to ask if it would be too forward of her to ask for an autograph. I told her to leave you the fuck alone. Anyway"—he fires up the engine, swerving in and out of car lanes more perilously than yellow cabs—"I just finished dinner with the D.A. He'll suspend Diego Discoli's sentence as soon as you pop over to meet him."

I nod even though I feel like shuddering.

"You have a meeting with him at his home the day before the show begins. The package should arrive by then. Troy confirmed he's expediting it," Dean says, turning left after Union Square Park.

"Where the hell are you taking me?"

"It's Friday night. We're going out to celebrate!"

"Celebrate what?"

Dean's already incandescent eyes blaze brighter. "My little deal. Your incoming commission. Chase's acceptance. Getting rid of Josephine's PI. The start of the show. There are so many things to celebrate."

"I don't feel like celebrating until it's all done."

Dean places his hand on my arm. "The Masterminds never fail."

I sit up so abruptly I fling his hand off me. "Never *failed*. Past tense. Troy got kicked out of Duke, remember? He's now a construction worker. He could've been so much more."

"He's content with his life."

"If he's so content, why did he agree to run an errand for you?"

"To help you. I told him your situation was serious."

I rub my hand over my forehead. "Well now, I feel awful. I didn't want to drag anyone else into this."

"That's what friends do for each other, Brook. Remember when you and Troy hauled my ass out of the ocean and trussed me up like a turkey after I od'd? I would've drowned if it hadn't been for you guys."

I picture the horrific night, remembering the shouting, the crying, and the vomiting. It still gives me chills.

"Troy said you could have his share, too, by the way."

"I couldn't accept."

"Well, you talk to him about it, okay?"

"Okay."

"I heard you sold your Hamptons house. I loved that house! Did you get a good price?"

"Where did you hear about it?" I ask.

"Dom told me."

"Did he also tell you how badly my family's art collection sold? The fire-sale he organized—"

"Don't you dare put the blame on him. He could've refused to help you."

"Could he? Could he truly refuse to help me? I know too much."

"He treats you like a son, and this is how you repay him? By saying how calculating he is?"

"That's not what I said."

"That's what you meant."

I growl. "Shit, Dean! Running errands for the mob...that's not the life I want."

I expect him to go off on me again, or to kick me out of his car while it's still running. Instead, he says, "This is the last time. We won't involve you again. You can go and live your life. Maybe you can even buy that ranch in Montana you always dreamed about and start your eco-farm."

"My eco-farm?"

"Isn't that what you wanted to do?"

"I made that up when we had to come up with an innovative business plan freshman year. Can't believe you still remember."

"You and Troy are the biological brothers I never had." His eyes flash to my hand, to the pinkie ring he commissioned for the three of us at the end of our freshman year, the shiny tie that binds us. "Even though you speak of us in the past tense, we will always be the Masterminds. The trio who ruled the school. Who threw the best parties. Who came up with the most lucrative bets."

I stay quiet.

"You know what? I'm not giving you a choice. We're going out. You need to let out some steam."

He goes through a red light, not because he doesn't see it, but because he doesn't care. Cars screech to a halt around us. Some honk. Dean lowers his window and gives them the finger. As I watch the joy he gets out of being reckless and rude, the ring tightens around my finger.

EIGHT

AUGUST 16TH

JOSH

Something rings. It takes me a second to realize that it's my cell phone. I peel my eyes open, expecting sunlight, but my bedroom is dark. Who could be calling me at this hour?

Aster?

I sit up so quickly my head spins. I grip my lit phone and fumble to answer it, heart blasting inside my ribcage.

"Joshua Cooper?" a male voice says. *Not Aster.* I can't decide whether to feel relieved or alarmed.

"Who's this?" I say, walking to the bathroom and shutting the door.

"Dennis. From the motel."

I'm fully awake now, even though it's...I check the time on my phone's digital clock...4:13 a.m.

"You told me to call you if someone stopped by." He's whispering. "Mr. Mann just arrived with some lady. They're in the room together now."

she adds, leaning in closer. Her gaze snags on the seam. "Did you notice the tear?"

"A tear?" My stomach feels as though it's filled with ice cubes.

"Right here." She jabs the edge of the quilt with her index finger.

"Must be intentional."

"Perhaps," she finally says. And then her eyes light up like the blue flashers atop police cars. "I have just had a fabulous idea."

"What is it?" I shift away from her.

"We will include it in the auction test!"

I gulp. "She'll take it badly."

"To be sold by the Masterpiecers?" Josephine snorts, which makes her nose wrinkle. It's the only part of her face that creases since everything else is stretched tight, thanks to plastic surgery or Botox-infused night cream. "It will be *un honneur*." She crouches down and picks up the two corners resting on the floor and brings them back up toward the ones I'm holding. When she pinches the edges and tugs on them, they slip right out of my grasp.

I watch her fold the quilt like one watches a car cut across several lanes on a teeming highway. I need to get it back before the truth comes crashing out.

TEN

JOSH

It's been almost two days since my life spun out of control, yet it feels like minutes since Ivy phoned me...since I rushed over to her apartment and saw the crack in the windshield of Aster's car...since I spotted the blood and black hair stuck to the dark red substance...since I flung their front door open to find them huddled on the couch.

Aster's hair dripped from a shower. Her eyes were bloodshot. Her skin was white, paler than Heidi's. She barely reacted when I stepped in. She was still in shock. Ivy, though, hopped off the couch to hug me.

I never want to relive that night, but like a curse, it plays in a loop in my mind.

"If we get rid of the car, then—"

"Don't ask me to do this. I can't, Ives. I'm a cop."

"You're our friend. Before you were a cop, you were our friend," she said, tearing my heart in two. *"Please."*

"I can't."

"Then I'll do it." She untangled herself from me and walked toward the door but I captured her wrist.

"No. If you get involved, and the guy truly is dead, then you become an accessory to murder."

"But she's going to go to prison if...if he's dead."

"It was an accident," Aster said mechanically.

"I'm sure it was, Asty, but if he's dead, then he's dead. There will be charges and consequences."

"But he threatened her!" Ivy threw her arms in the air. Maybe for emphasis, or maybe to get away from me. "It was self-defense."

"Where did you hit him?"

Aster clasped her hands tightly in her lap, the tips of her nails ragged and brown, as though she'd tried scrubbing the blood off the windshield with her bare hands. "In the stomach."

"I didn't mean where on his body, I meant in what part of town? On what street? I need to call it in."

"Why?" Ivy asked.

"Because, there's a dead body in the middle of the road, one your sister put there, and if I don't call it in, and someone notices I stopped by your place after the crime—"

"The accident," Ivy corrected me.

I flinched. "After the accident, then that makes me an accomplice."

"The body's not in the middle of the road," Aster whispered.

"You moved it?"

"No. It's in a parking lot."

I slapped my forehead. "That's still the middle of the road." I took my cell phone out of my pocket. "What parking lot?"

"The motel off route 9."

I shut my eyes, and then opened them super wide. "Tell me it's not Troy Mann."

Aster looked up then. "He stopped by the pizzeria. I recognized him."

"Who's Troy Mann?" Ivy asked.

My phone rang. It was Dennis. After I picked up, he confirmed my worst fear. "Should I call the cops, Joshua?"

"I'll do it."

My hands shook as I spoke to dispatch. My voice too. The patrol car arrived minutes later. As old Mr. Mancini, along with the rest of the neighbors, watched on, a cop from the precinct ripped Aster out of Ivy's arms.

I didn't want to leave Ivy alone, but she forced me to go, so I trailed the cruiser. Shaking, I nearly rammed into its bumper. I drove too fast. Recklessly. Because I was a wreck.

From the car, I called Dennis back to ask what he'd seen. "I was fixing the ice machine in the back when I heard glass break. And then Troy Mann...he was just laying there, in the middle of the road."

"Is he dead?"

"As a doorknob."

"Doorknobs don't live, so they can't die!"

"I, uh...I meant he's dead."

"I got it." It wasn't fair to yell at poor Dennis, but nothing at that moment felt fair.

"They're taping off the crime scene now."

"Okay."

"And, Joshua...that lady friend of his was here again tonight, but I don't think they um...did anything. They only spent five minutes in the room. I checked my watch. Although maybe they had time."

"Did you give the cops access to 2B?"

"Yes. Was that the right thing to do?"

"Yes," I reassured him. "Did they find anything?"

"If they did, they didn't tell me, but I can go ask."

"No, no, don't. I'll call my partner to find out." Before I disconnected, I remembered to say thank you.

"You're welcome, Joshua."

I tossed the phone on the seat next to me and squeezed my steering wheel. The street blurred. I blinked. The road was sharp again. Too sharp. Like the pain inside my skull. Like the sirens outside. Like the red taillights of the cruiser. Like the fear in Aster's eyes when they hauled her away from Ivy.

FORTY HOURS LATER, the pain is still raw. Not only has Aster been placed in custody of the Department of Corrections, but also, Guarda put me on probation when I admitted that Aster saw Mann's file at my place. I'm too honest for my own good. At least, that's what Fred told me when he heard about it all.

My phone pings with a text from Ivy. *Are you coming?*

On my way now, I write back. At the same time I press send, my phone rings.

"Hey, Fred," I say. "Has the chief—"

"This isn't about your reinstatement, although I'm working on it." He's whispering. A door squeaks shut. His voice doesn't get any louder, though. "I just wanted to pass on something I overheard by the water cooler about your girl."

"What?"

"We got something from the tip line. The night of the incident, Aster was seen with a blanket on her lap."

"Okay...why is that important?"

"I'm not sure yet, but it wasn't found in the car. I just wanted to keep you in the loop."

"I appreciate it, Fred."

"Don't beat yourself up over this. I'm sure it's going to be resolved fast."

"I hope. Did they find anything at the motel?"

"Nope."

"Nothing in room 2B?"

"Nothing. How's her sister?" He's chewing something crunchy.

"Not great. I'm on my way to her now."

"Wish her luck for tomorrow. She's still going, right?"

"I think so."

More chomping. "I'll call you if I hear anything else."

I park in front of Ivy's apartment, then let myself in with my key. "Ivy," I holler.

She walks out of her veranda studio, limbs rigid. "We have a problem." The skin underneath her eyes is violet. "*I* have a problem."

"Related to Aster?" I'm praying she's going to say no. At this point, I'd rather discuss genital warts than the crime that went down in the motel.

She picks up the newspaper and shoves it in my arms, and then she wraps her long red wool sweater tighter around her.

"You knew there'd be some buzz around the murder," I say softly.

She unties her arms and jabs her finger at the mug shot of Troy Mann taken a year ago. "He's the guy who bought my quilt."

"Rewind."

Ivy paces the threadbare rug. "Remember when I told you I sold a quilt? He's the guy I sold it to."

"Shit. Why didn't you mention this before?"

"Because that's not the name he used when he introduced himself, Josh! He said he saw me on that *Masterpiecers'* feature and wanted to own something of mine before I became too big. If my quilt is found on him, then I'm as good as convicted too, right? Selling art to mob runners—or whatever he is—it can't be a good thing."

My saliva turns to cement.

"Do the cops have it?" She's standing right in front of me now, arms folded tight.

I shake my head. "No. Nothing was found on him."

"Fuck," she whispers. The word sounds ugly coming out of her mouth.

I wrap my arms around her shoulders and pull her in tight. "This is all my fault. If I hadn't left that file out, Aster wouldn't have gone after him."

"This is nobody's fault."

Her vertebrae jut out under my palms, even through her sweater.

"Should I still go to New York tomorrow?"

I want to say no; I want her to stay. For Aster...and for me. "Yes, dummy. You have to go. You have to kick ass and come back super rich so the three of us can retire somewhere tropical."

She snorts a laugh. "How very Mormon of you, Josh. Suggesting a *ménage à trois*."

I pull away fast. "I didn't mean it like that." My face is hot. "It was a joke."

Ivy smiles. "I know." She places her palm over my cheek. It's cold and soft and familiar. "I'm going to kick ass. I have to. I need to bail Asty out. And then I have to repay the loan I took out on this place." She sighs and lets her hand fall to her sweater.

She grips the hem and rolls it between her fingers like she used to roll the tiny quilt her mom made her eons ago. She took that thing everywhere with her.

"How's she going to survive in there, Josh? She's so fragile."

"I'll go see her. Every day. I promise."

She nods. After a long stretch of silence, she says, "I went to visit her today."

"And?"

"She looks like a ghost. I don't think she *was* taking her medication. I think she flushed it down the toilet. I went to speak to her warden. I asked him to put her back on it. He had a sister who was schizophrenic too. She ended up committing suicide." Her voice is barely above a murmur. "Like Mom." Her beautiful blue eyes blur with emotion. "I'm so afraid that's what Aster's going to do, Josh. So afraid. Especially now that she's in—"

I press her against me and rock her. "Shh...Don't think like that. Aster's not weak. She wants to live."

"Suicide is not weakness. It's despair."

"Let *me* worry about her, you hear? I'll be there for her every step of the way."

"But you have a life, a girlfriend, a job."

"You girls are my life." I don't add that I'm currently out of a job. As for Heidi, she detests Aster so fiercely that I worry it will impact our already brittle relationship.

As I hug my friend, my gaze wanders over the small room. How empty it will feel once she's gone. The red quilt Ivy turned into a bag is propped on the couch, full of clothes.

"What did the quilt look like? The one you sold Troy?"

"It was gold, lots of gold. Two people kissing. I made it for Mom. Right before she...right before she left us."

A thought knocks into me. The blanket Aster had on her lap...could it be the quilt Ivy asked me to locate?

PART 2
DURING

ELEVEN

Brook

Zara Mach's show was a success. And a pleasant distraction from the nightmarish quilt episode.

The second I step off my flight, my phone rings. No caller ID, so I assume it's Dean.

"I thought about it all night," he says. "I want to go search the twins' place. The stones *have* to be there."

"What if they're in her car?"

"It's been impounded, so if they are, we'll never get them back." He pauses. "But she wouldn't have left them in there. Right?"

"Right," I say, even though I have no idea. "Don't go yet. Let's wait until we get the quilt back. You know, to make sure we didn't miss them."

"I can go inside the vault tonight—"

"And set off the alarm?"

"I have Dom's code."

"Every time you input the code, it adds it to a log book. Dominic is supposed to be on the show all week. Visiting the vault is *not* a good idea, you hear me?"

"The D.A. warned me that either I get him the stones by next week or my client goes to jail for an extremely long time."

"Next week is plenty of time, Dean."

"Next week is tomorrow."

As I walk out of the terminal, someone calls my name. It's Dominic's driver, Carl. I nod hello and follow him to the parking lot.

"That PI Jo hired...I heard he lawyered up," Dean says. "I should've offered him my services."

"And become a public figure? Dominic wouldn't have approved."

"That's why I didn't do it. Wait. I got to take this call. It's Mom."

"Send Alaina my love." I hand my carry-on to Carl who sets it in the trunk of the Denali.

When I hear him ask this blonde girl if she wants to put hers in the back too, I slip my phone into the breast pocket of my jacket. My gaze jets over to the sign wedged in Carl's hand.

I read it out loud, "Ivy." Once her name reaches my eardrums, I snap my eyes up to her face. "Carl," I yell. I was just talking about her. What if she heard Dean say her name? "Get the girl another ride. Judges and contestants can't be seen together! Who was in charge of this planning?"

"Miss Raynoir, sir. She told me to pick you up since I was already at the airport."

She's trying to get me in trouble.

"This could've been a disaster. If the paparazzi—"

"You better get in the car, sir." Carl tips his head toward two men with large cameras. "They're here."

I lunge into the Denali. In the rearview mirror, I see Carl

push Ivy into the backseat of a black town car that has just pulled up.

How did I not recognize her when I walked out? I watched an entire feature about her. I let out a breath that sounds like a growl. Everything will be okay, I whisper to myself. A picture taken of me with a contestant pales in comparison to the shit Dean is going through.

That's all I can think about as Carl drives me back to my place. I shower and change and then return to the car to be driven uptown to the Met. When I arrive, I try to tell Dominic about the airport fiasco, but he's too preoccupied to listen. I eye Josephine, debating whether to confront her, but I'm not sure that would work in my favor, so I let it slide. Then the first guests walk in, and I slip back into the role of Dominic's assistant *extraordinaire*.

Between greeting people and leading them to the decked-out Temple room, I momentarily forget about Dean and his missing diamonds. Music and champagne and the aroma of the white roses gracing the round dinner tables smooth the ragged edges of my nagging thoughts until I am almost blissful. Almost because I haven't seen Chase yet.

A half hour of schmoozing later, Dominic asks me to take my place on the stage between the two floor-lit Egyptian arches. As I walk up, Lincoln Vega, the pretty blonde chalk artist struts in, her beaded dress glimmering under the strobe lights Jeb has trained on her. Behind her, Herrick Hawk enters, black hair teased and floral scarf knotted neatly around his neck. Nathan Stein walks in next, longish hair framing his face that looks drawn and tired, in spite of the make-up. And then I spot my brother, and my stomach does a backflip because he spots me too, but looks away almost instantly. Maxine Specter, the girl with the buzz cut and the massive Hamptons house walks in next. Jared J., the graffiti artist files in behind her, grinning to the crowd whose applause rise in tempo. And then Dominic's former beauty queen, no-talent-Maria, sashays inside the room, waving hello with a cupped hand.

They snake around the tables and climb onto the stage to take their assigned seats. Ivy Redd's chair remains empty. For the flimsiest second, I hope she changed her mind about competing, that she commanded the driver to do a U-turn on the highway, because having her on the show complicates everything.

But then Dominic's strident announcement rips my wishes to shreds. "Eight! Lucky number eight, you made it!"

I almost snort when he says *lucky*, but that's before I lay my eyes on her. As she carves a path toward us, I am mesmerized. She is stunning in her floor-length, blue silk dress, which makes me wonder if this is the same Ivy Redd I watched on the feature, the same girl I ran into at the airport.

When I feel Josephine's gaze on me, I throw my attention on a random table below. I keep my eyes averted throughout most of the introductions. When Dominic presents my brother, though, I jump to attention. Literally. I smile and sling an arm around Chase's shoulders but he shrugs it off. Selfishly, I want to grab the microphone out of Dominic's hands and tell the crowd that Chase is here thanks to me, but no one can know what I traded to get him on the set of this game show. No one besides Dominic, Dean, and my father. It shouldn't matter anyway. I didn't do it for recognition; I did it because it was his dream, and that's what brothers do.

I lift my chin and keep smiling as Dominic bombards him with questions. When it's over, I return to the gold bench where sitting next to Josephine suddenly feels more comfortable than standing next to Chase.

While Dominic introduces his beauty queen contestant, my gaze wanders off the screen displaying her hideous paintings and onto Ivy, on her sloping nose, her full lips, her startling pale eyes. Her wild hair has been tamed and drapes glossily over her sculpted shoulders. I've met many beautiful women, but Ivy is something else. She turns her head and catches me staring. Like a fifteen-year-old boy, I jerk my gaze away.

When she stands up to be introduced, I listen to her speak, and her voice echoes in my chest. It's calm and smooth, the sort of voice you want to listen to at night, in the silence of your bedroom.

After the presentations, I breathe a little easier, until Dominic informs me it's picture time. A group photograph means I need to spend more excruciating minutes trying to act like the poised judge the contestants must respect and fear. I don't think I could inspire fear in a mosquito.

When Patrick Veingarten claps a big hand against my back while saying, "If it isn't the Masterpiecers' most beloved graduate," I kick the awkward teenage boy out of me.

I smile. "You mean, the one who stuck around?"

Patrick chuckles.

"So what are you thinking?" Dominic asks, gesturing to the eight ornate golden frames.

"You'll see." Patrick's gaze perches on Ivy. He strides toward her and takes her elbow. "Let's start with you." I lower my gaze and try to stay calm when Patrick adds, "I hope my camera will do you justice."

I look up and see the sleazy fashion photographer whisper something else in her ear. When she laughs, I fold my arms in front of my chest.

"Let yourself go. Think languid, just pleased, but still ravenous. I'm sure you know how to do that," he tells her.

Asshole.

"Perfect...a true work of art," he adds a moment later.

Even though I have to agree with him, my blood warms at the way he's staring. As I wait to be directed, I concentrate on cooling down, but it backfires once Patrick puts me in front of Ivy, instructing me to watch her as though I'm appraising her value. Is he toying with me? Trying to make me look like the blubbering fool I've become around this nineteen-year-old girl?

"Brook, I'm sure your shoes are valuable, but eyes on Ivy please," he says.

Fine.

Slowly, my gaze climbs to her face. I take my time absorbing each detail, from her almond-shaped eyes to her bee-stung lips. If I were an artist, I would choose this girl as my muse. But even an artist could never do justice to such a face.

She flicks her gaze to mine. As I grind my eyes deeper into hers, my breathing turns raspier, heavier. Patrick gave me permission to admire her, so that's what I'm doing...admiring her.

TWELVE

JOSH

I rush through the mall toward the food court where I was supposed to meet Heidi almost an hour ago. I pray she's still there. My cell phone ran out of battery after my stopover at the prison, where I spoke with Aster and with the woman who's going to conduct her psychiatric evaluation. The shrink pummeled me with questions about the relationship between the two sisters. She sounded skeptical as to whether they were as close as I "made them out to be." And then she asked me about their mother, and I explained that she drowned back in March, and was never kind to Aster.

"Sorry I'm late," I tell Heidi, as I swoop down in the plastic chair next to hers, and peck her lips.

She places her forearms over a magazine. Her skin is creamy and sprinkled with freckles that darken in the sun. The first time I saw Heidi was at a pool party. She was lying on an inflatable raft shaped like a doughnut, with her legs draped over the plastic frosting decal. She has beautiful legs, but it was her floppy sunhat that drew me in. She seemed so much classier than all the other girls in their teeny bikinis and oversized sunglasses.

"It's okay. I was busy." She tips her chin toward the magazine, which makes her purple-framed glasses slide down. She pushes them back up.

We're trying to make our relationship work, even though she was pretty reluctant to meet me. I try to grab her hand but she pulls it away.

"What's going on in"—I glance down at the cover of the glossy tabloid—"Angela Discoli's life?" I peel the magazine off the sticky table and stare at it, feeling suddenly lightheaded. "That's Angela Discoli?" I ask out loud even though I know the answer.

"Uh-huh. You know her?"

Does seeing her in bed with a man count as knowing someone? "Can I borrow your phone?"

"Sure."

"I'll be right back," I say, squeezing her sparkly Hello Kitty rubber case between tense fingers. When I'm far enough away from her, I dial Fred's number. "Fred?" I say, but he hasn't picked up yet. I carve my hand through my hair and start pacing. Suddenly a voice says *hello*. "Fred! It's me. Josh."

"Oh. Hey, buddy. What's up?" I hear his wife chattering in the background and a cartoon running.

"Fred, I've just discovered something big."

"What?"

"The night before Troy Mann died, I found him at the motel with someone."

"You didn't mention that."

"Because I thought he was having an affair, but I don't think that's it. The woman I saw him with, guess who she was?"

"Who?"

"Angela Discoli!" I must say it way too loudly because Heidi perks up at the name, even from the distance.

Fred doesn't say anything.

"Fred?"

Still nothing, so I move over a few feet, bumping into a potted plant. The connection must be bad.

"Fred, can you hear me?"

"Yeah, yeah, I heard. I was peeing and thought I'd spare you the sound. Forgot to take my phone off mute. So Troy was screwing Trashy Discoli?" He doesn't mean trashy as in bimboy; he means it as trashy. The Discolis are the largest waste collectors in Indiana. That's their official business. Their unofficial business is laundering money.

"Her engagement just made the cover of a magazine, so I don't think that's it."

"Women cheat. It happens."

"My gut tells me there's more. She wasn't even undressed when I came in." I pace the shiny floor. "What if the affair was a cover-up? What if she was giving him stuff to move?"

"*Oh.*" Silence, then Fred says, "I should call the chief."

"Okay. Will you tell him it was my theory?" I hold my breath and cross my fingers until he speaks.

"Yes, Coop. I'll tell him. This could be huge."

I get goose bumps, because if I'm right and Troy was moving stuff for the Discolis, life in prison is the least of Aster's worries.

Brook

I negotiated with Dominic about using my own clothes for the show. I have a wardrobe full of fitted dress shirts and tailored suits I bought to complement my status in the art world, a wardrobe that will soon go to waste.

I would gift some suits to Chase, but my little brother is a few inches shorter than I am, and broader in the chest and shoulders. Plus, he would never accept a gift from me. It would be like accepting a gift from your wicked stepmother.

When I arrive at the Met, I climb up the three flights of stairs to the contestant quarters. The first person I run into is Ivy. I see her from behind, but I know it's her from the perfect curves on display in her white outfit. The irony that I'm dressed all in black while she wears only white isn't lost on me: the devil and the angel. Sadly, that's not far from the truth.

"Hey, Ivy," I say, catching up to her.

She spins around. She seems hesitant to engage with me, and almost fearful, so I smile, hoping it will ease her tension. She studies my face for a moment, then returns my smile.

"And here I was afraid I wasn't recognizable like this." She points to the thick white make-up smeared over her face.

I chuckle.

"So what are we doing today?" she asks.

"Can't tell you."

Her eyes spark. "Really? Not even a hint?"

"Not even a hint." Time stills as I take her features in one by one.

She tips her chin down, and the faintest blush stains her cheeks under the heavy white grease paint. "I should go eat something."

I swallow hard, then gesture to the enclosure in the fabric wall. "After you."

Ducking, she walks ahead of me and straight toward the buffet.

"Morning, everyone," I say. I'm cheerful until I notice my brother's face is painted white like Ivy's, and he's wearing the same outfit as she is. And I suddenly remember why. I don't feel chirpy any longer, yet I keep up the smile and friendly banter until the make-up artists barge in for last-minute touchups. My cue to go find my spot next to Dominic in the grand hall where the row of vaulted ceiling windows have been obscured.

"They're on their way," I tell him.

Dominic beams at me, and then he grins at the crowd below. "Lights out," he orders.

Whispers and sharp intakes of breath arise from the dark pit of onlookers filling the titanic stone hall. And then the click of shoes on the winding staircase behind me replaces the noise from below. Like everyone else, I watch the eight hopeful contestants descend into the darkness. As Dominic introduces the first test—performance art—Ivy gasps. I want to reassure her that the next eight hours should be easy.

For her.

Not for me.

Watching her in a soundproof box staring only at my brother—her mission for the next eight hours—will be some version of hell. When Dominic describes how intimate it is to make eye contact for so long, my dread increases.

"Can I get a countdown?" he asks as the contestants find their stages.

Neither Ivy nor Chase seem eager about their task. As they take their seats, I step up to the large glass box, along with a couple dozen spectators. A drone camera buzzes over the box, capturing footage from above.

Ivy shifts in her transparent plastic seat. She's uncomfortable. I'm not sure if it's from being watched or the proximity with my brother. I suspect it's Chase's presence. Or perhaps I hope it's Chase. Her gaze travels over the miles of faces surrounding her. When it glides over mine, my heart holds still. I'm expecting her eyes to drift right off, but they don't. She looks at me, and I look at her, and even though there are hundreds of people around us, it feels as though we are alone.

"*Three...*" The chanting startles me. "*Two...*" Still, she watches me. "*One...*" I fold my arms in front of my chest. "*Showtime!*"

Her eyes settle on Chase.

My brother scowls. He enjoys challenges, and being locked in a box staring at a girl is not challenging. I bet he finds it terribly boring. I observe his face. Every feature is pinched, down to his lips, which are pressed together as tightly as a Ziploc baggie.

"So that's her?" someone breathes in my ear.

I jump. "You came."

"Wouldn't miss the first test," Dean says, staring at Chase, then at Ivy.

Placing my hand on his shoulder, I guide him away from the girl inside. We thread ourselves through the swarming crowd who gobble down buttery pastries and sip coffee from fancy porcelain cups, discussing the fabulousness of Dominic's imagination.

"Did you tell Dom about the...*doughnuts?*" I ask.

Dean snorts, but I can tell he's not amused by the way he fingers the gold tie bar his father bought him when he graduated high school, along with a hundred Hermès ties. He readjusts the perfect silk knot. "They called me," he says as we approach Lincoln's stage. His gray eyes gleam silver in the overhead lights, then flicker as one of the soap bubbles Lincoln blows pops right in front of his face. As she brings her outsized bubble wand back up to her mouth, she grins at me, her Lolita-pink lips stretching wide. "I told them we didn't receive the package yet."

We both stay silent for a minute.

"They're probably still in the quilt, right?" he asks.

"Probably." *Hopefully...*

Madame Babanina, who hadn't spotted me yet, trundles toward me, shoving people out of her way.

"Crap," I mutter.

"You can say that again," Dean says, but he's not talking about the crazy divorcée in the leather pants and see-through blouse who's obsessed with me; he's talking about his missing package.

"Brook, my love, I looked everywhere for you." She pounces on me, kissing both my cheeks, hopefully not leaving lurid pink stains behind. I wipe my skin when she turns toward Dean. "And who's this handsome boy?"

Dean slaps a smile on his face, picks Madame Babanina's hand up, and pulls it to his lips. He grazes her knuckles with his mouth, which fills her face—or what's visible of it underneath her long, thick bangs—with a blush. "Dean Kane, Brook's closest friend from Duke University," he tells her. Although he releases her hand, he doesn't release her gaze. "And I'd like to assure you that I'm very much a man, not a boy."

She throws her head back in laughter.

Dominic notices and makes a beeline straight for us. "Madame Babanina, you made it!"

"Of course I made it. I wouldn't miss the show I'm sponsoring," she says, with an upward twist to her lips.

"Of course not," Dominic says with a tense smile. "Dean, may I have a word with you?"

As the two of them walk away, Madame Babanina laces one hand around my bicep and brings her plump mouth toward my ear. "He's cute, your friend." With any luck she'll find him cuter than me. "He looks like a young Dominic."

"Did you hang your new—"

"He has the same round eyes."

"A lot of people have that eye shape." I drag her toward Herrick, who's buried in dirt up to his neck.

"Are they related?" she asks, trying to catch a last glimpse of them.

"No."

Finally, she stops prying and moves her pink lips closer to my ear. "I heard Dominic and Maria"—she tips her chin toward the beauty queen who's attempting to knit—"I heard they had a thing...is that true? Is that why she's here?"

"Well, I don't think she's here because of her talent."

Madame Babanina cackles again. Many people turn to stare. Thankfully, Ivy doesn't turn. I don't want her to get disqualified.

FOURTEEN

JOSH

I read Heidi's tabloid and find out that Angela Discoli's engagement party is taking place at three o'clock this afternoon at her parents' estate.

So here I am, dressed like one of the wait staff thanks to a bill with Benjamin Franklin's face on it. It's expensive, risky, and uncomfortable, thanks to a jacket two sizes too small, but I want to know her reasons for meeting up with Troy Mann at a motel. Since I think she won't want her fiancé to find out about her rendezvous, I'm planning on blackmailing her into a confession. I used to be a good cop, one who played by the rules, but that was before I lost my badge and found out that my friends had tangled with the mob.

I've seen satellite pictures of the estate on the Internet and photos of it in the magazine, so I know it's huge, but I was not expecting rolling hills, a car path edged with cypress trees, and a house modeled on some French chateau. It's preposterous, but I could totally picture myself living there. I'd add water-slides to the winding outdoor stairways and a moat-style pool around the house.

A woman with a head mic, a pink floral dress, and an armful of white helium balloons steps in front of me. "Where do you think you're going?"

I hope she's talking into her mouthpiece, or to the six other people around her, but I doubt it, since she's glaring at me.

"Wait staff goes through the back of the house," she says. "They don't come up the main hill."

My shoulders tense, stretching the already tight fabric. A tiny ripping noise reaches my ears. I try to relax before the jacket snaps off me like some two-cent Chippendale suit. "I was looking for the way to the back."

She sighs, annoyed. "You were briefed during the rehearsal engagement party."

"I couldn't make that one," I say. "My hamster died." *I couldn't think of another animal, could I?*

She scrutinizes me from top to bottom, then, handing her balloons to her assistant, she flips a few pages on the clipboard wedged underneath her arm. "What's your name?"

"Stuart Mason." I hope the guy I paid gave me his real identity.

She studies her list. When she nods, I can almost hear my muscles loosening. After pointing out the correct path, she grabs her balloons and starts tying them to the tree branches. "One hour till the guests arrive! Hurry up, people," she yells as I scurry away.

I walk back down the hill and find the narrow road bordered by the property's wrap-around wall. Moss and clumps of purple flowers sprout out of small cracks, making the high gray boundary less forbidding. I cross paths with other waiters. Most are jogging, lugging trolleys of food and decoration. I latch on to a trolley to melt into the workforce. After rolling it into the house, I stare around. When I see waiters collecting trays of drinks, I fall in line and grab one myself. Thankfully, I worked a couple weddings back in college, so I can balance a tray.

Fingers spread wide underneath the center, I rest some of the weight on my shoulder and walk up the stairs to the main hall where both families are posing for pictures. I look for the bride, but she's not there. I find a teenage girl playing with her cell phone and ask her where I can find Angela.

Barely looking away from her screen, she points to the huge staircase covered in a yellow carpet with blue flowers. "Second door on your left."

I trot up the stairs, nearly crashing into Angela's mother. Only one glass tips over, but thankfully, it doesn't spill on the mom's pink rhinestone dress that makes her look like an overgrown disco ball.

"Sorry, ma'am, I was told to bring refreshments up to the bride," I say, righting the glass.

She pats her puffy peroxide 'do. "Who told you to bring some up?"

"The planner, ma'am."

She inspects me through narrowed eyes ringed in black makeup. It's not flattering. "Well, don't spill any on her."

"Yes, ma'am."

As she starts down the stairs, I walk to the door the girl indicated. I would've barged inside if I wasn't a hundred percent sure Angela would call one of her bodyguards and have me shot on the spot. I want an explanation, not an early death.

A woman is working on the bride's light blonde hair, something I had stupidly not anticipated. Since asking her to leave would alert the household, I walk over to Angela and slide my tray too close to her stylist's arm. Sure enough, the woman's wrist collides with one of the glasses. I pretend-catch it, but make sure she still gets a hefty dose of orange juice on her.

"What the hell? Are you an idiot?" Mumbling angrily, she walks toward the adjoining bathroom to wash her hands.

Angela looks away from the flat-screen TV on the wall in front of her. "I know you." Her dark eyebrows slant toward her perfect nose.

"I just met your fiancé. Nice guy. Nicer than Troy."

Her eyes spring wide open. She remembers me. "What do you want?" She toys with the diamond necklace around her neck. The stones are so huge they seem fake, but she's a Discoli, so they probably aren't.

"Why were you meeting with Troy?" I don't add *in the motel*, because her stylist is walking back over. I'm allowing Angela to retain a bit of dignity. If she doesn't cooperate though, no more Mister Nice Guy.

"Angela, you want me to call security?" the stylist asks, backing up toward the bedroom door. She bumps into the bed and falls on the red satin cover.

"She calls security and I signal the team I have waiting just outside the property wall."

Angela snorts. "Do you even have a warrant?" Her voice isn't loud, but it's sharp.

"I do. I can go get it if you want, but that would mean going downstairs and alerting your family—"

"Wait outside," Angela tells her stylist.

"No way." I nod toward the far wall. "Wait in the bathroom and close the door."

She scampers back into the adjacent pink marble room, shuts the door, and spins the lock.

I'm still balancing the tray, so I set it down on the desk next to a bunch of eye powders and sparkly goo.

"Troy and I were in love." Her voice is as strained as my squashed shoulder blades.

"Seriously?"

A tear rolls out of her eye and curves down her pink cheek.

She takes a tissue and blots it. No other tear slips out. When Aster cries, she has tons of tears. A single tear seems calculated.

"I met him when he worked for Dad."

I'm letting her think I believe her pathetic lie. "What did he do for your father?"

"He got us contracts with private companies."

"Is that what laundering money is called nowadays? Getting contracts?"

Angela's now perfectly dry eyes narrow. "You have some nerve, Officer. I'm cooperating, and you accuse me and a dead man of corrupt dealings."

"Why did you meet him at a shitty motel? You obviously have money."

"Because I didn't want anyone to find out about the affair. If I went to a nice place, I'd be on the front page of some trashy tabloid right now."

I don't remind her that she's already on the front page of a tabloid. "If he hadn't died, were you going to call off your engagement?"

"It's arranged, so no. I don't have a choice."

I startle. *An arranged marriage?* I didn't even know modern Americans organized those anymore.

"Are we done?" she asks.

"Troy Mann bought a quilt from an artist called Ivy Redd. Do you know anything about it?"

Her pupils pulse as though two tiny grenades exploded inside.

"You do know about it..."

Her features contract into that sophisticated, impenetrable mask again. "You mean"—she raises a pointed finger to something behind me—"one of *her* creations?"

I turn around to find Ivy on TV looking pale and electrocuted. On the bottom of the screen, I read the words, *5th hour of Performance Art Test.* "Yes."

"He was going to buy me one as a wedding gift, but I didn't think he got around to it."

I study her face, but can't tell if she's bluffing.

"Why did that psycho sister of hers run him over?"

I squash my impulse of defending Aster by muttering, "He threatened her."

"What was she doing in the parking lot of the motel?"

"She was—I'm the one who's asking the questions. Not you."

The door of the room flies open. Two large men with earpieces march in. I check the bathroom door, but it's still closed.

"This is my grandma's room. She has an emergency buzzer near her bathtub," Angela says, smiling brazenly at me. "Ray, any police activity outside the property walls?"

Keeping his eyes glued to me, he dials a number, raises his cell phone to his ear, then shakes his head.

Angela's grin broadens. "Look who's lying now," she says sweetly. "Take him away."

The two piles of muscles stalk over to me and grab me under my armpits. The waiter uniform that feels like a strait-jacket finally rips, which is a relief, but it's short-lived. As they haul me toward the door, I wonder if they're going to dump me in some landfill next to a bunch of other corpses.

"Ray, I'm feeling generous today," Angela says, stroking her necklace. "I might not be in such a generous mood next time, Officer, so make sure there is no next time."

I have zero desire to see her again, yet somehow, I sense I will.

Brook

While I meander through the maze of galleries, the camera crew rushes past me, almost knocking me over. Maxine Specter, aka Daisy after the alcoholic shots that gave her the courage to enter the art competition, solved her riddle with impressive celerity. It was almost as though she knew exactly which piece she was searching for. Growing up with an art background probably helped. It hasn't helped my brother; at least, not yet.

As I penetrate one of the galleries, I freeze. Ivy is sitting on a bench, alone, eyes closed. I watch her. Her lips move and her head bobs.

I walk over to her and sit. "Think synonyms," I whisper, because I sense she needs help.

Her eyes fly open. "Trying to get me eliminated?"

"No. Synonyms are the foundation of a riddle. It's a fact, not a clue."

She studies me. I suppose she's debating whether to trust me. "Who solved theirs?"

"Believe it or not...Daisy."

"Daisy?"

"I mean Maxine."

"No, I know who Daisy is. I'm just surprised—I thought it would be your brother."

"He's still searching."

"He'll get it soon enough."

"He *is* pretty obstinate."

"I can tell," she says.

"This is his chance to get what he wants."

One side of her mouth lifts. "If he wins, will he be allowed to attend the Masterpiecers, or does he just get the hundred grand?"

"He'll be allowed to attend."

"Won't that destroy the school's policy?"

"It will complicate it," I say as Ivy stares at the Jackson Pollock in front of us. "Is your sister also artistic?"

"No. Not in the least."

"You don't talk about her." I keep my gaze on the painting.

"I came to compete in an art show, not to discuss my family."

"Fair enough."

"Now can you please leave so I can concentrate?"

My insides harden from her dismissal. "I'll be quiet." It's lame, but I want to stay next to her a moment longer.

Suddenly, she jolts to her feet and runs a shaky hand through her long, blonde hair. I peer behind her. My brother is standing in the doorway.

"How are you holding up?" I ask, rising and walking over to him.

"I thought the contestants weren't supposed to speak with judges or people from the audience." The vein on Chase's temple throbs.

"I can ask how you're doing."

"Is that what you were asking Ivy? How she was *doing*?"

I grind my teeth. "Yes. I wasn't giving her any clues, if that's what you're worried about."

We eye each other for a long moment. There are so many things I'd like to tell him but can't, because of rules and because of pride. Mine and his.

Loud applause cuts through the quiet gallery.

"Another winner. You two better hurry up," I tell them, brushing past Chase.

I don't turn around, although I think I hear Ivy leave. Lincoln is being interviewed when I reach the gallery. She found her riddle. J.J. runs in to announce he's uncovered his too. As I stand next to him in front of the Persian rug he needed to find, Ivy waltzes in.

"Ivy? Did you solve yours?" Dominic asks.

She starts from the sudden attention, but then she smiles. It doesn't reach her eyes.

"Almost." The smile falters once the audience turns away.

She glances at me, and adrenaline spikes through my veins. She needs help, but I can't give her any. I'm useless. I trail her with my eyes as she leaves.

My brother solves his riddle next.

Come on, Ivy.

When the camera crew angles their cameras toward one of the entrances, I hold my breath. It has to be her.

It's not.

It's Nathan.

But then she appears next to him, cheeks bright. "I got it!" she yells, but it's too late.

It's fucking too late!

I despise Nathan in that moment. Until he gives his answer and it's the wrong one. Then I could just kiss him.

"I'm sorry." Dominic pats him on the back, then turns toward Ivy whom he gestures forward. "What do *you* have for us, sweetheart?"

She walks over to us, shoulders held stiffly back. She comes to stand between Dominic and me, and I swear I can sense her heart thundering inside her chest. Our hands are inches apart. If I shift mine, I'd touch hers, but I stay immobile and hold my breath.

"*White Flag* by Jasper Johns," she says, her voice steady.

Yes. Yes!

But then Dominic hisses, and asks her if it's her final answer, and I think she got it wrong. But she couldn't have gotten it wrong for Jasper Johns's *White Flag* was one of the riddle answers, and it wasn't given yet. Could it have been Nathan's riddle? Was she supposed to find the—

Clapping erupts.

Dominic was toying with her.

I take Ivy's hand and pump it into the air victoriously. She turns to smile at me, and her eyes glisten.

"Good job, Redd," I whisper.

"Thank you."

I hold her gaze a while longer, and I clutch her hand until it becomes inappropriate for me to keep it nestled in mine.

***

THAT EVENING, after the dinner festivities, Dom asks me to accompany him to the post-production area to review the footage of the contestants' private dinner. They're aware cameras are recording them, but they don't know those cameras pick up sound.

"What are you doing, Brook?" Dominic asks in a quiet voice.

"What do you mean?"

"With Ivy. What are you doing with Ivy?"

"I'm being nice."

"This isn't you being nice; this is you flirting with a contestant. It's unprofessional, and it's not acceptable."

I bristle and turn defensive. "It's because I feel guilty, all right?"

Dominic sighs and plays the segment Jeb has kept for him to watch before running it on live TV.

Ivy's leaning back into her chair, arms folded tightly. She's glaring at someone. When I discover that someone is my brother, I smile smugly.

"I didn't rig the competition. I was chosen," she says. *"Based on my application. On my skill. But perhaps you did, Chase. After all, your brother's a judge. How difficult could it have been for him to get Josephine and Dominic to endorse your application?"*

"You don't know the first thing about me and my brother," he says.

"I know he got into the school, and you didn't."

"Because he was older. He applied first."

She leans forward. *"Is that the reason, or is he just better than you?"*

"Is that what Brook was telling you during the riddle hunt? That he's better than me?"

Dominic glances at me, but doesn't speak. He doesn't have to. I know what he's thinking. "I didn't help her, Dom."

"You swear?"

"Yes."

"Cheating, Redd?" Lincoln asks, dragging my attention back to the flickering screen.

"Of course not!" she says.

"Then why were you talking with my brother?" Chase asks.

"We were talking about you," she says.

"We were," I tell Dominic.

"Brook was telling me how badly you wanted to get into his school. Basically, he pleaded with me to let you win," she says. *"How's that for fraternal love?"*

I frown. "No. We spoke about school policy."

"Wouldn't be surprised if he came to all of you at some point to ask you to go easy on Chase," she adds.

Chase is going to detest me now.

Dominic places his hand on my forearm. "Will you still feel guilty when she destroys your relationship with Chase?"

"It's already ruined."

"This show can salvage it, but only if you stay away from her. He's the one you're cheering for, not some girl from the Midwest."

A hush falls over the contestants' table and over the small, dark room.

"If you forget again, I'll remind you," Dominic says.

I nod stiffly.

"We're getting the piece back tomorrow," he tells me, and it takes me a second to realize he's talking about Ivy's quilt.

"During the auction?"

He nods.

"Dean shouldn't—"

"It won't be him. I don't want Jo sniffing around him."

"I wonder what they'll have us do tomorrow," Lincoln says.

Dominic stares at her. "They proved the white supremacist rally pictures were fakes."

My eyes grow wide. "How?"

"Apparently Kevin was deployed at the time the pictures were taken. Did you know that digital pictures have a date stamp in the metadata?"

"It was Dean's idea."

"If you delegate a job to someone, and the job is poorly executed, don't blame the emissary." His voice is low, but far from soft.

Of course. Dean can do no harm. But according to his logic, Dominic shouldn't be blaming me. After all, he's the one who told me to get Kevin Martin eliminated after I confirmed that he wasn't just a retired sergeant.

"What do you want me to do about it?" I ask.

"Nothing. I'm taking care of it this time," Dom says, as Jeb penetrates the post-prod area.

"Should we air the segment, Mr. Bacci?"

"No." Dominic pats my arm on his way out. "I got to the bottom of the story, and it's not at all what it sounds like."

I tense up.

"But the audience would love it. Our ratings would go through the roof."

"No," Dominic says, blunting Jeb's enthusiasm. "It's too personal."

Sometimes, I can't tell if Dominic is my protector or my executioner, since he's capable of both.

JOSH

On one of the gym's wall-mounted TVs, Ivy has just walked onto the podium to present the first piece she has to sell. The quilt she described to me, the one with the gold fabric representing two people embracing. The water I'm drinking spurts out of my nose. I sponge it off with the towel hung around my neck. Fortunately, there aren't many people around the gym at this time of day. Most people are at work, which is where I would rather be, but lifting weights takes my mind off my dire situation.

"Shit," I say, wiping my forehead with the damp towel. How did Troy Mann's quilt end up in New York, on the set of *The Masterpiecers*?

I rush to the locker room to shower and change. I don't bother drying my hair since it's pouring outside. Taking cover under my gym bag, I jog to my car and drive toward the prison. I don't think to call ahead to get a meeting. I don't think about anything besides the quilt. By the time I reach the gates, I'm convinced Aster sent it there.

At the front desk, I ask to see her.

"What's your relationship to the prisoner?"

"I'm the investigating officer," I say, squeezing my car key into my palm. "I came to visit Miss Redd on August 20th. You probably have it in your records," I add, pushing myself on my tiptoes to see past the glass wall surrounding the desk.

The woman is slow to check, but the inspection pays off. She nods and radios in one of her colleagues to lead me into the visitation area. Dread pulses through me as I enter the bleak room with the barred windows overlooking the barbed wire fence and the purple-gray sky. Raindrops splatter against the glass, making the atmosphere sort of relaxing, although relaxing is a big word to use for this place.

The door buzzes and Aster barrels through, cheeks flushed. "I need you to check my sister's bank account," she says, dropping into the chair opposite me.

"Hello to you too, Aster."

The bones in her face press against her skin. "I think Ivy was paying Mom's bills."

"Swell. Means you don't have to pay them."

"That's not swell! She lied to me, Josh."

"How?"

"She never told me about the money."

"Why are you so worked up about it?"

"Because—"

I cut her off because right now, her mom's institution bills and the apartment deed are at the very bottom of my worry list. "How did Ivy's quilt end up on the show?"

Aster's pin-sized pupils throb against their sky-colored background. "Ivy's quilt? I have no idea."

"Want to know what I think? I believe you found it next to

Troy's body and sent it there. I believe it's the one you used as a *blanket.*"

She turns pale, like the time she ate bad chicken and threw up in my car.

"You're not denying this?"

She studies her lap or her socks. "No. It was a blanket."

"Aster, you're lying. Did you follow him from your house? Is that it?"

"I...he..."

"Asty, please tell me the truth," I ask in a soft voice. I can tell she's worked up and on edge.

"Okay, fine. I saw him at our house. I saw him go inside, and then I followed him back to the motel."

"Thank you for trusting me."

She looks up. "You mean, for always lying?"

My forehead furrows. "What? No. I never said that."

"The baby was real."

"I know."

"I never lied about the baby."

"I know."

"My doctor told you what I asked her to tell you. I was trying to protect you."

I play along. "I know you were, Asty."

"I didn't make it up. I felt it move. I saw it move. I was throwing up every morning."

"Are you taking your meds?" I ask her.

"No, it wasn't."

I'm not getting through to her. I squeeze her arm. She flings my hand off. "What wasn't?"

She's trembling. "It was real."

"Let's not talk about the baby anymore. It always makes you sad."

She stands up. "I need to go." Tears cling to her lashes, then tumble down her caved-in cheeks.

"Don't be sad."

"Be like what?"

I sigh. She's hearing another conversation in her head. "Just stay."

"And be interrogated and mocked? No, thank you. I'd rather go hang out with people who don't think I'm crazy."

"I never said you were crazy."

"You didn't have to say it." She stares at me with wild eyes. "Don't bother coming back here anymore."

"I'm going to come back. I'm in charge of the case."

She blinks, and more tears slide out. This time, I capture her hand. As I look at her face, her features soften. She's back.

"Before you go, can you tell the warden to inform the guards that I *am* allowed to watch the show whenever I want?"

"The warden would never listen to me."

"He did the first time around."

Maybe she's not back. "What are you talking about? What first time?"

"Ivy told me you got me that privilege."

"The warden? I've never even met the man."

"If *you* didn't talk to him, then who did?"

"Ivy went to see him. She probably—"

"I'm not crazy," she shrieks.

My heart jumps. I long to hug her to me until my Aster comes back, but this Aster...she'll fight me. Causing a scene will attract unwanted attention. What if I'm asked for my badge? What if they never allow me to return? I can't take the risk.

"Got it?" she asks, before returning into the entrails of the prison.

I stay sitting for a long time, staring at the space she occupied. Finally, hunching over, I cradle my forehead in my hands. Her condition is worsening. After her mother's death, her shrink told me trauma could aggravate the schizophrenia. I didn't want to believe it at the time. I wanted to believe she would overcome it and turn back into the girl with pigtails I plucked from the sea of multicolored plastic balls, the girl I spent my weekends chasing through the vast sunflower field bordering my grandparents' home, the girl whose laughter bubbled out of her mouth and spilled into her eyes.

I pray she's still somewhere in there.

Sighing, I realize I didn't get a straight answer from her. I still don't know if she sent the quilt or if it was Troy. Deep down, I think she shipped it, but when? She hit him around 10 p.m., and I got to their house an hour later. No post office would be open at that time. Unless she already had a stamped package, but why would she?

I slap the table because nothing makes sense. I feel like it should.

SEVENTEEN

Brook

I watch the slow drizzle of coffee, and slender threads of steam drift out of the espresso machine. The smell is intoxicating. If I close my eyes, I'm back in Durham, drinking iced Americanos and shoveling omelets with hash browns after a night of too much everything. Troy and Dean are there, sitting in front of me in the Union, planning out the next campus-shattering party.

The machine clicks. I'm no longer in North Carolina, no longer planning parties, no longer with Troy and Dean. I'm in New York, in my parent's apartment where I grew up, about to watch the press conference during which Ivy must deny her involvement with Kevin's doctored pictures.

And Troy is dead.

"Brook, honey, let me take care of the coffees," Carmelina, my parents' live-in housekeeper, says, bustling into the kitchen.

"I've got it."

She stares at me through bifocals that make her eyes look like vast, grassy plains. "You work too much. You need to rest."

If I rest, her salary won't get paid. Knowing Carmelina, who's been with us for over two decades, she'd probably insist on staying, but one of her kids just lost his job. She can't afford to work for free.

"Are you staying for dinner tonight? I'm making your favorite tamales."

"I have to get back to the museum, but as soon as the show's done, I want tamales."

She strokes my cheek like she did when I was small, when she helped me fall back asleep after bad dreams.

"Your mother told me about Troy. It made me so sad." Her thick lenses magnify her tears.

I swallow.

"The young should not die young." She lowers her hand. "Now, go sit. I'll bring your coffee." She all but shoves me out of her kitchen.

Snatching a tissue from the shiny metal box by the home phone, I return to Dad. He glances at me, and his face, already contorted with stress, warps even more.

"Pollen allergies," I lie. I'm not sure why I do. Perhaps I don't want to burden him with *my* grief.

We listen to the reporter who's summarizing the Kevin fiasco before Ivy's arrival.

"Did she alter those photos?" Dad asks me.

"No."

"You know who did?"

"No."

His eyes linger on my face, but he doesn't ask again. "How's Chase?"

"He's doing well. He floored Dominic at the auction."

"I saw," Dad says, smiling, but the smile doesn't smooth out his worry lines. "Every day, I fear an *artistic* test. He'd be elimi-nated for sure. He has as much talent as I do."

"There'll only be one, and it should be pretty easy." With Dominic, we designed this year's tests according to Chase's strengths.

"Thank you," Dad says.

"For what?" I stare at the crosshatched silver pattern on the pastel rug instead of at Dad.

"You know for what," he says. "I had a box of cigars sent to Dominic. Did he get them?"

"I'll ask."

Suddenly, the reporter whirls around, along with the crowd assembled on the Metropolitan Museum steps. I lean forward in my seat. Ivy steps out of the museum, flanked by Dominic, Josephine, and two lawyers. Her blonde hair seems lighter in natural sunlight.

Carmelina walks in front of the TV, sets down the platter, then moves to the side to watch the news with us. "I don't like her," she says after a bit.

"You don't know her, Carmelina."

"Her sister killed Troy."

"*Her sister*. Not her."

Both Carmelina and Dad eye me.

"She looks sad," he says, perhaps to deflect the strain in the room.

"She lost her mom recently, and her twin's clinically insane."

"Poor girl," Dad says.

Carmelina folds her arms in front of her. "You should be even more careful, then."

"She's just a contestant, Carmelina."

"Is she?" she asks.

Dad is busy tweaking the volume with the remote control, so I don't think he picks up on Carmelina's insinuation.

"I watch the show, Brook," she adds in a hushed voice. "I see."

My palms turn clammy. I grab my cup of milky coffee and it almost slips out of my hands.

Ivy's rehearsed speech echoes in my mind. Her voice gives me shivers. I'm afraid that Carmelina, who keeps swaying her gaze between Ivy and me, will spot the goose bumps on my forearms.

"Isn't Aster a Photoshop whiz?" a reporter asks Ivy.

Ivy wipes her forehead. Her hand doesn't shake, but she doesn't answer him for so long I can tell she's shocked. Her silence grows, becomes deafening. It's Dominic, of all people, who jumps to her rescue, defending Aster Redd. As he stares into the camera, I flinch.

Maybe he'll blame me. What's stopping him, after all? And technically, it would be true. But he simply apologizes to Kevin Martin for the injustice that was caused to him and publicly invites him to compete on the show.

My tepid coffee goes down the wrong pipe. I cough, then try to wipe the brownish spray from my white shirt with the used tissue I tucked into my jeans.

Carmelina leaves, returning a moment later with a clean shirt. "Here. Give me your shirt. You shouldn't let coffee stains set in."

I unbutton it and hand it over.

"You weren't aware he was going to be invited to compete?" Dad asks once she's gone.

I shake my head, too stunned to speak. Dominic has just invited a private investigator on the show. He'll get caught. *We'll* get caught. My boss puts his arm around Ivy's rigid shoulders and steers her back into the museum.

"The bank is going to repossess the apartment."

"What?" I snap out of my dazed state. "But they already pocketed the Hamptons sale." I stare at the empty walls on which used to hang masterpieces. "I thought we didn't owe them that much anymore."

Dad places his elbows on his knees and cradles his forehead.

"How much do we still owe, Dad?"

"Seven million."

"Seven?" I gasp. "I thought it was just one. When did one become seven? *How* did one become seven?"

He lifts his head up to look at me. "Back taxes. I...forgot...to declare a few sales."

"Forgot?" I yell.

His Adam's apple jostles up and down in his scruffy throat. "The apartment is worth seven million dollars. So that should settle it." Dad runs a hand over his nascent beard. In the past, he was always impeccably dressed and groomed. Now he wears high-waisted jeans and forgoes shaving. "What am I supposed to tell your mother?"

"How about the truth?"

His brown eyes are red and swollen with dread. "She'll leave me."

"She won't leave you."

"She will. She's already threatened to leave. She says I've changed."

"Stop letting yourself go, then. Woo her back."

"With what? I have no more money. I've bankrupted our business. I've left you and Chase with nothing. What sort of father am I? What sort of man am I?"

I touch my Dad's hand. "What about selling Mom's jewelry? Her engagement ring—"

"I will *not* sell your mother's things." He shakes his head, and his still-dark hair flutters around his ears. "She's already lost one house, soon two."

"So what are you planning to do? You can't borrow money

to keep up appearances. And I don't have enough to lend you, not even if I sold my Zara Mach piece."

He digs his knuckles into the inner corners of his eyes. "My life insurance policy. There should be enough in there to keep her—"

"Shut up, Dad."

He jerks. How could he not? I've never spoken disrespectfully to him. Then again, he's never suggested suicide to finance our family's lifestyle.

I stand up. "I have to get back to work. I'll find a way. In the meantime, talk to Mom. You can both move in with me until we can figure something else out, okay?"

I dash past Carmelina who stands in the doorway of the kitchen, rigid with terror.

When I get home, I dive into the pool of the apartment Dominic lends me as part of the package of working for him. Lap after lap, I think of ways to right my father's wrongs.

Ideas, all terrible ones, coil through my brain like a cloying song on repeat. The only way for me to help my parents is to continue laundering money through art for Dominic and Dean. The ties I'd felt loosening snap back into place. When I reach the point of physical and mental exhaustion, I climb out of the pool and grab a towel.

My cell phone rings. No caller ID.

"I shredded the whole fucking thing. They're not in there!" Dean yells, and I realize he means the quilt he bought at the auction, and it makes my stomach sour that he destroyed it. "She fucking stole them. The crazy bitch stole them! Or her fucking sister. Have you searched her yet?"

"Not yet."

"What are you waiting for?" he hollers.

I pull the phone away from my ear. "I was waiting for you to look through the quilt," I say calmly, "but I really doubt—"

"I heard about your little crush."

I freeze, and the towel slips out of my hands. "I don't have a *crush*."

"Whatever, Brook. I personally don't give a fuck if you do. All I care about is getting my diamonds back. If I don't get them to the D.A., he's going to convict my client. So go through her room and fucking help me, man. Fucking help me before they off me."

"Don't talk like that."

"I'm not exaggerating, Brook."

"I know I mentioned this already, but, now that he knows, ask Dom to cover what they're worth until we can find them."

"He doesn't have that sort of cash on hand. And taking a sum like that out of the bank...it'll raise eyebrows. He's already being monitored. He doesn't need to arouse more suspicion."

I step inside the penthouse and slide the door closed.

"Tomorrow, there's a pool party at your place," Dean says.

"There is?"

"Yeah. So everyone can blow off some steam. Anyway, when the contestants show up, go back to the museum and comb through her room. And if you don't find anything there, you get your ass home and frisk her. I want those fucking stones."

When he hangs up, I realize his problems are bigger than mine. Dominic phones me soon after to inform me I'm going to be hosting a pool party the next day.

"I heard," I say.

Dominic doesn't say anything for a long time, but he's still on the phone. I can hear him breathe. "We're taking the contestants out to the restaurant tonight. Dress casually."

"Okay."

"I'll see you later."

WHEN I ARRIVE at the museum dressed in black jeans and a blue shirt, Dominic and Josephine are informing the contestants about Kevin Martin's imminent arrival at the same time as J.J. is wishing everyone goodbye. He scored the lowest on the auction test. When he hugs Ivy, she tenses up in his arms. I wonder if she would tense up in mine.

I'm standing next to her when he walks off. She watches him for a long time.

"You need to get ready," I tell her.

"I'm going."

"Always hard to see someone lose," I say, because she's still surveying the doorway.

Her gaze shifts to me. "Actually, I was thinking the opposite."

When she walks away to get dressed, I find myself frowning at her frostiness. But then I remind myself of what winning this competition would mean for her.

"Brook, who is this Elise Frothington?" Josephine asks, sidling in next to me.

"Huh?"

"The woman who bought Ivy's quilt. I feel like I have seen her before, but cannot put my finger on where." She studies my face with her hawk-like eyes. "Who is she?"

"Probably a collector," I say, to lead her astray. "Or a sponsor."

"This is the first event she attends."

"Maybe the others bored her."

"*Peut-être.*"

Lincoln plants herself right next Josephine. "The clothes on this show are so gorge." She palms her purple suede skirt. "I want your life, Miss Raynoir."

"I am certain you do," Josephine says, as the rest of the contestants arrive.

There is no seating arrangement at the Italian restaurant,

yet I find myself next to Ivy. Dinner starts out nicely, especially when she snaps at my brother a few times. I shouldn't enjoy it, but I do. However, she suddenly asks me about the tear in her quilt, and the anxiety I thought I'd gotten rid of in the pool is back with a vengeance. Even Dominic grows fretful. His unease increases when Josephine asks if he's found out the source of the slanderous e-mail.

"It was sent to Brook." Perspiration beads on his forehead.

"It was encrypted," I say, when her attention lands on me.

"Can you forward it to me, Brook?"

"Sure. Remind me tomorrow," I say. The hacker Dean used was smart enough to encrypt it since we guessed the police—or Josephine—would eventually subpoena the e-mail. If only the Photoshop guy had been as smart.

"I do hope we find who sent it." She folds her napkin neatly next to her plate and rises. "*Bonne nuit*," she tells everyone, and then leaves just as Ivy returns from the bathroom.

Even though Dominic put the blame on me, he's acting more nervous than I am. Then again, I'm drowning my anxiety in wine. I've clearly had too much when I dare ask Ivy if she has a boyfriend. When she says no, I think it's a good idea to slip my palm over her lap. Not only does she cross her legs to shift my hand off, but Chase, who's seated on her other side, observes the whole thing. I glare at my empty glass of wine, wishing I could blame it for my lack of judgment, but alcohol only enhanced my stupidity.

EIGHTEEN

JOSH

I watch Ivy's press conference from my parents' couch. Mom kneads my hand throughout. I'm too nervous to tell her to stop. The implications reporters raise unsettle me so much that I don't eat a bite of the roast she's prepared.

When Heidi meets me at my place later that night, she's in a good mood, but I'm not, and my bad mood ends up spoiling our evening. She knows it's because of the twins, even though she doesn't ask. I bet she's afraid that if she mentions either of them, all we'll talk about are *them* for the rest of the night. Which is probably true. But avoiding uttering their names doesn't make my concern for them fade. If anything, it makes me retreat deeper into my mind. Heidi is pissed and settles in front of the TV to watch this alien sci-fi show I can't stand. I mean, come on, *all* the characters on the show are whiny and purple.

I go to bed before her but don't sleep while she all but

snores next to me. All night, I stare at the red digits on my alarm clock. I try counting my breaths, holding my breaths, pushing air out of my lungs, keeping it in. Nothing knocks me out. At five-thirty, I roll out of bed and go to the gym. I lift weights until my shoulders cramp and my muscles tremble, and then I buy a protein shake from the tiny concession stand on my way out.

Heidi is blow-drying her hair when I get home, whirling a thick brush through her dark blonde locks that look shot with copper and gold.

"Where were you?" she asks, setting her tools down.

"I hit the gym. Do you have time for breakfast?"

"I need to be in class in a few minutes." As she sits on the bed to tie her sneakers, she's quiet.

"I'm sorry about last night. I—"

"It's not just last night, Josh. It's all the time. Since Aster—"

I close my eyes. *Don't go there, Heidi.*

"Since Troy died," she says, "it hasn't been the same."

"I know but I care so much about you. Before all this blew up, we were good, weren't we?"

"We were."

I kneel in front of her and take both her hands in mine. She stares at me through her purple glasses. "Give us another chance. Please."

She sighs.

"I'll do better. Give me a chance to do better."

Her brown eyes become shiny. "Okay."

I shoot up so quickly that we rock backward onto the bed. Her shiny hair fans out around her head, making it look as though she were lying in a pool of melted metal.

I cup her freckled cheek. "You're so beautiful."

She giggles, so I pay her more compliments. It's the least I can do after being so distant with her. Even though she complains that she's going to be late for class, I make love to her, and it's amazing and liberating, and when she suckles my neck just as I'm finishing, I groan with pleasure.

"We should do this more often," I tell her, lying on my back with my arms cradling my head.

She slips her pink thong and jeans back on.

"Like right now. I'm ready," I say.

"I need to get to school." She climbs on top of me for one last kiss. "Dinner tonight?"

"As long as we have a do-over," I say with a wink.

"It's a date, mister."

She grabs her bag from the chair and slings it across her shoulder. "Pick me up at six? I'll be at the dorm."

"You got it."

I don't move for a long time after Heidi leaves. I feel too good to move. I haven't felt this good in days. At some point, I pass out and nap until a strident car horn startles me awake. I peel myself off the bed and take a much-needed shower. Although visiting Aster in prison is the last thing I want to do right now, it's also one of the only things I have to do. So I get dressed and head out, blasting music to make the drive out of town feel less ominous.

Instead of leading me to the visitation area, they upgrade my visit with Aster to the room they keep for attorney meetings. I take a seat on one of the iron chairs and look at the glass wall. A prison guard with a belly hanging over his belt and a mean scar through one of his eyebrows brings Aster to me. When she spots me inside, her blue eyes grow wide with alarm. Her mouth moves with words I can't hear. The guard shoves the door open, then shoves her in.

"You got fifteen minutes, Officer Cooper, then I need to take her to her shrink appointment."

Aster resembles a broomstick with her bristly hair and emaciated body. She jumps when the door shuts behind her. "Wh-what's going on? Is it Ivy?"

"Sit down."

With shaky hands, she pulls out the seat in front of me and sits.

"Aster, did you doctor the photos of Kevin Martin?"

"Who?"

"The contestant who was eliminated. Did you do it?"

"No. Why?"

"Because the media is claiming you might be behind the fake pictures."

"They're fake?"

"Are you playing dumb?"

"No!"

"Wasn't Photoshopping part of your job at the ad agency?"

"Yes, but I didn't do it."

"You promise?"

"Yes! Anything else you came to accuse me of?"

I rub the side of my neck. "How did the quilt end up—"

"Is that a hickey?" she exclaims. Her hands have stopped trembling.

"What?"

"On your neck."

"Oh, that...I cut myself shaving." Heat fills my face.

"Are you seeing someone?"

I breathe slowly, hoping to delay the inevitable. "Do you really want to know?"

Her lower lip wobbles. She bites down hard on it, then releases it and murmurs in a tiny voice, "Since when?"

"Let's not talk about this—"

"Since when?"

"A month." The lie pops out of my mouth. It's been two, but one might hurt less.

"Is it serious?"

"Aster," I whisper softly.

"Well, is it?" She's no longer whispering.

"I don't know."

"Do I know her?"

I rub the spot on my neck Aster is still gawking at.

"Who is it?" she asks.

Honesty is the best policy, right? But what if she goes after Heidi when she gets out of here? I'm an asshole. Aster isn't a murderer. I mean...in normal circumstances. How can I even be entertaining such thoughts? I'm a despicable friend. "Heidi," I blurt out.

"The floozy from Dairy Queen?"

"Don't call her that."

"You're the one who told me she slept around. She's going to give you HIV."

I forget about the hickey and about keeping my temper under control. "Goddammit, Aster! You and I are no longer together. Don't you get it? You are my *friend*."

Aster bobs in her chair, forward and backward. Her mother used to do that when she became angry. The only person who could calm her down was Ivy. She would whisper words in her ear and hold her hands without ever breaking eye contact. She called it "grounding."

I hesitate to reach over the table to ground Aster. She'll most certainly pull away. If only Ivy were here. She'd know what to do. Then again, if Ivy were here, she'd slap me for my insensitivity. I should've kept my yap shut.

Aster is somewhere else. Her eyes are glazed over like the top of Mom's mini donuts that the neighborhood kids love. The door of the visitation room opens and the fat guard steps into the small concrete chamber to collect Aster. I bet he eats tons of donuts.

"What happened?" he asks me.

Our private lives are none of his business. "Is she taking her medication?" I ask instead.

"Yeah."

"It must not have taken effect yet."

He snorts. "Because you really think medication can do much for her?"

I glower at him, animated by a strong desire to punch him. "I'll be back tomorrow. Can you tell her that, once she calms down?"

"Sure."

I stand up and wait for another guard to collect me. A short woman with a long braid down her back arrives a few minutes after Aster is taken away. She leads me back through the musty prison corridors.

My car feels like a toaster oven. As soon as I get the motor running, I pump up the air conditioning until it's louder than the music. I raise the music. Unfortunately, all the noise blasting around me does nothing to quiet my conscience, which is telling me what a total prick I am. It repeats it all the way back into Kokomo. And shrieks it even louder when I park in front of the ad agency where Aster used to work.

I take the elevator to the third-floor offices. Everything is white and clean and smells like air freshener. The receptionist, who sits behind a curved desk that resembles an outsized boomerang, recognizes me right away. She hops out of her chair and wiggles over to me on heels she's obviously not used to.

"How is she? We're all so worried. Did she really do it? Poor little sweetheart." The sentences pour out of her so quickly that I don't have time to answer any of them. "Good riddance. The criminal not Aster. Can't believe she's being convicted for it? What do you guys think at the police department?"

She's stopped talking so abruptly that I imagine she's taking a breath, but she looks at me expectantly.

"It's a complicated case," I say.

"I'd go visit her, but I'm scared of prisons. I've heard about the stuff that goes down in some. Even in the visitation areas. Besides, she'll be out soon, right?"

"We're working on it."

"I watch Ivy. I vote for her everyday. Everyone in here does. And all my Facebook friends and Twitter followers are voting for her. If they don't, I unfriend them."

Maybe I should vote against Ivy so this woman unfriends me. She's one of those people who posts something every hour on the hour, even during the night, be it pictures of cats, quotes about Jesus, or videos of babies burping.

"Wait"—she arches her unnaturally black eyebrows—"why are you here?"

"Um." I stare away from the pink bow with the articulated skeleton clipped into her black hair. "I need access to Aster's computer."

"Is this for the police investigation? Are you subpoenaing her computer? Are you taking away all our computers?"

"Just Aster's." I don't mention I have no police jurisdiction to back up my request.

She breathes a sigh of relief. "Of course. Come with me." She waddles all the way to the back of the open-space layout of the agency. Curious faces pop out from behind computer screens, but quickly duck back.

She taps on the keyboard and enters the company passcode. "All yours." She returns to her desk to greet a deliveryman who's just arrived. I bet she would've stuck around and looked over my shoulder if he hadn't.

I'm not great with computers, but I know enough to locate picture files. I sort them by date and open each one. None of them correspond to the black-and-white pictures of Kevin Martin that were leaked on national TV. I do find an entire file on Ivy's quilts. I click through them. I find the one she gave me: three shadows made of small rectangles. It's supposed to represent us, but sort of looks like my parents' shower tile. But prettier.

As I look through the folder, I come across the quilt Ivy sold Troy. I stare at the embracing figures for a long time, wondering who they're supposed to be. Did my friend have a lover? No, I would've known. It must be an idealized vision of love. That's what artsy people do. They represent ideas. Or maybe it's her mom and dad? I right click on the mouse and print out the image. The printer roars to life on the other side of the room.

I close all the open windows on her computer screen and go collect the printout. As I roll it up, two of Aster's colleagues stop by to ask questions about the case. I tell them I'm not at liberty to discuss it, because technically I'm not, and because they're busybodies. Unlike the receptionist with the skeleton in her hair, they don't care about Aster. And even her, I have my doubts. She cares too much about everyone.

In the elevator, I slip my phone out of my pant pocket to call Fred for news, but an e-mail makes me forget about my partner.

Josh—

The quilt is here...was here. It's the one I auctioned off. There was a rip in it. I think Aster did it. Can you find out why?

How did Ivy send me an e-mail? I thought she wasn't allowed access to the Internet. I shake my head. That's not what's important. What's important is that there was a rip in it.

I get an awful feeling in my gut that Aster wrecked the quilt to punish Ivy for leaving her behind. That must be why she sent it to the art school. To show Ivy how torn she was herself about being abandoned.

Brook

Ivy is inside my bedroom. She's been inside for a while now, so I knuckle the door.

"Everything okay?" I ask.

"Y-yes. Almost ready."

The door swings open and Ivy steps out. She's wearing this tiny turquoise bikini that shows off her perfect body. I'm tempted to throw a towel over her, so that nobody else can see how incredible she looks.

"That's a nice color on you," I end up saying, because I've been staring too long at her *not* to say anything.

She lifts her eyes that look as turquoise as the beads sewn on the bikini. "Thanks."

I look away from her so she doesn't think I'm sleazy, especially after last night at the restaurant. My gaze locks on the pile of clothes she's left on the armchair beside my bed. A piece of black lace sticks out.

She turns her head, but I wrap my fingers around her arms to stop her. I don't want her to see what I'm looking at.

"I'm going back to the museum to greet Kevin. Save me a swim, okay?"

"Brook? Your phone keeps—" My brother's voice makes Ivy jump away from me.

Great timing, brother.

"I'll see you outside," Ivy mumbles, stepping past me, and past Chase, who's still holding my phone out.

I swipe it out of his hand.

"It's Mom."

"You're not allowed to take phone calls," I say.

He snorts. "I didn't take it. You have Caller ID." He shakes his head.

We stare at each other for a long while. I can find no trace of the little boy I used to build Lego fortresses with, of the younger brother I would smuggle into R-rated movies when he was still a pre-teen, of the one I'd cover for when he was late coming home from dates with Diana.

Diana.

After their breakup, she came over to my apartment to vent. Chase showed up, supposedly to ask me for advice. He hadn't asked me for advice in years. Anyway, after seeing her, he ran off assuming things, and I was too offended to set him straight.

I walk into my room and slam the door closed behind me. For a moment, I just breathe. Then, when I feel somewhat calmer, I twist the lock and walk over to Ivy's clothes. There isn't much fabric to look through. I swallow hard when my fingers brush her underwear. I need to stop fantasizing about a girl who obviously doesn't like me. I fold everything back and peer inside the bag she brought with her, but it's made of mesh. Not exactly conducive to hiding things. I'm about to leave when I spot my iPad on my nightstand. I unplug it and slip it inside one of the drawers in my bathroom. I can't have contestants using it.

When I leave my bedroom, Chase is no longer in the hallway. He's lying by the pool next to Ivy. *God, is he flirting with her?* I walk up to the sliding glass windows. I can't hear them, but I can see them talking.

She doesn't like him, I reassure myself.

She doesn't like me either, though.

Heart twisting in my chest, I turn away from the pool deck and call my mother back.

"What is going on?" she yells.

"On the show?"

"Not on the show. In our lives. These two men are here from the bank. We are being evicted. Evicted, Brook!"

"Is Dad there?"

"He went out earlier, and now he's not answering his phone." My mother is hysterical. "Can you please come here? Honey, please..." She sobs.

"I'm on my way, Mom."

The elevator takes forever to go down seven stories, and the ride uptown takes even longer. I call Dominic to tell him I have a family emergency.

"Kevin's flight has been delayed anyway. Can you be at the museum in about an hour?"

"I think so."

"Good. Call me if there's anything I can do for your parents."

By the time I get home, Dad has returned too, sweaty from a jog. "You said we had two months," he's telling the bank emissaries.

"I'm sorry, Mr. Jackson, but you must take this up with your account manager. We received instructions this morning."

One of them, a young guy in a suit that's too shiny to be of good quality and a tie with an awful pattern, gawks at me. "Aren't you...?"

"On TV? Yes. Where's my mother?" I snap.

"In the living room."

Dad looks up. His dark eyes are wide with anguish, but it's nothing like the anguish lodged in my mother's face.

I sit down beside her. She leans into me and cries. As I confess everything Dad should have told her, mascara runs down her cheeks.

"How could he not tell me? How could *you* not tell me?"

"Dad was protecting you."

"You don't protect a person by not telling them the truth. Lies make people vulnerable!"

I attempt to calm her down, but it backfires. "He was trying to find a solution."

"And what? I wasn't smart enough to help?" Now, not only is she furious with Dad, but she's furious with me.

"Honey, would you like Carmelina to pack your suitcase?" Dad asks, standing in the doorway.

Mom's green eyes blaze and her mouth flattens until almost no more lip is visible. "How dare you," she shrieks, grabbing a picture frame and chucking it at him. It hits the wall, making the glass shatter and rain down over the worn parquet.

I'm so stunned by her violent reaction that I stiffen. Dad gapes at Mom, then looks down at the broken object. It's as broken as he is...as our family has become.

"I can pack my own suitcase. I have to get used to it now anyway, don't I?" She leaps off the couch and stalks off toward their bedroom.

Things crash and break inside. Ghost-faced, Dad looks to me for help, so I go after my mother inside the gray velvet room. She's staring at the mosaic of pictures of us nailed into one of the walls.

"Mom," I whisper as I wrap one arm around her slumped shoulders.

She leans into me and weeps. The top of her head fits right underneath my chin. It's fit there since I was eighteen.

I stroke her back and she quiets down. She still cries, but they're silent tears.

"I sent Sandra a message. I'm going to go live with her," she whispers, her voice cracking.

"Or you can come stay with me." Not that staying with her younger sister is a bad idea, but I want her to know I'm there for her too.

"You're in the middle of a show, Brook."

"Well at least let one of the chauffeurs drive you over."

"I don't have much of a choice, do I? One of my credit cards was declined this morning. I bet none of them work now."

I sigh.

"I knew things weren't great when we had to sell the beach house, but this"—she gestures around her—"this goes beyond my wildest imaginings." She turns toward me, swiping her palms across her cheeks, smudging the trails of mascara and staining her cheeks gray. "What else don't I know?"

That I've done bad things to keep her and Dad afloat, things I could get convicted for. I feel a presence behind me and turn to find my father standing in the doorway. "Nothing else."

My mother stares at my father for a long, hard time. Decades of shared history and unspoken blame pass like an invisible current between them.

"I'm going to my sister's place," she finally tells him.

"I heard."

"Alone."

"I understand," he murmurs.

"Alone?" I ask, because I didn't realize.

"I need time to think," she says.

Dad hunches over.

I swing my head between both of them.

"Where are *you* going to stay?" I ask Dad.

"Larry offered to lend me his guest bedroom."

That's bound to be weird for Chase since Larry is Diana's father. Then again, living with his ex-girlfriend isn't a permanent arrangement.

Dad gazes at Mom. "When I find a job, I'll start looking for a new apartment."

"A job?" I say stupidly. "Doing what?"

"Whatever I can," he says softly.

She can't leave Dad. Not right now. Not ever. "Mom—"

"Do we have anything left to give Carmelina?" she asks.

Dad takes a few crumpled twenties from his wallet.

"That's it? That's plain insulting." Mom's tone is so harsh it makes Dad shrivel. She walks to the closet, to the safe bolted into the floor.

When I was young and she opened it, I would dig through her jewelry, pretending I was a pirate who'd just unearthed a bounty. Which reminds me of the diamonds I should be searching for in Ivy's room. Screw those diamonds.

"My jewelry is still here." She sounds surprised. She yanks out the open boxes she uses to store her big rings and twinkling earrings, and tosses them on the bed. The stones glitter like the glass that shattered earlier. "Sell them, Henry. Sell everything. And give it to your sons."

"But—"

"I don't want any of it. I don't need any of it." She stares at the glistening pool of jewels, bends over, selects a necklace with a heart-shaped diamond, and walks out of the room.

"That was the first present I ever gave her," Dad croaks. His eyes shine as brightly as the pile of baubles.

"I can't," Carmelina says from somewhere in the apartment. "I can't."

A tear rolls down Dad's cheek. When Mom returns, necklace-free, she asks Dad to leave.

"Carmelina will call you when I'm gone," she says. Her green irises look phosphorescent against their red background.

Dad scrambles out of the bedroom, and I dash out after him, afraid he's going to do something stupid. He trips over the rug in the living room and falls, crumpling to the floor. Glancing back at me with wet eyes, he hoists himself up and limps out of the apartment. Waves of dread slam into me, fill me, rock me. I have just witnessed the fall of a great man.

I can't decide whether to go after him or return to Mom.

"Brook," she calls out, making my choice for me. "Don't tell Chase. I don't want him to worry."

I nod.

"I know it's his birthday the day after tomorrow. Tell him Sandra broke her ankle and I had to go help her out. And tell your father not to burden him with anything."

"How—How long will you be gone?"

"As long as it takes. Will you come out to see me after the show?"

I nod.

"Can one of Dominic's drivers truly take me out to Rhode Island?"

"Yes."

She walks over to me and hugs me tight. "I love you so, so much, honey. I'm sorry you have to go through this. If only I'd known, we could have made plans. Instead—" She breathes in through her nose. It makes her nostrils flare.

"I'm worried about Dad."

She doesn't say anything.

"Are you leaving him?" I ask.

"For a while."

"So not for good?" I feel like a seven-year-old kid, scared his mommy and daddy might not love each other anymore.

"After thirty years, you don't leave someone for good on a whim."

My throat hurts too much to speak.

"Now, go," she tells me.

"The car's downstairs when you're ready."

She tries to smile, but her steel-gray cheeks barely crease with the dimples she passed on to me.

I start walking but turn around. "You'll be okay?"

"I'll be fine. Go."

So I do. On my way out, I find Carmelina sitting in the kitchen, sobbing. "I can't take this."

Like my mother, I try to smile but just can't. "You'll break Mom's heart if you don't."

"But it's yours. For your girlfriend someday."

I shake my head. "I'd have to find a girlfriend first." I go over to her and kiss her cheek. "Give me news from time to time, okay?"

"You too."

I nod and leave. I call Dominic to ask him about using a car to take my mother to Rhode Island. Like I thought, he accepts. He tells me to hurry to the museum. After giving instructions to the driver who brought me uptown, I hail a taxi. Thankfully, the cabbie doesn't recognize me, so the ride crosstown is quiet. I attempt to phone Dad. Several times. He never picks up. Fear twisting in my gut, I tap my phone against my jean-clad thigh and instruct the cabbie to go down into the parking lot.

"It's restricted for show personnel," he says.

"I am show personnel."

"Oh." His eyes dart to his rearview mirror as he drives down the ramp. The security guard stops us, but then sees me and waves the cab through. There is only one other car parked in the underground lot—a silver Ferrari.

Gulping, I pay the cab driver and hurry into the museum and up to the contestants' quarters. The makeup room is dark. I try a switch but still no light comes on. I turn the flashlight on my phone and walk through the black space, hoping there is electricity in the tent, but it's even darker in there. A creak makes me jump.

I lift my phone and shine it right into Dean's face.

"You scared the living daylights out of me," I hiss, clapping a hand over my chest.

His eyes gleam in the darkness, more silver than gray. "I found one."

He grabs my wrist to angle my phone's light on his other hand. A small porcelain box rests in the middle of his palm. With his thumb, he flicks it open. Inside shines a diamond twice the size of the heart pendant Mom gave Carmelina.

"Ivy had it?"

"Yep. Sewn into the lining of her bag."

"Just one?" I'm still whispering even though Dean isn't.

"Don't have to whisper, man. I cut the power and no one's around. And yeah. Just one. She probably brought it to New York to sell it. Wouldn't risk flying with all of them."

"So you think she knows where the rest of them are?"

"I do."

"And if she doesn't?"

"Then her sister definitely does."

"I'm going to give this one to the D.A. as a guarantee that the others are coming, then I'm leaving for Indiana."

"To see the Discolis?"

He snorts. "Hell no. I value my life. I'm going to offer my services to Aster Redd."

"You're what?"

"I'm going to become her lawyer."

"But—Won't that look suspicious?"

"I'll tell her she's my pro-bono case of the year."

"But it's a public trial. The Discolis are bound to find out."

"You are so naïve sometimes." He belts out a sinister laugh.

"I won't actually go to trial. I only want the location of the diamonds. You're going to inform Ivy I'll be representing her sister, and then you're going to introduce me to Ivy. I'll work both sisters until I can find my stones. Because I *will* find my stones. Mark my words."

His phone beeps, which makes me jolt.

"Relax," he says without even checking it. "I'm tracking the car Dom sent to fetch Kevin. This was to tell me it's ten minutes away." He smiles. "Things are looking up for us. You might just get your commission after all."

Right, my commission... "What about the pictures?"

"You mean, the ones Sergeant Martin's wife doctored to get her husband disqualified?"

"What are you talking about?"

"I'm talking about the fact that I am a mastermind, and a mastermind finds a solution to every problem."

"Why would she ever consent to take the blame?"

"Why does anyone ever consent to do something?" When I don't come up with the answer, he tips his head to the side. "Why did *you* accept to help us? Besides for our undying friendship, that is."

Something in the way he says the last part irks me. "Money," I admit.

"Bingo. It's magical. I might've also dropped a hint that her husband was gay and sleeping around while in Afghanistan."

"What?"

"Yep. I did some homework on our little undercover buddy. His wife was plenty happy to sign the confession and take my money." He puts his hand on my shoulder and squeezes it, the same way Dominic does when he wants to give more weight to his words. "Heard about your parents. I was poor once too. Until I found my fairy godfather. Dom will take care of you until you can bounce back. Just like he took care of me when he found out about me."

TWENTY

JOSH

My coffee slops out of the Styrofoam cup as I hit the brakes a little too roughly. The security chain-link gates of Aster's prison just stalled at the halfway mark. Even though my car is small, it's not narrow enough to slip out, so I wait until the guard stationed by the DOC's only entry point can fix it. I blot the stain off my navy pants with an old napkin. It's not too visible.

As I wait, I take my small pen and my little spiral notebook out of my shirt pocket and jot down everything I learned before I forget.

- Aster put the quilt back inside the envelope she found it in. It was already addressed to New York: to the Masterpiecers.
- There were diamonds inside, or so Aster told me. She said she left them inside.

- Angela Discoli must have given Troy the diamonds. She must have hid them inside the quilt (that's why she was nervous when I asked her about the quilt). NOT WEDDING PRESENT.
- Aster thinks her sister is involved, but she's not. Right?

I stare at my little checklist until the gate screeches back to life. The armed guard gives me a thumbs up and I go through, fingers tapping my wheel, but not in time with the music blasting out of my speakers—in time with the hectic pace of my heart.

When I get on the highway, I call the police station and ask to speak to Chief Guarda.

"I'm sorry, Cooper," the officer on the phone tells me, "but he's in a meeting and can't take your call."

More like doesn't want to talk to me. I try calling Fred but he doesn't pick up either. Annoyed, I fire the car in the direction of the precinct. I have information they'll want. Which means they'll have to see me. I still want to be reinstated, but right now, it's not about my badge. It's about dismantling an organization that stretches far beyond my reach. Which is something I can't do by pursuing my little investigation alone. I need higher help, and I'm not talking about God, although a divine intervention would be much appreciated.

I park in my old spot and race into the precinct. I don't stop by the dispatch desk, even though the cop on duty—the one I had on the phone—shouts out my name, yelling for me to stop. I run up the stairs to our first-floor offices, and barge into the conference room just as the guard catches up to me.

He digs his fingers into his waist, panting. "Cooper...come on...stop."

The chief rolls the tips of his mustache between his fingers. "I tried...to...stop him."

"Didn't do too good a job now, did you?"

The officer releases his waist, and straightens up. His complexion goes from red to white in under a second. The fear of losing his job is scribbled all over his face. I'm tempted to pat his back and welcome him to the badge-less club, but don't. Picking on another officer is not my style.

"I have something big for you," I tell the chief.

He studies me, still stroking his mustache.

Fred's tiny eyes, which usually look sunk deep in his tubby face, seem to protrude as he stares at me.

"Close the door," Guarda barks, still looking at me.

My rainbow of hope sinks so quickly through me that I expect to see it pool around my leather shoes, multi-colored and foolishly shiny.

Bowing my head, I start to turn around, but the chief's voice stops me, "Not you. It's the other imbecile I want out."

I snap back around like a rubber band, head held high again.

I'm back!

After the door closes, I take a breath and recite the bullet points on my spiral notebook to Fred, Guarda, and the female officer they replaced me with. No one speaks after I finish enumerating my discoveries. When the chief pushes himself back from the table, I anticipate he's going to walk over to me and pat me on the back. Instead he crosses his legs and leans back. Not the ecstatic, proud reaction I expected.

"By running your little investigation, you disobeyed direct orders, Cooper," he says.

"I—"

"Let me finish. You knew about Angela Discoli's meeting with Troy Mann and you didn't tell us."

"I didn't know who she—"

"I said let me finish," Guarda snaps. "You penetrated the Discoli compound without backup."

I curl my fingers into fists to keep myself from asking how he knows that.

"You keep visiting Aster in prison, posing as a badge-bearing officer. I heard you even dropped by her office yesterday to look through her computer. And now you dare run into my precinct and interrupt my meeting."

I gulp and shut my eyes, bracing myself to be ripped a new one. Instead, there's silence. It echoes louder than the chief's barking.

Finally, his voice rings out again, "What do you have to say for yourself?"

I don't dare open my eyes. I don't dare speak. I barely dare breathe.

"Cooper, I'm allowing you to talk, so talk."

I crack my lids open. All three are gaping at me. "You took me off this case because I was careless about Troy Mann's file. I deserved what I got. I'm not disputing this. However, this is *my* case, and it's become even more so now that it reaches into my private life. Aster and Ivy Redd are my friends, and I can't stand around and do nothing. So whether you want me involved or not, Chief, I will be involved. The moment I figured out who the girl in the motel was, I told Fred. And then I went to visit her because I wanted to understand what she was doing with Troy Mann. She said they were lovers. Maybe that's true. I don't know. What I do know is that she startled when I spoke about the quilt, so I understood that was important to the investigation. And now I know why. They used it to transport diamonds to New York. What I still don't understand is who they were trying to pay off, or what they were buying. And that's why I came here. Because even though I can keep investigating on my own, I don't want to. I want to work with a team. I want to work with you again. You told me you don't play by the rules. Well, apparently, I don't either."

I watch Guarda's lips. I'm waiting for them to curl in displeasure, but instead, they curve upward.

"How long did it take you to come up with that speech?" he asks.

"Uh. I...I came up it with it n-now."

"Well then, bravo. It deserves some applause." He claps.

Hesitant at first, Fred and the blonde chime in. When Guarda stops, the two others stop.

"Sit. We have a lot to discuss," he says.

I scramble into a chair.

"This is going to be hard for you to hear, but if you're going to be part of this task force again, then you need to be aware of our suspicions."

"Okay." My leg shakes and my foot taps the ground.

"We don't think your friends are that innocent."

"What?"

He rocks against the springy backrest of his chair, bobbing like the baby-pink awning of Mom's bakery when there's a lot of wind. "We have two theories. One, that Ivy knew about her quilt being used to launder mafia goods, and that her cut was getting a place on the show."

My mouth gapes. I should snap it shut, but I can't, so I let it hang open.

"And two, that Aster, who's a little genius with computers—but you know that already—well, we think that she forged those pictures to get her on the show."

"I checked her computer."

"We know. We collected it from her office. It's being picked apart as we speak."

"She didn't do it. I checked all the files."

"Did you check the deleted files?" he asks. "Did you check her emails? Did you check the ROM memory?"

"No. I—"

"Well, we are. We're covering all our bases. And Ivy is being interviewed this afternoon by our liaisons in New York."

"Interviewed?" I repeat stupidly, picturing my poor friend in an interrogation room.

"We want to find out how many players we're dealing with."

They're making a mistake. Ivy and Aster are not involved. *Right?* But what if they are? Ivy really wanted to get on that show, and Aster would do just about anything to help her sister. A chill spider-crawls up my spine. "Do you know what the diamonds were used for?"

"Little Diego, Angela's youngest brother, has been convicted in New York for killing a prostitute." Guarda grins. "Although I believe that's the slightest of the crimes that make him rotten, at least he was caught. I'm willing to bet you anything those diamonds are going to pay off a prison guard to help him escape. We've informed the warden at his jail, who says they've tightened security."

"But who at the Masterpiecers is connected to the Discolis?"

Guarda pinches his lips so hard it looks as though he's vacuum-packed them. "The agents in New York are working on that. They don't care to swap info."

"Wouldn't working together be more beneficial to the case?" I ask.

"Why don't you go ahead and tell them that?" he says, his voice as tight as his lips. Slowly, he unseals them. "We don't need them, right, team?"

Fred and my replacement nod.

"*They* need *us*. It might take them a while to realize it, and until they do, we're pursuing our investigation. All they have right now are a bunch of puzzle pieces. What we have is a picture that's missing a few corners. About one of those corners,

Claire...have you made any progress tracking down Elise Frothington?"

"Elise Frothington?" I ask.

"She's the woman who bought the quilt at the show's auction."

Claire tightens her long, blonde ponytail. "From the footage I received, she arrived at the museum in a taxi cab. I ran the plates and got us a name and number. Apparently the cabbie picked her up from the Four Seasons Hotel, where she was checked in under Elise Frothington and paid cash. She checked out right after the auction was over."

"Cooper, Claire, get everything you can on this woman, down to the brand of toilet paper she uses to wipe her ass."

I give a jerky nod.

"Fred, you get me an update on Diego's criminal case proceedings, and phone the prison. See how he's behaving." He rubs his hands together excitedly. "Finally, we're getting somewhere."

We *are* getting somewhere, but it's not anywhere I want to get to if the twins are truly, knowingly involved.

TWENTY-ONE

Brook

When two detectives waltz into the museum after today's test, I assume they're heading for me. I back up into the crowd, bumping into someone. The detectives don't even look my way. They approach Ivy, and then they take her away. Being the coward that I am, I don't try to help her. I stay frozen and quiet, unlike Dom, who stands up to the detectives. And then I flee to the second floor and pace the empty galleries even though I'm supposed to be working the crowd below. I can't bring myself to head downstairs and make small talk.

I twirl my phone between my fingers as I stare at the shadowy paintings around me. I crossed paths with one security guard, but it was two galleries down from where I am now. No one is watching me here. I find myself in front of Jasper Johns's *White Flag*, and it reminds me of Ivy. Everything is starting to remind me of her. I drop on one of the benches and yank at my hair in irritation. I would shout or punch something if I weren't afraid it would trigger an alarm.

I should go to the station and confess, but that would mean bringing Dom and Dean down with me. And my parents...what would they do if I were to go to prison? Because that's probably where I'd be sent. After all, I received mafia money. I accepted bribes. Chase would hate me because the show would probably be terminated if Dom were to be convicted. And Ivy...she'd be free, but she would despise me too.

I am *so* close to cracking.

Even though I try to bite back my anger, it rips up my throat and through my parted lips. I ball my fists and punch the bench. Screw the security cameras. Screw everything and everyone!

I call Danny the driver and ask him to go pick up Ivy. "Phone me when she's in the car with you," I tell him before hanging up and calling my father. "Hey, Dad," I say, attempting to temper my voice to sound normal. "How's life at Larry's?"

"Can I call you later? I'm in the jewelry district," he says. He's pawning off Mom's jewels. Which is good. At least he's not dangling off the Queensboro Bridge.

"Sure." I hang up. "I'm fine. Thanks for asking," I mutter after ending the call. I shouldn't be bitter with Dad, but I can't help myself. No one cares about me.

My phone rings. I stare at the screen. When Diana's name pops up, I'm tempted to let it go to voicemail, but maybe talking to someone on the outside is exactly what I need. "Hey, there," I say.

"Brook Jackson, what the hell is going on?" she shouts.

"You mean, Dad moving in with you?"

"Yeah. *That.* And on the freaking show? What the hell is happening on the freaking show? One of the contestants just got *arrested?*"

"She didn't get arrested. She was taken in for questioning."

"For what?"

For nothing. "They're still looking into those doctored photos."

"How's Chase doing?"

"He's fine."

"And you?" she asks, her voice softer. "How are you doing?"

I was wrong. Someone does care about me. My brother's ex. "I'm okay."

"You don't sound okay."

"You can tell over the phone?"

"Brook, I've known you for-freaking-ever. Your father's here with me, your Mom's in Rhode Island, and you're hosting a super messed-up show. Don't pretend you're okay. At least not with me."

Silence stretches between us, interrupted only once by a car horn. Diana must be walking around the city. I lean forward and hang my head in my free hand. I close my eyes, wishing I were outside too...wishing I were far away.

"Is Chase talking to you at least?" she asks.

"No."

"Does he still think—"

"That we hooked up? Yeah."

"Now would be a good time to tell him the truth."

"I'm sick of having to explain myself to everyone."

"So you'd rather let him assume things?"

"He wouldn't believe me, Diana."

"Then I'll tell him."

"I thought you never wanted to speak to him again."

"Your dad is living at my house. I don't think I'll be able to avoid Chase once the competition is over."

My caller ID beeps. Danny's calling. Ivy must be on her way back. "Diana, I have to go. I'll call you soon, okay?"

"Call me whenever you want."

"Whenever I can," I correct her. Perhaps, if I were to go to jail, Diana's father, who's an extremely successful hedge fund manager, would bail me out. The thought winches up the hem of the bleak veil that has settled over my future.

Danny informs me that he's just dropped Ivy off, and I sprint down the large stone stairs into the almost deserted lobby. I spot Ivy entering the elevator and run faster, just managing to slide my hand between the closing doors.

Cara, Ivy's assistant, blinks at me.

"I need a word with our contestant," I say.

It takes her a moment to figure out that I'm dismissing her. She steps out of the elevator while I step in. As the elevator begins to rise, I tug on the red emergency lever.

Breathing hard from my run, I finally wonder what got into me to trap Ivy in a steel box. She must think I'm crazy.

"What?" she snaps.

But I'm not crazy. I'm concerned. I want her to leave the show. Staying will only make things worse for her. "Dominic's worried about you," I lie. "He's worried you have a lot on your plate. Perhaps too much. He thinks that maybe you should..."

"Maybe I should what?"

I gaze at the floor. She's angry—and rightfully so. I flick my eyes upward but still can't bring myself to look straight at her face. *Stop being such a coward...* Slowly, very slowly, I lock my eyes on hers. "He thinks that maybe you should drop out."

"Drop out? Of *The Masterpiecers*? No...no way. I want to stay. I *need* to stay."

"Ivy, you're doing well, but—"

"But what?"

But bad things are bound to happen if you stay. "But there's a lot to think about. Between the media, and Kevin, and your sister. You should see what's being written up in the newspapers." I'm a wuss, that's what I am.

"I'm bringing the show bad press. Is that what you're getting at?"

"Well...not exactly." I rake my shaky fingers through my hair. "Yes."

She tilts her head to the side. "Don't you know journalists love scandals?"

"I know that, but—"

"They don't intimidate me, Brook. And neither does Dominic. I'm sorry about the bad press, but I'm not leaving the show. This is my one chance. Maybe you don't understand because you've never had to worry about where your next meal came from, but I *can't* drop out. And I'll say this again however many times I need to: I had *nothing* to do with Kevin's pictures." She shakes her head, and her glimmering hair flutters against her bare, burnished shoulders. "You know, for a second there, when you cornered me, I thought you were going to ask me how I was doing. I thought you were worried about me. But I guess people like you, like Dominic, like Josephine, only worry about themselves."

"Don't say that." I jolt forward. "I *am* worried about you. The situation sucks, Ivy. Really, it does."

"I'm still not leaving. If you want me out, you'll have to disqualify me."

She shouldn't want to stay; she shouldn't want to endure the media scrutiny and the nastiness everyone on the show doles out on her!

"That wouldn't be fair," she adds, her voice raspy.

Life is not *fair, Ivy.* That's what I want to tell her, but perhaps I should let her dream. Just because I'm living a nightmare doesn't mean she has to take part in it. I could protect her from now on. She's so close I can feel the heat from her body seep into mine. I can hear her heartbeats thunder in the silent, suspended space.

"The public's vote counts for something," she says. "Now, can you please switch the elevator back on?"

Before I let her leave, I need to know what the detectives

wanted, but instead of asking her point blank, I mumble a stupid question, "Could Aster have had anything to do with Kevin's pictures?" A question I already know the answer to.

"I doubt it."

"But you're not sure? She's your sister—"

"If I remember correctly, you had no clue your brother entered the competition," she counters.

I frown. "I did know. His girlfriend told me."

"The one you screwed?"

Shocked that Chase would confide something so intimate to her, I blurt out, "You know about that?"

"Yeah."

I breathe in slowly. And breathe out even slower. Anger at my brother fills me so quickly that I want to punch the wall. My hands turn into fists. Dean used to tell me that my brother was a spoiled brat. The few times he came over to visit me at Duke, if he didn't want to do what we had planned, I'd cancel everything for him. I never felt it was a great sacrifice on my part, but Dean saw it as such because, when I returned to New York during holidays, Chase wouldn't alter *his* plans for me.

Thinking about Dean reminds me about the conversation we had yesterday afternoon in the contestants' tent. "I have a great lawyer."

"Are you threatening me?"

I blink. "I meant for your sister, Ivy."

"Oh."

"And he'd be free."

"Really?" She bites her lower lip. In the darkness, her teeth seem phosphorescent against her red mouth. "Is he free even if I decide to stay on the show?"

"Yes."

"Does he work pro bono?"

"No. He's a friend."

"Why would you do that?"

I swallow. Hard. "So you can forgive me for being disrespectful toward you."

"I don't know what to say."

"Just say yes, and I'll make the call."

As I tug the lever back up to free her, she releases her lip and lets out a smooth breath. "Okay."

The lights snap back on, blindingly bright. I lift my fingers to her face and brush a strand of hair off her cold cheek.

"I'll give him a call right away," I murmur.

I tuck the pale strand behind the shell of her ear that's as soft as peach fuzz.

"Thank you," she whispers back.

The elevator doors open. For a second, I hold my breath, hoping she won't step out, wishing there existed a button on the elevator dashboard marked *Elsewhere*.

But there is no magic button.

And wishes don't come true.

Her black lashes swoop down over her glorious eyes as she turns and walks away.

TWENTY-TWO

JOSH

I grab the Chinese take-out Heidi asked me to pick up. It smells like hot oil and sweet garlic. Before I've even made it to my car, a spot of grease blooms on the brown paper bag. I wince, reminded of my awful Hamster days. Fatty Chinese food was my favorite back then. I pull an old newspaper from my trunk, lay it on the passenger seat, and position the grubby bag on top.

As I pull out of the Panda Express parking lot, my phone lights up with a call from Mr. Mancini, the twins' nosy neighbor. I bet he wants to ask me if Aster killed the guy in cold blood, or maybe he wants to complain about the noise his upstairs neighbor's baby makes at night. I'm not a disturbance cop, yet that's how he's treated me since I got my badge. When he calls me again, I assume it's more important than the kid who doesn't sleep through the night.

"Hello, Mr. Mancini," I say politely. "How can I help you?"

"You have to come over right away."

"Did something happen?"

"Would I call you if nothing had happened?"

Yes. "What is it?"

"I can't tell you over the phone. Never know who's listening."

No one is listening. "Can it wait until tomorrow morning?"

"Sure, but the person could be gone by then."

"What person?"

He grunts with impatience. "The one inside the twins' apartment."

"There's someone in their apartment? Who?"

"Would I be calling you if I knew who it was?"

"I'll be there in a few minutes. Stay in your house, okay?"

"Yeah yeah. Just hurry."

So I hurry. Even though I don't have flashers on my personal car, I drive as though I've turned them on. I even go through two red lights. When I come to a stop in front of Mancini's ground-floor apartment, my tires screech.

Before my finger grazes the doorbell, he unlocks the door, holding a rifle in his liver-spotted hands.

"I loaded my hunting rifle," he says, swinging it toward me so I can see it.

I drag the nozzle away. "I'm sure that's unnecessary."

"You have your gun?"

I tap the holster at my waist.

"What is that? A Colt?" He wrinkles his long nose. "I'm keeping mine. Now, let's go." He shuts the door.

"But—"

"Don't you dare tell me to stay inside. *I* saw the intruder, so *I* get to go too."

I open my mouth to say *no*.

"I was a bank manager back in the day," he says, "and we had a hold-up once. And I saved everyone because I brought my shotgun to work that day. And before you ask, I have a license to carry." He's breathing so heavily that his nostril hairs quiver. "The only reason I called you is because I know you got a key to the Redd girls' place."

I nearly snort, but stop myself because Mr. Mancini has narrowed his fog-colored eyes.

"Now let's stop making a spectacle of ourselves. Go open the door."

I dig my keys out of my jeans' pocket. "If we find anyone," I whisper, "you can't shoot them."

"Stop your yappin'. We're gonna be found out," he hisses.

Grabbing my gun, I plunk my key in the lock and twist it. I push the door open carefully, senses on high alert. Gun pointed, I scan the dark living room with my eyes and my ears. No sound. No movement.

Tailed by Mr. Mancini, whose rifle is hazardously swinging this way and that, I creep toward Ivy's studio in the veranda. The place is a mess. All the drawers have been tossed. Fabric litters the floor and her sewing machine is toppled over. The room reminds me of our lawn the night me and my buddies decided it would be fun to TP the large oak tree in our back-yard. It had been much less fun the following morning when Mom asked me to clean it all up—even the pieces stuck in the top-most tree branches.

Something crashes. Like glass. Heart punching my ribcage, I run out. Mancini is cursing. "Knocked this vase over with the barrel of my rifle."

I widen my eyes and fling my finger against my lips. Stealthily, I check the two bedrooms in the back. I don't have to open any closet doors as they all hang open already. Clothes are everywhere. The dresser drawers have been pulled out. I race to the small bathroom, the last room in the house. I flick the light on.

The cabinet is wide open and the medication bottles have

all been opened and emptied. A rainbow of assorted pills surrounds the tossed toothpaste tubes and face creams on the yellow bathmat. I crouch down and pinch the expensive perfume bottle I gave Aster at Christmas. I hold it up to the light and whirl it around slowly, looking for prints. Nothing. The person was wearing gloves. I lay the bottle back on top of the messy heap. Mancini is standing in the narrow hallway behind me. He peers into one of the bedrooms.

"You think it's a random break-in?" he asks.

"No."

"Anything missing?"

"I don't know." The scattered pills draw my attention. Whatever this person was looking for could fit inside a pillbox— *The diamonds!* I squeeze both sides of my face with my palms, before rising from my crouch.

"What's the point of entry?" Mancini asks.

"Aster's window," I say without hesitation.

I traipse back down the corridor and straight into Aster's room where the butterfly wallpaper has turned yellow and is peeling off the walls. Her hung window is closed, but when I tug on it, it slides right up. "The lock's been broken for ages."

"Not too smart of Aster to leave it broken."

"The only option was to change the whole thing, and that was expensive."

Mancini stares around the room. "She kept it the same."

"The same?"

"As her mom. I came over ages ago. The girls were seven or eight at the time. I helped her fix a leak. It was before she turned loopy. Whatever happened to her? She still in the loony bin?"

"She passed away five months ago."

"Oh. I didn't know."

I cock an eyebrow. The man who knows everything didn't know the twins lost their mother?

"Is that where they took Aster? To the batty house?"

"Aster's in jail. Don't you read the papers?"

"I've been feeling under the weather. You know, pancreatic cancer." He shrugs as though he told me he had a common cold.

"I'm so sorry."

"At my age, it progresses slowly, so I'll probably die of natural causes."

"Do you have any family, Mr. Mancini?"

He rotates his knobby fingers around the barrel of the gun. "I had a daughter." A few tears trickle into his wrinkles. I turn around so he can wipe them. He sniffles once, then clears his throat. "We should call it in."

"We should," I say, holstering my gun.

"Well, what are you waiting for?" He's back to being his usual sweet self.

As I take out my cell phone, he leans against his big gun, which he's rested on the floor like a cane.

"Don't you have a radio-thingy?"

"Not in my off-duty vehicle."

I call the station to report the robbery. Fifteen minutes later, a cruiser careens onto the street. Claire and Fred step out of it. They interview Mancini, and then Claire walks him back to his place and calls another unit to come and run prints and document the break-in.

"Is anything missing?" Fred asks me before the crime scene technician arrives.

I shake my head no. "But it's a mess, so I can't tell. And I tried not to touch anything, but my prints are already everywhere."

"Don't worry, Coop," he says, staring at my hands that I have clasped together.

They're shaking. I'm shaking. I hadn't even realized it. I stuff them inside my pockets and watch as both cops weave around the apartment.

"You think it's connected to the case?" Claire asks, squatting to inspect the pills on the bathmat. Her blonde ponytail swooshes around her shoulders as she straightens back up.

"They were looking for the diamonds," I whisper.

"Didn't Aster say they were in the quilt?" Claire asks.

"I think she lied to me." I grab my car keys out of my pocket and make to leave but Fred stops me. "I need to go see her, man."

"It's the middle of the night. They probably won't let you see her. Besides, what are you planning to do? Threaten her until she breaks? Think this through, Coop."

"I need to know where she hid them, so I can check if they were found, before more people rummage through her stuff."

"Visiting her in the middle of the night will freak her out. And freaked out people don't confess. Especially..." Fred's voice dies off.

"Especially what?"

"Especially if those people are...unstable."

Although I wince, Fred's right. If she lied to me, then her mind isn't functioning right. The real Aster, the one who takes her medication, she trusts me.

Brook

As the contestants build art from sand and grass and wood, I stare out at the ocean that rolls gray-blue waves onto the shore. I've been to better beaches, I've looked out on more beautiful seas, but being whipped by salt spray and briny sunshine feels, nonetheless, incredible. I can almost forget the show is under scrutiny, that my family is destitute, that my parents split-up, that a PI squats a few feet away weaving a rope while surveying Ivy.

"A thousand dollars for your thoughts?" Dean asks, sidling in next to me with the stealth of a wildcat.

"A thousand dollars would be nice right now," I reply, keeping my gaze on the frolicking waves.

"Here," he says.

I glance down at his outstretched hand. "I was kidding, Dean." We're standing far enough away from the crowd that no one can see the flattened and folded hundred-dollar bills. As he tucks the money back inside the pocket of his pricey pantsuit, I ask, "So what's the plan? You have one, right?"

He stares out at the ocean, which makes his eyes appear steelier, in spite of the bright sunshine. "I didn't find anything last night," he says, instead of answering my question. "I looked everywhere. I checked the freezer, the oven, their underwear drawers, the pill bottles...you should see how many they have. Pills for everything. I even brought some back." He shakes something. I see the name Aster Redd on the label. "A few of these can knock someone unconscious almost instantly."

I look up at him. "Dean..."

"I'm not going to use them on myself," he says, thinking I'm calling him out on his drug habit. I'm not. Although it would be nice to see him sober. "I'm going to slip some in Kevin's drink. Get him to talk. And then I'll plant the bottle somewhere easy to find. When he comes out of his medicated stupor, he'll have forgotten about me, but he'll have this little reminder." He jiggles the bottle. "It'll get him off our scent." His eyes are wild, like the foamy crests in the distance.

"If you do that—"

"It will get him sniffing around Ivy instead? That's what you were going to say, wasn't it?"

"He's already convinced she's involved."

"Better her than us, right? Besides, if she's innocent, she'll manage to prove it."

I want to tell Dean to go to hell with his pills and Machiavellian plan, but Dominic is staring at us and so is Josephine who's giving an interview. A soft breeze makes her white-blonde hair flutter around her long, pallid neck.

"Introduce me to Ivy tonight, okay?" Dean says.

I drag my gaze away from Josephine. Even though it kills me, after a stilted moment, I nod. "Be careful. There are cameras everywhere."

Far behind Dean, Ivy spins blue beachgrass around slender twigs. She's concentrating so hard that she's biting her lip.

"Josephine asked about Elise Frothington," I tell him.

"Dom told me. She won't find anything. And even if she does, my mother's allowed to purchase art."

"She is, but not under an alias. Why couldn't you have paid someone else to buy it? Someone *not* related to you."

"Because the only person I trust entirely is my mother."

I cast a sideways glimpse at him. I sense there's an insinuation. However peeved I am by it—after everything I've done—Dean is right: his mother would do absolutely anything for him. And not just because he's secured her a generous alimony and a mansion in Palm Beach.

"Where's your ring?" he asks.

I stare down at my bare pinkie. "I forgot it at home."

"You forget it a lot these days. Are you embarrassed to be associated with me?" He fiddles with the gold bar that holds his poppy-red tie flat against his dress shirt. For all the confidence Dean exhibits, deep down, he's insecure.

"I can't believe you're wearing a tie here," I say, to change the subject.

"After six years, you can't believe it?" He smiles, but it seems contrived. "I just spotted Kelley."

"Who?"

"Kevin's lawyer."

"Here?"

"Yeah. As your sugar mama's guest. Dom told her to invite him so I could speak to him."

I bristle. "Madame Babanina is not my sugar mama."

Dean's smile grows wider, taunting. "Perhaps you should ask her to be. You could use a sugar mama right now."

"No way."

Dean chuckles, squeezes my shoulder, then trots toward Mr. Kelley, a ruddy-faced man seriously lacking a neck.

ALTHOUGH I KEEP an eye on my friend throughout the afternoon, I don't see him again until after Herrick gets eliminated, until after I offer Ivy thirty thousand dollars to buy her web—money I don't have.

Her eyes shine at my proposition. When I feed my fingers through hers to shake on our deal, the beach empties. It's an illusion, I know, but what an illusion it is. I wish we were the last ones left on this beach, just me and this beautiful barefoot girl dressed all in white.

"What are we shaking hands to?" Patrick, the photographer, asks, intruding on our moment.

Startled, Ivy pulls her hand out of mine.

"I've just bought my first Ivy Redd piece," I tell him, trying to slow my thundering heart before he can capture it on camera.

Thankfully, he snaps a picture of her—not of me. The flash makes her blink.

"The web?" he asks.

"The Web," I repeat, smiling down at Ivy. "Shall we call it that?"

"Sure."

"I might not be the first owner of a Redd original, but I'm certainly the luckiest because I saw it come to life under my very own eyes. How many collectors can claim that?" I tell Patrick, all the while watching Ivy.

She's looking beyond me now, at Kevin and Mr. Kelley, who are talking with Dean. His gaze slides to mine and he tips his chin. He wants me to bring Ivy over to him. I grip her arm gently, which makes her look away from the three men. I don't want to take her there. I want to drag her off the beach and tuck her away somewhere safe until the night is over...until the show is over. But of course I can't do that. She'd think I was a psycho.

Goose bumps rise on her skin under my palm.

"Excuse us, Patrick," I say, still holding on to her. "I have someone I'd like to introduce to my contestant." Hoping the goose bumps are a reaction to my touch, I rub my thumb over her soft skin, but stop when we reach Dean. And then I let her go. "Ivy, I'd like you to meet Dean Kane, my dear friend and the lawyer who will be defending your sister."

She frowns as she shakes his hand.

"And this is Mr. Kelley," I tell her, gesturing to Kevin's lawyer.

She politely shakes his hand too.

"I should get back to Madame Babanina. She doesn't like to be left alone," Kevin's lawyer says. "Mr. Martin, I am deeply sor—"

Kevin, whose chin is tucked into his neck, doesn't wait for him to finish his sentence before traipsing away. I eye Dean whose lips cock up on one side with a shameless smile.

"Brook, may I speak to Ivy privately? I'd like to discuss her sister's case," he says.

"Sure, but don't bore her with too many details."

I watch them set out along the beach and keep them in my line of vision until they return. This might make me an awful friend, but I don't trust Dean with her. Later, when she parts ways with Dean to sit at the contestants' table, I take a much-needed break from spying and head to the luxury port-o-potties, where I am ambushed by the divorcée. She comes at me so quickly and so suddenly that I find myself locked in her embrace. I try to press her away, but her hands tighten around my back, her sharp nails ploughing into the fabric of my shirt like the talons of a vulture.

"Madame Babanina, please..." I try to say, but she squashes her lips against mine.

I was taught to be polite, but I don't feel like being polite right now, so I shove her off.

Although her bangs cover her forehead, I can tell she's frowning.

"I'm sorry, but I have a girlfriend," I lie.

She smirks. "And I have a boyfriend. Two even." She raises her face toward mine again and plants a short kiss on my lips. "I don't mind."

"I do."

"What a shame. What a shame." Keeping the smile up, she winks and walks away.

I'm so stunned it takes me a moment to gather my composure. And when I do, I almost wish I hadn't, because in front of me, knee-deep in the ocean, my brother has his arms wrapped around Ivy's waist.

And he's kissing her.

My heart holds still, and then it shatters like the frame Mom threw at Dad. I tear my gaze away, but still I see their kiss. I recede into the shadows and stagger away from them, from the crowd. Minutes later, when I think I've succeeded in escaping everyone, I come across Kevin and Dean sitting on the beach, sipping drinks and chatting like old friends. I crouch behind a sand dune to stay out of sight.

Fireworks explode overhead. It's the fireworks I organized for Chase's birthday. My present to him. I hope he hates them, because I certainly do. Everyone on the beach is staring heavenward except Kevin, who's now slumped against Dean's shoulder. Even though more rockets erupt overhead, I keep my gaze on Dean, who is struggling to stand. He pulls Kevin up and slings his arm around his shoulders, then slowly, losing his footing a few times, he walks over to the ocean.

What is he doing? I scream inwardly.

A chill inches up my spine as he wades into the surf, dragging Josephine's private investigator along. When Dean lets go of Kevin and the big man topples facedown into the water, I rocket out of the sand dune. Kevin floats away, drifting atop the waves like an unmoored boat.

He's going to drown!

Dean rubs his hands against his suit that is soaked up to his knees. He scans the beach, and his eyes lock on mine.

No. NO! Killing the PI wasn't the plan! My angry, appalled thoughts teeter on the edge of my tongue, but don't spill out.

As though he didn't just drown a man, he pulls out his checkered pocket square and polishes the pill bottle. Then he drops it on the sand, and plods unhurriedly back toward the thick crowd who's too mesmerized by the glittery sky to realize what's happened.

I tear my gaze off him and stumble across the beach, eyes skirting the water for Kevin, hoping that it's not too late to save him. Between the people swimming and the darkness, I can't him pick out. What I can pick out is the incriminating prescription bottle. I swipe it as the first scream pierces the night.

JOSH

"You know, you're making one of my childhood dreams come true," Heidi tells me, as we hop over a stream.

"You dreamt of sexcapades as a kid?" I tease.

"No, silly. Camping."

"You've never been camping?"

"Never."

"So this will be a first for you?"

She nods.

"I like firsts."

She rolls her eyes. I try to kiss her, but instead I stub my toe against a rock and rock backward, taking Heidi down with me. My enormous backpack breaks my fall, and my body cushions hers. I readjust her tilted sunglasses, then wrap my arms around her and enjoy the moment.

She grins down at me. "Nice move, hotshot. Have you been practicing?"

"Yep. At the precinct. On Fred. He's a bit harder to catch, though."

She laughs. She's never met my partner, but knows his weakness for junk food.

I smile, bring her face closer to mine, and place a chaste kiss on her curved lips. "You're real pretty, you know that?"

"I know. Guys throw themselves at me all the time. It's exhausting." I can see her wink through her dark shades.

"At least you're not vain."

"At least there's that."

She kisses me, and her tongue slips into my mouth and caresses mine. Everything in me tightens and hardens, and if it weren't illegal to have sex in a public place, I would have my way with Heidi on our shaded patch of hill underneath the purpling sky with the gurgling stream in the background.

"Should we pitch our tent out here?" she asks, coming up for air.

"Yes." I stand up abruptly, fueled by the idea of getting our shelter up to pursue our make-out session in private.

"Never seen anyone so excited to build a tent," she says, latching on to my extended hand. I pull her up, and she dusts the back of her bare legs and the bottom of her khaki shorts with her freckled hands.

"Setting up camp has little to do with my *excitement*."

She whistles a song as I pull the lightweight dome tent out of the backpack and toss it in the air. It opens up and clicks in all the right places.

While Heidi secures the pegs into the ground, I unroll the blow-up mattress and puff air into it.

"Stephanie told me she was selling Troy's Cadillac. I know you have a thing for vintage cars—"

"I'm not interested." My stomach churns at the mention of Troy Mann.

Heidi nods, but her mood turns gloomy. I tuck a loose

strand of hair behind her ear. "For the rest of this weekend, let's not talk about anyone but ourselves, deal?"

She hoists up a small smile. "Deal."

"Did you bring the sleeping bag?"

She taps her rucksack.

I shove the puffed-up mattress inside the tent and cover it with the sleeping bag. When I crawl back out of the tent, Heidi's popping the lid off Tupperware containers and setting them out around a bottle of wine.

"Did you cook?"

"In my dorm room? No. But I tried to buy wholesome stuff since my boyfriend worries about what goes inside his body."

"I'd rather not revisit my Hamster days. Shoot me."

"And I'd rather do other things to you than shoot you."

Grinning, I hold the tent flap up. "Then after you, *mademoiselle*." I don't think I pronounce it right, but it makes the corners of her mouth lift as she crawls inside. I scuttle in after her and zip up the tent.

When she tugs off her tank top before I even have time to lie back, I think sacrificing my cell phone and access to the news for two days is the smartest decision I've made in my life. At any rate, half of me thinks so.

ON SUNDAY MORNING, the sky cracks open and our little tent is battered with so much rain that the air in the tent turns suffocating. In minutes, Heidi and I are packed up and running toward the campsite facilities.

"You kids forget to check the forecast?" the guy behind the desk asks us the second we step inside. He sports a beard my father would kill for, dense and evenly trimmed.

"Yeah," Heidi says. Her long hair is stringy with water that's bleeding into the collar of her tank top.

"Want to rent one of our cottages?" he asks. "I got only one left."

"How much is it?" I try not to make a habit of digging into my savings, but if it can buy me more time with Heidi, then—

"A hundred and twenty bucks. You gotta pay up front."

"What?" I choke. "A hundred and—" My voice dies off when I sense Heidi's disappointment. "Is food included at least?"

"No, man."

"Can you make it a hundred?"

"No. If you don't take it, someone else will. At a hundred and twenty bucks," he repeats, leaning his beefy forearms on the wooden desk. A barbed wire tattoo wraps around one of them.

"One-twenty is perfect," Heidi says.

I wrench my gaze off the guy's inked arms and onto Heidi's hand that's brandishing a credit card. Before Tattoo can grab it, I say, "Put that away, will you?"

After I pocket my receipt and the key to the cabin, I study the layout map scotch-taped to the counter. The door chime rings and a couple that resembles drowned rats dashes in and asks for a cabin.

Tattoo hoists up an eyebrow. I'm expecting him to say he doesn't have any, but instead he says, "Got one last one."

"Last one, my ass," I mutter as Heidi shoves me out of the cabin.

We take shelter under the roof that juts a couple feet out.

"Where's our cabin?" Heidi asks, scanning the campgrounds hidden behind sheets of rain.

"Fifth to the right."

The people who came in after us peek outside. "We're better off waiting it out in here. Did you hear what happened on *The Masterpiecers* last night?" the woman says right as the door seals shut.

My ears prick up at the mention of the show. I touch the doorknob to find out what happened, but Heidi claps my arm.

"You promised."

"But what if—"

"What if Ivy got disqualified?" she supplies.

That's not the thought that entered my mind. Granted she doesn't know about my investigation.

"Will it change anything if you find out tomorrow?" Her lips are squashed together as though she's just sucked on a Sour Power Straw.

With a sigh, I release the doorknob. I pray Ivy hasn't been disqualified, and then I pray even harder that nothing bad happened to her. What if—

"Race you," Heidi says, grabbing my hand and jerking me into the rain.

Shoving all the *what ifs* out of my brain, I run along.

Brook

Even though I tried to sleep when I got home from Fire Island, I couldn't. Every time I shut my eyes, Dean was there, leading Kevin into the foamy water, pushing him under. After tossing and turning, I get up, pull on a pair of swimming trunks, and dive into the cool water of my pool. I swim until I'm exhausted, until my muscles hurt more than my head, until I've rinsed Troy and Kevin's blood off of me. No one was supposed to die, yet two people are gone. How many more before this is over?

The sun crests on the horizon, tingeing the city orange and pink and the dark waters of the Hudson River navy blue. Below me, the Highline is coming to life as New Yorkers ford the suspended deck, walking by landscaped clusters of flowers and trees, clutching thermoses of coffee and pastries wrapped in paper napkins. I enjoy the view from up here, just like I enjoyed watching my stick insect slink around his terrarium.

As I pour myself a bowl of cereal, my mother calls. She heard the news. She's horrified. I bet she'd be even more horrified if she knew it wasn't a suicide—that's what it was ruled after Kevin was fished out. I ask her when she's coming home. Instead of answering, she tells me to wish a happy birthday to my brother.

Right...

Even though I have no claim to Ivy, I'm pissed that he kissed her. He should've known, should've sensed I liked her, but my brother only feels what he wants to feel. If he knew me at all, he wouldn't still be convinced I hooked up with Diana.

Dominic phones to tell me we are taking another day off filming that will end with a dinner at "the place I'm lending you." Granted, it's not *my* place, but *the place I'm lending you* sounds downright threatening, like he's reminding me yet again of all he's done for me...all he's still doing for me. Before hanging up, he asks me to pay Patrick Veingarten a visit.

"Review the pictures he took last night. In case you find anything incriminating we can hand over to the cops," he adds, even though he's actually telling me to check for any damning picture of Dean and Kevin.

I walk uptown. It's long, but pleasant and loud, almost loud enough to mask the noise in my head. Birds chirp while people do the same on their cell phones. Metal shop curtains creak up and delivery trucks beep into tight, illegal parking spaces. I'm surrounded by so much life, and yet I'm filled with so much death.

On my way to Patrick's, I pass by the Met, which is still decorated with the outsized publicity banners for the show. In the warm breeze, they puff up like the sails on a ship. There are three: one of Dominic, one of Josephine, and one of me. Seeing my face up there had felt like a leap in my career. What a leap it was...straight into a sinkhole that sucks me under a little more every day.

The block teems with news vans and hordes of teenage fans, yet no one notices me. I speed-walk the last few blocks to the brick firehouse Patrick's turned into his studio and ring his doorbell. Not too long after, the door sweeps open.

"Dominic informed me you were coming. Come in." He leads me into the living room. His freshly shaved head reflects the sun pouring through the round skylight "You want something to drink?"

I sink down on the couch. "No."

Patrick's bare feet plod over the vintage tiles that are cracked in spots. "I know why you're here," he says, taking a seat across from me.

I link my fingers together. "Dominic wants to see if you captured anything..." I can't find the word, but Patrick finds it for me.

"*Peculiar?* You can say that."

My mouth feels as hot and dry as the air outside.

Patrick grabs his laptop from the coffee table and powers it on. Once he stops clicking, he rotates it toward me. In the background of one of his shots stand two shadowy figures. Even though they're grainy, they're recognizable. "I'm guessing that's your friend Dean, right?"

I wet my lips but don't talk.

"And that looks a hell of a lot like Sergeant Martin, doesn't it?"

Again, it's not a question.

He flicks through two more shots. One of Dean entering the water with Kevin and one of Dean in the water, alone. And then he closes his laptop and reclines in the high-backed chair he bought from a flea market. He told me all about it during a photoshoot once, so damn proud of his purchase.

"Tell me, Brook. Why should I turn these pictures in to you

instead of to the police?" he asks. "It looks to me like the cops could make great use of them."

I drag my knotted fingers through my hair and sigh deeply. "Your career...it took off thanks to Dominic, didn't it? When he let you be the official photographer of the first *Masterpiecers'* competition three years back, right?"

This time, it's Patrick who stays silent.

"Don't do this for me. Do it for him."

"We'd be covering up a murder," he says.

"An alleged murder," I correct.

"Come on, Brook. I'm not an idiot. Kevin was murdered!"

My eyes go wide when I hear the words spoken out loud.

"We'll pay you."

"I don't want money. I want to know *why* I'd be doing this?"

"Kevin was a PI. Josephine hired him to nail Dom for something, anything, so she could get his job," I say. "You know the art business...it's not always black and white. Dom could've lost everything."

"So he told Dean to kill Kevin?"

"No. Dean chose to. He was trying to protect Dominic."

"Why?"

"I can't tell you."

"Oh, we are *way* beyond keeping secrets from each other, Brook. You're going to tell me right now, or I am leaking these."

"You wouldn't..."

"Do you want to test me?"

Although this is not my secret to tell, it's also no longer my secret to keep. "Dean is Dominic's son."

"Dominic has a kid?" he exclaims.

"Dominic has a kid," I repeat. Once it's sunk in, once Patrick has stopped blinking as though he has dust in his eyes, I add, "Do you have any pictures of Kevin running into the water alone?"

"One. But it was a while before the fireworks."

"Can you darken the sky and add some fireworks?" I ask.

"Brook..."

"If you do this, Patrick, Dominic will give you that private show you've been dreaming of. I'll see to it myself."

The sigh is replaced by a rapid intake of breath.

"It'll double your pictures' worth. Probably even triple it."

Patrick grimaces. He's going to accept. No one turns down easy access to fame and fortune.

I didn't.

"This"—he gestures between us—"this never happened. You got it? 'Cause if it does, Brook, I'll hang your ass right next to mine, and I don't mean on some pretty gallery wall."

I extend my hand to shake on another dangerous deal.

WHEN I LEAVE PATRICK'S, I walk for hours. I don't answer my father's phone call. I'm in no mood to meet him and Chase for lunch. If only I could walk to another town...or to another state. I bob along with the throngs of people clouding Third Avenue. No one recognizes me. After crossing Lexington, I amble through Grand Central, itching to buy a one-way ticket to anywhere, but it's an illusion to think I can escape.

An attractive illusion...

Dominic phones me. Did he sense what I was considering or does he have someone tailing me? I spin around and scan the enormous marble hall, but there are too many people to single out a tail.

Finally, I pick up the call.

"I'm on my way to your house. Apparently you're not there," he says.

Sighing, I say, "I'm on my way."

As I start weaving back through the mass of travelers, Dominic fills me in on Ivy and Lincoln's run-in with the press on the Brooklyn Bridge. Apparently Lincoln insinuated Ivy had a hand in Kevin's death. Detectives are heading over to my house to interview her again. My heart starts pumping, with contempt for Lincoln, with grief for Ivy, and with anxiety for myself. By the time I arrive downtown, I'm drenched in sweat and racked with tremors. Barely acknowledging the camera crew, I steal into my bedroom to shower and change. I don't usually pop pills, but I find a leftover Xanax and swallow it with a mouthful of cold water.

The water slackens the tightness in my shoulders, but does little to level my raging nerves. I pull on a white shirt and a pair of pants, then wander into the hallway. When I find Lincoln standing by the guestroom door, I shoot her a dirty look.

"Is she in there?" I ask, reaching for the handle.

"Yeah. And she's *super* pissy."

"Justifiably so, don't you think?" My hand shakes so badly I have trouble wrapping my fingers around the slender piece of metal keeping me from Ivy.

"Whatever," Lincoln says, blowing a strand of wheat-blonde hair out of her green eyes.

I'm about to tell her to go away when Dominic barges into the apartment through the front door that is wide open since it's part of the "set."

"Where is she?" he asks, his haggard gaze darting over mine. The skin underneath his eyes is puffy and dark, like mine. I wonder what state Dean's in. I can imagine him sprawled out on his thousand-thread comforter, comatose from snorting too much cocaine.

"In here," Lincoln says.

I draw the door open, and Dominic trundles in the bedroom ahead of me. Ivy is curled up on the bed. She looks so fragile and so small. Dominic lifts her feet to make space to sit, then asks me to leave and close the door. I listen to their muffled conversation until Dominic's lawyer and the two detectives erupt into the apartment. My trembling, which had lessened, starts up again. Every nerve in my body twitches at the sight of the two law-enforcement agents. Even my eyelids.

"Where's Ivy Redd?" the female detective asks, looking tightly at me.

My pulse jackhammers as her partner sizes me up too. "Here," I say, hoping my voice doesn't crack.

I press the door open. The two detectives and the Master-piecers' lawyer troop in. Ivy is sitting up in bed, with her legs gathered against her. Her light blue eyes appear leaden. When they alight on me, my breath hitches. The detectives ask her about Kevin, about her whereabouts, about her drinking. I try to concentrate—what they're saying is important—but their words bounce off my eardrums.

When Ivy says, "He stole something from my room," I snap to attention. Is she talking about me?

I blink and stare at Dominic whose face also spasms.

"Are you sure?" he asks.

Ivy nods.

"What was it?" he asks.

Don't say a diamond!

"A piece of jewelry," she says.

"Why didn't you come to me with that? Or to Brook?" Dominic asks.

My shoulders jerk. I press them back until the blades touch and I've somewhat contained the juddering.

"Can you pull the camera footage?" Dominic asks me.

"There's no camera in the hallway," I say.

"The angle of the one in the living room should be wide enough to see if anyone went into her room." Dominic's fore-head glistens with sweat. "This is just absurd! I swear, the show's cursed this year."

"Can we get back—" Detective Clancy begins, but Dominic interrupts her, "When did you notice the theft, Ivy?"

"The night Kevin arrived."

"And you're sure it couldn't have happened before he got there?" Dom asks.

"I'm sure. It was still in my bag when I left for the pool party."

Dominic slaps his thigh. "Absurd, I tell you. Brook, pull the footage of that day."

I swallow hard. "I'll phone Jeb."

"What were you doing in the ocean last night?" Detective Clancy asks Ivy.

"In case you didn't notice, there were a lot of people in the water," Ivy says.

"Yes, but what were *you* doing?" McEnvoy, the detective with the premature gray hair, asks.

A knock resounds in the room.

"Come in," Dominic says.

The door opens, and my little brother treads in. From the sour look on his face, I can tell Dad told him something. What? I don't know. But something. And for a millisecond, I feel better because I'm no longer the only one in the sinkhole. But then that feeling dissipates when Chase provides the detectives with one of Patrick's pictures—one of him and Ivy kissing. It's her alibi; while Kevin Martin drowned, she was busy swapping saliva with my brother. My stomach clenches, so I shut my eyes and work on erasing their kiss from my retina...from my memory.

"Will that do, detectives? Can I be dismissed?" Chase asks.

McEnvoy rips the picture from his partner's hand and ogles it. Then he flicks his index finger against it. "How do we know this hasn't been doctored?"

My brother's jaw clenches.

"Shut up, Austin," Detective Clancy mumbles, eyes flashing over the room. "Thank you for your time, Counsel,

Mister Bacci, Mister Jackson. Miss Redd, I'm sure we'll see each other again soon."

"Why would we?" Ivy asks.

"Just a hunch," she says.

Ivy blanches.

"Let me walk you out," Dominic suggests, ushering the lawyer and the two detectives out of the bedroom. Chase leaves right after them.

I need a stiff drink or I'm going to unravel like the black thread Troy stitched through Ivy's quilt.

"Brook," she calls out.

Wincing, I turn back toward her. Her skin looks like porcelain, like those hand-painted dolls Diana collects. She has an entire shelf of them. I remember lying in her bed about a year ago. She'd needed to discuss Chase's problem with expressing emotion, and apparently I was the right person to talk to about it. I'd stared up at those dolls, wondering how their unblinking ogling didn't freak her out.

"I have a paper to give to Dean. It's for Aster's trial." She slips her hand into her pocket and holds out a folded sheet.

I don't know what I was expecting, but not to be a mule for Dean. Though isn't that what I am? *All I am...* "Okay," I say, taking it from her fingers.

Her nails are shiny red. And long. She has beautiful hands. The sort of hands I would give anything to feel wending through my hair and caressing my bare skin.

I take the paper and tuck it inside my back pocket. "So you and my brother, huh?"

"There is no *me and your brother.*"

"But the picture—"

"Pictures lie."

My pulse thrums with hope. *Stupid hope.* I lower my gaze from hers. "Kevin's personal effects are being packed up as we speak. I'll have the cleaners check for jewelry. What was it exactly that was stolen?"

She hesitates. Will she tell me the truth? Does she trust me enough?

"A necklace," she says.

The answer is *no*. Ivy Redd doesn't trust me. "Can you describe it for me?"

"It was a diamond pendant. I kept it in a porcelain box."

I look back up at her. "Why weren't you wearing it?"

"Because the show lends the jewelry. I thought my stylist would make me take it off."

"You should've left it at home then."

"I don't have a safe at home."

Then where did you put the others? I don't say this out loud, although I think it so loudly I think she'll hear me. I study her face, and my gaze is inevitably towed down to her lips, which she moistens with the tip of her tongue. I find myself leaning in, craving to close the distance between our mouths.

"Sorry to interrupt, Mr. Jackson, but we need to get Ivy ready for dinner," her stylist says.

I jolt away from her as though electrocuted.

"Already?" Ivy breathes, eyes cemented to mine.

God, don't look at me like that...not when others are around.

I shut my eyes to sever our connection, and then I nod and leave without turning back. I head to the terrace that's set for dinner and pour myself a glass of wine. I walk to the transparent railing and stare out at the sun setting over the Hudson River. The dark waters are thick with color—peach and gold and sapphire. As I sip my wine, they brighten and dance on the choppy surface, magnificent and vivid and full of life, a piece of art more glorious than any that graces a wall. But it's transient, and when I take my place next to Ivy at the dinner table, the colors have dimmed, smudging together, their glory tarnished by the absence of a sun.

The camera crew's bright lights fall on Ivy, even though she needs none to shine. Unlike nature, she is as stunning in darkness as she is in daylight.

Dominic begins dinner with a toast. "To Kevin, who we hope has finally found peace."

"Amen," I say at the same time as Josephine.

"*And*, to the most eventful, and surely the most memorable, competition." He smiles. How he can smile right now is beyond me. "And to the last two tests! We're raising the stakes."

"Shh...Dom," Josephine says. "Don't give it away."

"And to Chase's birthday...a happy one this time," Dominic adds as servers bring out little glass bowls of gazpacho.

"I'd also like to propose a toast," Josephine says. "*Plus de drame*. No more drama. Okay, Brook?"

Fear blooms through me. I down my glass of wine. I don't look at anything but my wine for the remainder of dinner. The line of liquid decreases then rises almost as fast, then dwindles again. When Josephine excuses herself—apparently she needs an early night—Dominic tugs me aside.

"Pull yourself together," he whispers.

"I'm trying."

"By drinking your weight in wine?" He snorts. "You should be sober, Brook. Alcohol makes people slip up. This is not the time to slip up."

After chastising me some more, he asks about Ivy's "missing jewel." And I tell him what she told me.

"I don't think she knows about the others," I murmur, watching the crew pack away the equipment.

"I'll inform Dean," he says.

"About Dean, Patrick asked—"

"If he was my son. I heard. He already called me to schedule his *big* show."

I cringe.

Instead of asking me what I was thinking, Dominic

squeezes my shoulder. "You did good, kid...you're doing good," he adds as an after-thought or as an encouragement. I don't feel like I'm doing good. "Two more days."

"Two more days," I echo.

A tight smile curves his lips right before he leaves.

I return to the table that's been cleared. "Dom has agreed to let all of you hang out a while longer. To decompress," I tell Chase, Ivy, and Lincoln.

Chase eyes me. "Is that what *you're* doing?"

"If you were under the stress I was under, little brother, you'd—"

"I just think you should quit while you're ahead."

Did my father not tell him about our family's situation? "Why don't you mind your own business?"

Chase walks over to one of the lounge chairs.

"Well, this isn't awkward," Lincoln says. "I'm going to go powder my nose." She rises and heads inside.

"I feel like I'm missing something," Ivy says.

Fueled by all the alcohol I ingested, I observe her unabashedly. "Josephine doesn't like me."

"I don't think she likes anyone."

"Yeah, but she really has it in for me."

"Why?"

"Because she's afraid Dominic's going to promote me," I tell her.

"So what if he does?"

"I'd be taking her place."

"Ah. I can see how that would be a problem." She runs her tongue over her lower lip, making it glisten.

I contemplate her mouth. "Remember that day at the airport, when you arrived at the same time I did?"

"Hard to forget when someone treats you like dirt."

"Josephine orchestrated that."

"If you have proof, then she can't use it against you."

I lean in closer. "Exactly."

I lift my hand to tuck a strand of hair behind her ear.

"You shouldn't do that," she says.

"Do what?"

"Touch me. I'm a contestant."

I drop my hand back onto my lap. "Right."

"Crap. Now Lincoln's going to tell the press that you and I are hooking up," she whispers in my ear, tipping her head toward her nemesis.

Pleasure shoots through me. And power. There's not much I can fix right now, but this is within my means. "Watch me take care of that." I stand and walk over to Lincoln. "Want to go for a swim?"

She nods.

"Anyone else up for a midnight dip?" I ask loudly, hoping Ivy will come inside the pool too.

"I think I'm over midnight dips," she says.

I cover my disappointment with a hefty wink.

I change quickly into swim trunks. When I step back inside the darkened living room and spot her lying down on the lounge chair next to Chase, pieces of my heart flake off. I'm suddenly animated with the need to break something. My gaze brushes against the clear, bubble-shaped vase propped on my coffee table. I reach out for it as a hand skims over my back.

Lincoln stands there in a skimpy bikini. "When they said dinner was at your place, I hoped it entailed swimming."

To help Ivy, I was going to kiss Lincoln, but now, it won't be just to help her. I make a fist and dig my nails into my palm. Now, it will be to begin to forget her. She wants Chase; she doesn't want me.

TWENTY-SIX

DAY 8

JOSH

"The wife did it," the chief says, trundling into the meeting room on Monday morning. Claire and I are nursing mugs of hot, watery coffee, and Fred is nursing an extra-large glazed donut. "It's always the wife."

"Did what?" I ask.

"She killed her husband?" Claire asks.

"Which wife? Which husband?" I ask.

"She wasn't on the beach with them," Fred says.

"Someone died?"

All three pairs of eyes converge on me.

"Where did you spend your weekend? In a cave?" Claire asks.

Not too far off. "I was camping."

"Kevin Martin drowned on Saturday night, Coop," Guarda explains, while I stare at him wide eyed.

So that's what that couple was talking about in front of the cabin.

"Yeah...shocking," he says.

And crazy. And unsettling. Ivy must be beside herself.

"And Kevin Martin's wife is the one who tampered with the pictures of him," Guarda continues.

"So Aster is no longer a suspect," I say more than ask. Even though I'm furious with her because she lied to me about the diamonds, I'm relieved she didn't cheat to get Ivy on *The Masterpiecers.*

Guarda tosses a photocopy of what looks like a note on the table. "I went to high school with her lawyer, Mr. Kelley. He sent me this little nugget."

Fred picks up the sheet and scans it, then hands it over to Claire. I get it last. It has a few grease smudges, which makes one of the words hard to read.

"However, she is *not* the one who killed her husband. It was a suicide." He flicks a picture of Kevin running into the water, fireworks exploding over him, reflecting in the ominous black water.

Claire snorts and twirls her mug. Her fingers are thick and her nails are wide and cut off at the cuticles. They look like foreign hands that have been attached to a random body. "That's a pretty drastic move. End his life because of heartache and shame."

"Shame is a huge suicide factor. Depression's number one, but humiliation is right up there," I say.

"Look who's brushed up on his psychology," she says.

I stare down at the brown liquid that reminds me of the pond the twins' mother drowned in.

"Shut it, Claire," Fred says.

Claire grumbles, "Geez. I didn't know it was a sore subject."

"Chief, may I be excused? I'd like to go see Aster. Ask about those missing stones. I have a hunch she took them out of the quilt and hid them somewhere."

"I don't think today's a good day for that."

"Why not?"

"You haven't heard?"

"Heard what?"

"That Aster was locked in a freezer?"

"What?" My hands jerk, which makes my coffee tip over. A brown river flows toward Fred. It stops next to his empty plate. "Is she okay?"

"She's alive."

Ice shoots up my spine. "Was it an accident?"

"Apparently. But it's prison...if you get my drift," Guarda says, while Fred blots the spilled coffee with a paper napkin.

"Do we know why the wife confessed, Chief?" Claire asks. I'm not sure whether to feel relief at the change of subject or irritation.

I want to know more.

I want to know everything.

I want to know which cruel, nasty person could do this to my Aster.

"The wife felt guilty, and wanted to make things right by confessing. Kelley's going to pay her a visit tomorrow. Cooper, want to join him?"

I nod, even though my mind is on Aster. She must be terrified. And what was I doing while she was going through hell? Showing Heidi I could survive two full days without a phone and without Internet. I proved my point, but I also proved I was a great big idiot.

"Fred, what's the status on Diego Discoli?" Guarda asks.

"He's still locked up, but his trial's been postponed."

"Can you find out why it's been postponed?"

Fred nods, and carrying his plate with the small pile of sopping brown napkins, he walks off toward his desk.

"Claire, any leads on Elise Frothington?"

On the TV behind the chief, Lincoln, the pretty blonde contestant on the art show, is apologizing for having blamed Ivy for Kevin's death.

"What the?" I exclaim, walking up to the television screen.

"Ivy, I regret the terrible confusion my words created," the blonde is saying. "I didn't mean you any harm."

"*Ivy* was accused of murdering Kevin?" I shriek.

"Where the hell were you camping, Josh? Under a rock?" Claire asks.

"I turned off my phone," I say, although I shouldn't have to explain myself to my replacement. I'm sort of pissed she's still even on this task force.

Guarda stands next to me as the news channel replays some footage of the night on the beach, shots of Ivy and Kevin together at different moments of the evening.

"That's Kelley," Guarda says, pointing to a man whose head seems screwed right into his torso.

"Who's the guy next to him?" I ask. "The one with the red tie? I've seen him somewhere."

Guarda cocks an eyebrow. "Apparently, he's your girlfriend's lawyer. Dean Kane. Kelley says he's an arrogant prick."

"My—Aster doesn't have a lawyer."

"Are you sure?"

I squint at the screen, as though my retina could run some fancy face recognition system—which it can't, because I'm not a robot, *and* I don't have any fancy spy glasses, although I've been writing them on my Christmas lists since I was six.

"Where have I seen you, Dean Kane?" I ask out loud. When it hits me, I run to Fred's desk, swipe the Discoli file that he has opened in front of him, and run back, flipping through it until I find a picture of the same guy. He's wearing a grass-green tie in this one. I jam my finger on the picture. "He's Diego's lawyer!"

Guarda stares at the picture, then stares at me, then stares back at the picture. Claire's gaze follows the same trajectory.

"Shit," Guarda whispers, eyes and face glowing from the discovery. "Dig up everything you can on him."

Animated by the conviction that Dean Kane is one of our missing puzzle corners, we spend the next hour researching him, and boy, do we find *a lot* of stuff. A young nobody who went from living in a trailer park in Naples, Florida, with his mother, to an all-star Duke University graduate turned lawyer to the rich bastards of the world. In a society column, there's a picture of him in a tuxedo standing next to a woman who looks to be a decade older than him. Instead of a bow tie, he sports a hot-pink tie. How many ties does this dude own?

"Blow the picture up," Claire says, leaning over my shoulder, chomping on a piece of gum that smells like cough syrup. "Well hello, Elise."

I eyeball the woman holding Dean's arm. "No...no way."

The caption on the bottom reads, *Dean Kane and his mother, Alaina Kane.*

Claire must have told the chief and Fred to come over, because they're both there, pressing in.

"Troy went to Duke University. That's how they know each other," I say as Mann's file swims through my mind.

Guarda sucks in a breath, then straightens up. "It's time we call New York."

He's the first to leave, and then the two others peel themselves away from the space around me. Buzzing erupts inside my skull, or perhaps it's inside the room. I look at the phone on my desk and pick it up to call Aster's jail. After they authorize a visit, they ask me to hold for the shrink.

"Joshua Cooper?"

"How's Aster?"

"The nurse told me she was okay, considering. Look, I've been—"

"Just okay? Who did this to her?"

"She says it was an accident."

"Yeah, right."

I hear the shrink sigh. "I wanted to speak to you about something else."

"Can you make sure she's not returned with the rest of the prison population? I want better protection and better care. This *accident* is unacceptable! Actually, transfer me to the warden right away!"

"Officer Cooper, please. I have an urgent matter to discuss with you."

"More urgent than my friend's well-being?" I snap. "I don't think so."

"Were you aware that Ivy made her sister sign a document that gives her power of attorney over her?"

"What?"

"Aster signed it without understanding what it meant."

I want to say *what* again—scream it.

"Aster's lawyer emailed it to me this morning."

"Her lawyer?"

"Yes. A Mr. Kane."

I cradle my head, then glide my fingers down my face, squeezing it. Both my head and heart throb long after I hang up with her.

I realize I didn't get to talk to the warden. I'm about to dial the prison again when my phone rings. Maybe I can get a tête-à-tête with the warden after I see Aster.

"Officer Cooper," I say in an exhausted whisper.

"We were told you were the person to contact about the recent burglary at the Redd apartment."

"Yes. And you are?"

"The crime scene technician."

"Did you find anything?"

"Unfortunately, nothing besides your DNA and the twins' DNA. Whoever the perpetrator was, they were careful."

Of course they were. I'm not surprised by the news, but I'm irritated by it.

"You may clean up the apartment now as we are closing this case," the person on the other end of the line tells me. "Have a nice day."

Grumbling to myself, I pick up my cell to tell Heidi not to wait up for me tonight just as Angela Discoli waltzes in—or rather is escorted in by Claire. I jog to the hallway down which they've just turned. They're headed to an interrogation room. Angela's gaze flicks to mine. She doesn't say anything, yet I can hear a thousand words in her hostile stare.

When the door clicks shut behind both women, I jog to the adjoining room from which I can hear and observe the interview. Fred and Guarda are already inside, standing next to the glass, peering in at the pretty blonde and the not-so-pretty blonde. *Sorry, Claire.*

"You didn't tell me you were bringing her in," I say, breathless.

"The motel clerk phoned the precinct. He said she was going through the room she'd used with Troy Mann."

Angela's livid blue eyes find mine through the glass. I jerk back, but then remind myself that all she is seeing is her reflection. She probably knows it's not a mirror, though.

"Miss Discoli, what were you doing at 10:35 a.m. this morning in room 2B of the motel off route 9?" Claire asks.

"I was looking for a lost earring," Angela says.

"An earring?"

"Yes."

"And did you find your missing *earring*?"

Angela smirks, and runs one of her manicured hands through her hair. Her large blonde curls shimmer.

"Definitely took after her mother," Fred says, "because her father is one ugly bastard."

"Why are the hot ones always conniving?" Guarda says.

"Not always," I say, just as a tinny voice says, "Who's hot?" Both Fred and Guarda stare down at the cell phone in my hand. "Josh?" comes the distant voice.

"Crap," I mumble. I dialed Heidi without realizing it. I lift the phone to my ear and retreat to the back of the room. "Hey."

"You forgot me," Heidi says, pain tingeing her voice.

"I'm sorry, babe."

Guarda glares at me.

Cupping my hand over my mouth, I add, "Look I can't talk right now, but I need to go to the twins' place tonight. Clean it up. I don't want them coming back to it looking a mess."

"Want some help?" she asks.

"You must have better things to do."

"Then spend time with my boyfriend?"

I chew on my bottom lip. I can't have her around because I'm not just planning on cleaning it up; I'm planning on finding those diamonds. Plus, she doesn't know it was tossed. "This is something I need to do by myself."

"Fine," she says in a tight voice. "Bye, Josh."

When I return to the interrogation, I ask Fred, "You think she was looking for the missing diamonds?"

"Yeah."

"Did you search her?"

"Claire frisked her. She didn't find anything."

"She could've swallowed them."

"Considering she was still unscrewing the showerhead when we found her, I'd put good money down that she didn't recover them."

"Chief, I'm going to see Aster. The DOC gave me the green light."

Even though his chin is tucked into his neck, Guarda nods.

"Is Claire going to ask her about Dean Kane?" I ask before stepping out.

"We're going to ask her about every fucking person in her life. I'll phone you if we get anything," Guarda says.

I pull open the door and rush out of the precinct toward my car. After pumping the music up, I set out toward the jail. Thirty minutes into the trip, I blow a tire. I slap my steering wheel before driving the car to the side of the highway. Then I mutter a long strand of ugly words. If my mom were here, she'd make me drop quarters into her curse jar.

I get out of the car, pop the trunk, and grab the extra tire and toolkit. This isn't my first rodeo changing a tire, but it is the first time I have to do it in ninety-degree weather on the side of a highway. The last two times were in town, and both times, I'd managed to pull the car into a parking lot.

I set everything out and begin to loosen the lug nuts when this idiot in a Range Rover drives so close to me, I can actually feel the boiling air vibrate against my backside. I jump up and give him the finger but he's already long gone. I bet he was speeding. How I wish I could've pulled him over and fined him.

I squat back down to finish loosening the lug nuts and then wedge the jack under the car body and begin cranking it. Something creaks and I barely have time to jolt out of the way before the jack shatters and my car comes crashing down.

"Fuck!" I explode. Another quarter pings into Mom's curse jar.

I yank my phone out of my jacket pocket to call AAA only to notice that it's run out of battery. I didn't use it all weekend! How could it have run out of battery? I kick the flat tire. Repeatedly. The nearest exit is seven miles away. *Seven miles!*

So many choice words fly out of me that the sound of a Vegas slot machine goes off in my scorched brain. Attempting to calm down, I stare at the highway and debate whether to walk the distance or get a ride. I'm already sweating profusely, so I decide to stick my thumb out. Even though I don't have my patrol car, I'm dressed like a cop. Someone is bound to pick me up.

Or not.

An hour slips by and I'm still standing there with my thumb out, and probably, with the sunburn from hell. Fourteen cars have passed me and none have stopped. They didn't even slow. People probably think I'm a fake cop, one of those who pull you over to rob you. Even though I'm tempted to sit back inside my broken-ass vehicle, and wait for traffic to pick up—I'm bound to find one nice soul then—I start walking.

And I walk.

It takes me almost two hours to reach the exit. I feel as though I've been dunked in a pool fully clothed. Every inch of fabric sticks to my burning skin. I start fantasizing about freezers and ice cubes. The fantasy eggs me on. When a gas station shimmers ahead of me, I blink to make sure it's not a mirage. It trembles in the stiflingly humid heat, but remains right there.

To say the teenager behind the counter is surprised when I walk in would be an understatement. His eyes bulge like anthills. "You okay, sir?"

"My car broke down seven miles back, and then my phone died, or maybe my phone died before my car broke down, and I don't have my police radio, so no, I'm not okay." I don't mean to be rude, but I am pissed at the world.

The teen jumps off his stool behind the cash register and brings me a bottle of cold water, free of charge. "You a police officer?" he asks, as I gulp it down.

"Yeah." I tap the badge hooked onto my belt. The metal part feels like it's just come out from welding and the leather around it is stewing in sweat.

The kid stares at it. "You can use the phone in the back, sir."

He leads me to a back room that's more of a closet than a

room, but who am I to complain? There's a working phone and fan. I grab the phone and dial AAA. After explaining where I left the car, I ask them to meet me at the gas station. Planting my face against the fan, I call the precinct and ask to be patched through to Fred. He tells me they got nothing from Angela, and I tell him I got nothing from Aster besides a blown tire.

"But guess who else went to Duke University?" he says.

"Who?"

"Brook Jackson."

I gasp, gulping down so much fan air I start coughing.

"They were all roommates their sophomore year," he continues.

I cough so hard I can't get any air in...I can only push air out. My lungs feel sore and compressed, as though Fred were sitting on them.

"You okay, Coop?"

"He's the—he's—" I hold my breath to calm the spasms.

"Yeah. He's the one linked to the Masterpiecers. Apparently, Josephine already had doubts about him. She even provided proof of his involvement."

"What did she have on him?"

"Don't know. The Feds wouldn't tell."

Damn Feds. "When are they going to arrest him?"

"Tomorrow."

"Why not right now?" I snap.

"They want to interview Dominic Bacci to see if he knew about it, or if he could give them more info. But don't worry. They *will* get him."

"As long as Ivy is out there, and he is too, she's at risk."

"Josephine asked the show's videographer to keep an eye on her. Apparently he's monitoring the security cameras."

"That doesn't reassure me."

After hanging up with him, I call the prison and ask to speak to Aster because there's no way I'm making it out to her jail before visitation hours end, but I'm told she's unable to speak at the moment. Shrink's orders.

"You don't understand. This is urgent," I shout into the phone.

"You take it up with the warden. I'm just following orders," the woman says.

"Patch me through to the warden then."

"Don't you use that tone of voice with me, mister."

The recycled air pulses up my nostrils. "I need to speak to Inmate Redd's warden. This is—"

"Visiting hours start at 8 a.m. tomorrow. Goodbye."

When the dial tone drones in my ear, I growl and throw the phone against the desk. The battery compartment cracks off and the batteries fly out. As I reassemble it, my fingers shake because putting this back together is easy. Putting my life—and the twins' lives—back together is beginning to feel impossible.

TWENTY-SEVEN

Brook

Lincoln is clingy the night of the art heist. It's partly my fault—I shouldn't have kissed her in my swimming pool. But Lincoln is the least of my worries. It's Dean who's at the forefront of my mind. I called him several times to find out how he was doing and what he was doing and didn't even get a text back.

"Any news from Dean?" I whisper in Dominic's ear after he's done greeting the director of the Museum of Modern Art.

Dominic smiles warmly at the retreating man. When he's not looking any longer, the smile washes off his face. "Not here."

"Did you tell him about the detectives?"

Dominic spears me with a dark look.

"Did you—"

He drags me toward the orchestra. The vibrations from the

brass instruments throttle my eardrums. "I don't want to worry him. Besides, it'll blow over soon."

I don't see how this is going to blow over; I only see how this is going to blow up.

"In other news, Josephine and I talked this afternoon. She admitted hiring Kevin to investigate me."

"She confessed this? To you?"

"Yes. She wanted to ask for my forgiveness. She realized she'd been wrong in assuming I was part of anything. She had the Masterpiecers' bank records pulled. Our school has done no wrong." Dominic smooths out my burgundy lapel. "I told her it was unacceptable and asked for her resignation."

Tonight, I didn't get to wear my own clothes. I had to match Dom. My get-up makes me look like I'm part of the circus. "So she's resigning?"

"She has to. After what she's done." Dominic smiles. "You can relax now. Everything's going to be fine, Brook."

I chew on my lip.

"How are your parents?"

"My parents? Uh...I think they're okay."

"Call them tonight. I'm sure they'd like to hear from you."

"O-Okay."

"Now let's go. Our audience awaits. And our contestants."

Sure enough, Ivy, Chase, and Lincoln are taking their places on the stage. Ivy is in black tonight, which makes her look elegant, but also in mourning. Even her face seems strained. She's still beautiful, but she doesn't glow like she did the first night she was up there.

As Dominic begins his show, asking the audience if any of them had guessed that today's test was an art heist, I stare at the Egyptian temples' floor-lit carvings.

Josephine is resigning. Everything will be okay.

The lights dim and the three screens hanging around the room light up with the picture of Chase. He's winner number one. I already knew that. He worked at Christie's, and that's where he chose to perform his art heist, so it was no surprise when he walked out of the auctioneers with his stolen piece tucked under his arm. He says they ate up his lie about our mother wanting to see the piece hung in our family home before purchasing it, but I'm pretty certain Dominic called ahead.

Ivy's hands wring together in her lap. She's nervous because she's not aware she's the other winner. The deserving winner. What a performance she gave in the Museum of Modern Art. To torture her, Dominic asks Jeb to play both her heist and Lincoln's before announcing the second winner.

I watch her performance again, and again I find it exceptional. From the camera hooked into her shirt, I see what Ivy saw when she stepped into the MoMA, when she rode the escalator up to one of the galleries, when she located the painted silk tissue installation she had to steal, when the museum-goers swarmed around her begging for autographs. In part thanks to her cunning and in part thanks to the accidental mob, she surreptitiously pocketed the silken prizes.

Her profile glows from the projection. When the drumroll resounds through the room, she sits up straighter, but there's the slightest quiver in her shoulders, as though the rumble were inside her. And then the room goes dark. I keep my eyes on her as she's plunged in shadows. When the screen flashes with her picture, her mouth curves with a smile that takes my breath away.

If only that smile were for me.

At least it's not for my brother.

Her delight is contagious and loosens the tendrils of angst that locked around me the day her quilt arrived empty.

During dinner—which the contestants attend tonight—I lope around the room, stopping by tables, making small talk with our clients and our benefactors, high on Ivy's bliss. I save her table for last. When I reach it, I slide my hands over her shoulders.

She tips her face up to mine.

"How many special orders have you received already?" I ask her, grinning.

"None yet."

Her skin is soft and warm. "What? What's wrong with you people? Grab her while you still can."

"We were waiting until dessert to ask such forward questions," the curator of the MoMA says with a chuckle.

Across the table from Ivy, Paul Willows—a blond art dealer who graduated from the Masterpiecers ten years ago and whose father Dad detests—leans back in his chair and folds his arms over his chest. "I'd like to buy your entire collection, Ivy."

I laugh. It's a nervous sort of laughter. I hate Paul. Paul is not touching Ivy's art.

"I'm serious. All of the pieces you've made," Paul tells her, keeping his eyes on me.

My laughter dries up, and my fingers tense against Ivy's shoulders.

"Have you signed with anyone yet?" Paul asks her.

"Signed? You mean with a gallery?" She sits up straighter and shakes her head no.

"But if she wins tomorrow, she'll automatically be represented by the school." If I could get my hands on a microphone, I'd shout it to everyone in the room.

"And if she loses?" Paul asks.

"She'll be represented by me."

Ivy tips her face up again, surprise etched in her blue eyes.

"Are you allowed to take on private clients, Brook?" Paul asks.

My fingers are so tight now they're probably bruising her skin. "Why don't we discuss this matter tomorrow, in private?"

"With pleasure. You have my number. Call me at your convenience."

Because I need to cool down, and because our conversation has created tension, I move away from the table, but keep my eyes on Ivy. When she stands, I wind my way back toward her. I find her talking to some overly done-up woman whose dress looks two sizes too small.

"Excuse me," I tell the woman. I surely know her, but I don't bother retrieving her name from the depths of my memory. "I need a word with my contestant." When she leaves, I say, "Don't sign with that guy, okay?"

Her unsteady breath tickles my jaw. "Are you really going to offer me representation?"

"I've been considering it."

"Are you allowed?"

I make up something about it being a clause I've asked the show's lawyer to implement in my contract. "I just need to get it past Dom."

"And past Josephine," she says.

"Josephine's opinion won't matter."

"It won't?"

"No. Soon it won't."

"Is she leaving the school?" Ivy asks.

"I wouldn't use the word *leaving*, but yes. Something like that."

"Was she fired?"

I've said too much. I need to quit while I'm ahead. "The heist was all Dom's idea," I say, before anyone overhears us.

"What an idea. Anyway, I should get to bed. Larceny is exhausting, isn't it?"

I gawk at her.

"Goodnight," she says, and turns to leave.

I start to follow her. I'm sick of this. So sick of all these secrets. I want to tell her everything. But of course, someone captures my arm and tows me back to discuss some emerging artist before tossing me to his friend like a chew toy. By the time everyone's done trying to scrape information from me about which rising star to bet on, Ivy's long gone.

My confession will have to wait until tomorrow.

TWENTY-EIGHT

JOSH

As the highway blurs past, I rub my temples to combat the headache that's made my skull throb since I found out about Dean Kane and Brook Jackson's friendship.

At least I'm not the one driving. I would've swerved into a ditch or rear-ended another vehicle by now. I flash my eyes to Guarda's friend, Kelley, Kevin's former lawyer. I met him two hours ago, when he came to pick me up from the twins' apartment to drive to Columbus, Ohio to visit the widow.

Apparently, we're not just going to offer our condolences anymore. Guarda thinks Dean Kane is behind the note she wrote her husband. He wants us to get proof so we have solid grounds for an arrest, because apparently being a Discoli louse isn't enough.

"It was her signature on the paper, wasn't it?" I ask Kelley as we pass the sign for Springfield.

"Yeah, but I don't know. Don't you think it was convenient?"

It is convenient. "But she confirmed she wrote it?"

"Yeah. But it ain't right. It just ain't right." With his polo shirt buttoned up to the top, he looks like he has no neck. "What were you doing at Ivy's place?"

"Cleaning it up. It was broken into about a week ago."

"For the missing diamonds?" he asks.

"Chief Guarda told you about the case?"

"My client drowned on a show that's being sniffed out by the Feds, so yeah, I know everything about your case. Did you find them?"

I think of the hours I spent rearranging the rolls of fabric, the bookshelves, the closets, the kitchen cabinets. Fruitless hours. I press my lips together. "No. I didn't find them." And I'd searched underneath their mattresses, in the couch cushions, in places even the intruder hadn't touched. "Dean was on the beach the night Kevin drowned, wasn't he?"

Kelley frowns. "He was. But he left after speaking with Ivy."

"Are you sure?"

"What are you getting at?"

"What if Dean had a hand in Kevin's death?"

"Kevin ran into the ocean. There was a picture of him."

"Pictures can be tweaked."

Kelley spins his face toward me so fast, the car swerves too. Horizontal grooves form on his forehead. "Guarda told me he requested more footage, but there wasn't anymore."

"Brook Jackson could've made it disappear."

Kelley glances my way again. And the car veers to the right, again.

As I seize the grab handle over my window, my stomach squeezes as though it's about to eject the lone granola bar I ate for breakfast. "Could we stop for a sec?"

"I was just about to suggest it."

I buy a sandwich and a cold Coke that help lessen the nausea caused by my lack of sleep and my surplus of stress. They do little to squelch the queasiness from Kelley's erratic driving. To avoid distracting him, I don't utter a single word during the last half hour of our trip. Instead, I pretend to sleep.

Kelley taps my shoulder. "We're here."

We've pulled up in front of a simple one-story house in a cookie-cutter neighborhood. Every home on the block is single storied and painted the same shade of carpet beige. Only the mailboxes planted by the driveways are different. The one in front of the Martins' home resembles a birdhouse. It's probably confusing for the postman...and for the birds.

We park the car on the street, then walk up to the house and press on the doorbell that chirps like cheery birds. *Obsessed much?*

There are no approaching footsteps, no movement of the doorknob. Kelley digs his cell out of his jeans and dials her number. The home phone rings. We can hear it through the plaster walls. At least it sounds like a proper ringtone, not some bird song. Not that I have a problem with birds.

As we wait, I slink along the wall of the house until I reach a set of windows that look into a kitchen. The phone's still ringing.

"Are you sure she's expecting us?" I ask Kelley.

His brow furrows. "Go round the back."

So I take off at a trot and travel around the house, peering into every window. Only her bedroom window is obscured by drapes. I knuckle the glass. She must be asleep. If I'd led someone to suicide, I'd be holed up to lose track of time, too.

I knock again. Harder this time.

I'm about to return to Kelley and suggest we kick the door down, when the shiny eggplant drapes tremble. A set of dark eyes stare out at me. Involuntarily, I jerk back. Mrs. Martin cracks the window open.

"Fuck off," she says. "I'm not giving interviews."

"I'm here with Mr. Kelley...your lawyer?"

The whites of her eyes are red.

"I'm real sorry for your loss, ma'am," I add, to make myself sound nicer, even though I don't think many nice things about this woman. She crushed her husband's hopes. Wives are supposed to be supportive, not destructive. My mother always champions my father. They're a team. That's what she told me once. Teammates in life and for life.

"Mr. Kelley's here?" Her face is mega white and her neck, too. The only color on her body is her neon yellow bra and panty set. "I'm comin'," she grumbles, shutting the window and yanking her curtains closed again.

I scurry back to the front door where Kelley is still waiting. I nod to him as the door swings open.

His eyebrows shoot up in surprise. "Mrs. Martin, I left you a message to tell you—"

"I've stopped checking my phone. Too many fuckin' messages," she says, tying on a silk robe.

Kelley shifts his weight from one white-socked-loafer to the other.

"Well, are you gonna come in, or you gonna stay planted out there?" she says.

His gaze dips to her inner thigh and that bright underwear of hers, which is totally exposed since she didn't tie her robe very tight. I don't think she notices since she doesn't adjust it, or maybe she doesn't care.

Kelley steps in, and I follow suit.

"I'm sorry, Mrs. Martin," he says.

"Yeah, yeah," she mumbles as she leads us toward the couch with a...*wait for it*...bird pattern on it. Various colored-glass birds sit on an otherwise empty bookcase. I wonder if she likes birds or if it was Kevin's passion.

"You didn't come here to tell me that, did you, Mr. Kelley? You came to ask me why I did it, didn't you? It's not a crime to write your husband a letter."

"But it is a crime to tamper with pictures," he tells her.

"I said I was sorry about that. You're my counsel. Why are you even givin' me shit about it?"

"Since I am your counsel, why didn't you come to me with your note? Why did you go to Dean Kane?"

"He came over and told me the Redd sisters were going to press charges if I didn't come clean."

My gaze drifts beyond her, to three packed suitcases. "Are you going somewhere, Mrs. Martin?"

Her ghost-white cheeks flare. "I was going...I was going to visit my mother out in Texas when I received the news of"—her voice catches—"of Kevin's crazy reaction to my letter."

Kelley reclines backward into the couch to dig something out of his jeans pocket. "So you *weren't* booked on a flight to Belize?"

She blinks. I blink too since he didn't breathe a word about it during the two-and-a-half-hour car ride.

"What? No." She shrugs, which makes the robe fall open even more. I really try not to stare.

Kelley points to the printout. "But it says here—"

"Okay, fine. I was going to go away. I wanted to leave Kevin. He cheated on me! And with guys. I should've known what he was..." She shakes her head and her hair whips her almost-bare chest. "Never wanted to have sex with me. Do you know how that feels? I started wonderin' if there was somethin' wrong with me. It effed-up my self-esteem. And before you ask, I didn't mean for my note to make him commit suicide. I'm not some cold-hearted bitch. But I did mean to hurt him. He hurt me so fuckin' much."

"Did Dean Kane give you anything in exchange for the note?"

"Yeah."

I scoot closer to the edge of my seat. *This is it.* The morsel that will help us put him away for good. I'm winded by how easy it was to obtain. I suppose wronged people have no trouble—

"He gave me five phone numbers. Kevin's lovers. You want the list?"

"I thought you modified those pictures because you already knew about his lovers."

She flushes again. "I only knew about two of them."

"Did he give you any monetary compensation for it?" Kelley says, disregarding her offer for the list.

"Are you askin' if he bought my confession?" She drums her hot orange nails against her bare knee.

"It's come to our attention that you've come into a bit of money recently."

She stops the drumming.

"Mind telling me where this money came from, Mrs. Martin?" Kelley asks.

The doorbell chimes before she has time to respond. It sounds like we're sitting in a huge birdcage. The pealing makes my temples throb. Not bothering to pull her robe closed, she walks over to the door and flings it open. The UPS man's gaze zeroes in on her bare legs and sticks there for an inappropriate amount of time.

Since he just stands there, she yanks the oddly shaped package from his arms and begins closing the door in his face.

He finally reacts. "I need a signature."

She takes the small stylus he hands her, signs his screen, then kicks the door closed. She walks back into the living room and plops the bundle down on the coffee table. "At least it's not flowers. I swear, if I get another condolence bouquet..." She picks up a pen and jams it into the sticky tape, then drags it the length of the package and underneath the flaps.

Black eyebrows pinching together, she takes ahold of what's inside and pulls it out. At first, I think it's a snake.

"What is this?" she asks, nose crinkled.

"It's the rope Kevin made on the beach," Kelley explains.

Her throat convulses as she studies her dead husband's work, and tears snake out of her eyes. She doesn't bother blotting them as she walks into the kitchen, still clutching the rope. From where I'm sitting, I see her pull open the drawer underneath the kitchen sink and release it into what I imagine is a trashcan.

She returns and sits back down, folding her legs and jiggling one of her feet. "Could we do this some other time? I'm not feelin' too well."

"Tell me where you got the thirty-thousand dollars and we'll get out of your hair."

She pinches the bridge of her nose. "From a Mega Cash scratchy ticket."

"You have it here?"

"No. You gotta give it in to win the prize."

"Where did you claim it?"

"I don't remember. I was so fuckin' excited that I walked into the first 7-Eleven and they gave me cash for it."

"That's interesting," Kelley says, leaning back into the couch. Kelley proceeds to explain that they wouldn't give her that amount in cash but would've had to write a check.

We caught her. But most importantly, we caught Dean Kane.

"So Dean Kane gave you money?" I ask, point blank.

"Uh. No. I won—"

"Mrs. Martin, please. Stop lying," Kelley says. "The more you lie, the less I'll be able to help you."

She stares at her lawyer, wide eyed.

"Now, tell me the whole truth," he says, and she does.

Dean Kane falsified those pictures to get the PI off the show, then paid her thirty grand to take the blame for them. We phone the local police to place Mrs. Martin under house arrest until we can get her testimony in writing, then we phone Guarda with the news that we can officially put out a warrant for Kane's arrest.

Once I'm done rattling on about what a genius Kelley is, and what a dumbass Kane is, he asks, "You sitting, Coop?"

The blood drains from my face, because no one asks you to sit to give you good news.

"Mr. Kane visited Aster's prison this morning, Joshua."

I swallow. He never calls me by my first name.

"He slipped an inmate a weapon. Told her to threaten Aster with it so she would cough up the location of his diamonds." He stops talking. I don't want a cliffhanger; I want the rest. I want the entire story. I'm about to tell him not to leave me hanging when he adds, "It did a lot of damage. She's in a coma."

I feel hot and cold, I sweat and shiver, and then I dash out of the living room and throw up in the flowerbed on the side of her house until I've poisoned all the flowers like Kevin's wife, Dean Kane, Brook Jackson, Troy Mann...like they've all poisoned my sweet Aster.

Brook

Finding the right words to confess everything to Ivy kept me up all night. Around sunrise, I turned off the TV, rolled off the couch, and went for a swim. The water invigorated me, and followed by a glass of iced coffee, I almost feel human when I stroll onto the set. I smile politely at Jeb's crew, then mingle with the audience until Ivy and Chase penetrate the Temple room for their final test: finding a fake painting. The catch: the gallery will be full of forged pieces.

Dominic chose this test because Chase would excel at it. I was enthusiastic when he ran it past me, but today, I wish the trial had been to create something, because then, without a doubt, Ivy would win.

As we walk toward the designated gallery, I look at Ivy, and keep staring at her long after we've arrived. Dominic introduces both her and Chase to the two art experts who are supposed to help them understand how to use the advanced technology laid out before them. Both experts are smart and trained at the Masterpiecers. I went on a date with one of them two years back.

When Dominic gives his okay to start, Chase all but pounces onto the one I'd wined and dined. He should've let Ivy pick first. I scowl at him, and he glares right back. This show did nothing to bring us closer.

Ivy is so focused that I don't get more than a fleeting glance from her. As Dominic speaks to me about his projects for the school come fall, I keep my eyes on her. At some point, she reaches for the x-ray binoculars at the same time as Chase. I half-expect my brother to swipe them, but instead, he grasps Ivy's hand, pries it open, and sets the silver binoculars into her palm. I stiffen as their fingers and eyes lock.

"I suspect those two like each other," Dom whispers. "They're rather sweet together, don't you think?"

I fold my arms in front of my chest so tight I'm cutting off circulation in my forearms. As Dominic explains how their budding romance will bolster the show's ratings, my hands go cold and stiff. He's aware I like Ivy, and yet he salts my wounded ego.

When Ivy and Chase walk up to us with their answers, I tell Ivy to come with me, but I never get to lead her out of the room. Josephine surges out of nowhere, flanked by Lincoln and a man she introduces as her lawyer. My heart hurtles around my chest like a trapped mouse.

Josephine asks to speak to Dominic in private. Seemingly exasperated, he latches on to her elbow and accompanies her out of the room. The contestants are taken away, and the ending of the test is delayed. The upheaval has caused a great amount of uneasiness within the crowd. My head buzzes too loudly to concentrate on their whispered hypotheses of what could be going on. As they're herded out of the gallery and out of the museum, Jeb latches on to my arm and guides me out too.

"What's going on?" I ask before taking the elevator down to the parking lot.

"Everyone's been asked to go home and change, and return at seven o'clock sharp."

My heartbeat picks up momentum. "Why?"

"For the concluding celebration," the short videographer tells me.

"But Josephine—"

"Came to speak with Dominic about her resignation."

"You know about that?"

"I know about everything around here."

Everything? I shiver.

"Go home, Brook. See you at seven."

Jeb unhands me when the doors open. I walk into the elevator, and as it dips below ground, so does my dread. It sinks through me and spreads until I shake so much that putting one foot in front of the other becomes a feat. On my way downtown, I replay Jeb's words, that this is about Josephine's resignation. If she wants her job back, making a spectacle of her demands might get Dominic to fold.

I take the elevator up to my penthouse and pace around it like a caged tiger. My mother phones to ask what's going on, and I tell her the two heads of the Masterpiecers have been on the outs.

"It's just an ego thing, Mom."

"Has Dominic offered *you* her position?"

"No."

"I heard rumors he was thinking about it."

"I don't want her position."

"Don't be a fool, Brook. If he presents you with this opportunity, you take it, you hear me? There's nothing left for you at home."

Her words make my throat tighten.

"How's Chase? He looked confident today."

The mere thought of Chase is like a tornado striking after a tsunami.

"Honey?" Mom says. "Are you still there?"

"I have to go," I whisper. "I'll come up to see you in Rhode Island tomorrow or the day after, okay?"

"Oh, that would be lovely. Bring Chase."

"Sure," I tell her, even though I refuse to take a three-hour car ride with my brother. I've seen enough of him these past few days.

After I hang up, Dominic calls to tell me Josephine decided not to resign.

"What was Lincoln doing there?" I ask him.

"She's Jo's new assistant. Birds of a feather, those two. But don't worry...I'm sure you won't need to see too much of Lincoln. Unless you *want* to see too much of her. I heard you two had a moment in your pool."

A beat passes. "You're misinformed, Dominic."

He makes a sound, like a grunt. "Anyway, wear a tux tonight," he says before disconnecting.

His explanation doesn't appease me. I lie down on my bed to mull things over, but end up sleeping. When I wake, it's a quarter past six. In a panic, I pull on my tuxedo and comb some gel into my hair.

"This is the last night," I tell my mirror image. "Last night."

Grabbing my keys and cell phone, I walk out my door and go down into the street where the driver who dropped me off is already waiting. Maybe he was always there. I climb into the car and send Diana, who's left me half-a-dozen messages, an emoticon of a thumbs up.

When I arrive at the museum, the driver drops me off in front of the mammoth entrance. Along with the other attendees, I make my way inside, dodging one question after another.

I spot Madame Babanina a few paces ahead of me, twittering with her high-society friends. Hoping she doesn't notice me, I hurry past them into the Temple room and make a beeline for the stage, watching the small entrance for Ivy and Chase. Without uttering a single word, Josephine sidles in next to me.

"Lincoln's a liar," I say. "You shouldn't associate with her."

"Aren't we all liars?" she asks, keeping her eyes on the entrance.

My heart jabs my ribcage. The temptation to get the hell away from these toxic people almost overpowers me, but again, I stay stoic, slap on a smile, and remind myself that in a couple hours, I'll be free.

Ivy steps into my line of sight, and my breath catches like it did ten days ago. Her blonde braid gleams as it dips over her shoulder and curves over one of her breasts. I hope she'll be able to forgive— My train of thoughts screeches to a halt when I spot her hand entwined with my brother's.

"We've made it," Dominic yells to the enchanted crowd.

I keep staring at Ivy's hand. She's released my brother's, yet I can't shake the image of their fingers overlapping. Josephine jabs me with her elbow. Rigid with rage, I glare at her. I hate her. With all my heart, I hate her. I also loathe Chase, and I don't like Dominic much either.

She tips her chin toward my right side where an assistant is extending two electronic tablets. Stiffly, I take them from him and carry them over to Ivy and Chase so they can write down their answers. I can't bear to look at Ivy, neither when I hand her the tablet, nor when I collect it.

Her hand shakes. If she'd chosen me, I would have held it.

My brother wins, and although I clap his back, I don't feel happy for him. My gloominess is exacerbated when I see Lincoln speaking with Ivy.

Her calculating green eyes lock on mine. Evil witch. "So you're working for the devil, now?"

"If Josephine's the devil, what does that make you, Brook?" She resents me for our meaningless kiss. "Enjoy your evening. I know I will." She winks and leaves.

"Did she really get eliminated yesterday because of...of what happened in your pool?" Ivy asks.

"Is that what she told you?"

She nods.

"She was eliminated because she was careless," I tell her, just as Madame Babanina locates me.

"Brook, dear, you look so handsome tonight," she says, not bothering to address Ivy. Perplexed by Lincoln's words, I don't tell her to leave me alone even though I'm screaming it inside my mind.

"So, this is goodbye?" Ivy asks.

Lincoln is whispering something into Josephine's ear. "I suppose it is," I say distractedly.

The divorcée's curvy bangs bob against my jaw as she slides her hands around my arm. "I have someone I'd like you to meet. He'd like to start a collection, and I was thinking who better to advise him than—"

I start to shake her off when the entire room goes eerily quiet. The lights flare overhead, and then the detective with the prematurely graying hair bursts into the room.

"FBI," McEnvoy yells. "Nobody move!"

Madame Babanina drops my arm and slinks to the back of the room, along with a large chunk of the crowd.

His partner, Clancy, pops into my line of sight, also in navy and yellow FBI garb. She walks straight up to me. "Brook Jackson, put your hands where I can see them."

Terror flares through me. I rock back.

"Hands up, Jackson, now," she repeats.

In slow motion, I raise my arms. I look for Dominic but instead find Josephine beaming with a savage grin.

"Brook Jackson, you are under arrest for colluding with

wanted criminals, trafficking stolen goods, and laundering money for the mafia."

"What?" I yelp. "This is fucking ridiculous."

Josephine waves her hands in the air. In one of them, she clutches the empty, torn package Ivy's quilt arrived in.

"What the hell is that?" I ask, even though I know exactly what it is. Frantically, I search for Dominic. I can't find him, goddammit! I glare at Josephine as the room fragments around me. I listen as she accuses me of using art for terrible things. I can't decide whether to yell or bawl. Finally, I spot my boss.

"Dominic, tell them this is a misunderstanding," I plead.

Slowly, hunched over, Dominic shakes his head and walks away. *He walks away!*

"With these rights in mind, do you wish to speak to me?" Clancy asks me.

I swing my face toward her. "I'm not speaking to you, or to anyone else here. I want a lawyer. Chase, call Dean right away!" Might as well take him down with me.

"Dean Kane?" McEnvoy asks.

"Yes!"

"Doubt Mr. Kane can represent you as he'll be needing his own defense." McEnvoy glances at Ivy when he says this. "Once we catch him."

"What are you talking about?" I ask in a shrill voice.

Clancy moves toward Ivy. "Ivy, why don't you come with me?" she says, her voice low.

"Wh-why?" Ivy stutters.

She looks around. Agents are escorting the agitated audience outside.

"What happened?" she asks.

"Your sister was attacked."

She pales. "Attacked?"

Clancy nods.

"Is she...is she alive?" she asks, as Chase winds one arm around her waist. I glare at his arm.

"She's in a coma," Clancy says, then tells her that Dean gave one of the other inmates a blade to attack Aster.

"I don't understand," Ivy says, but I do.

I squeeze my eyes shut.

"Why did Dean order the hit?" Ivy asks.

"To retrieve the diamonds Troy Mann hid inside your quilt."

"Diamonds?" She looks genuinely surprised.

"Dean and Troy were working together."

"But then that would mean—" Ivy swings her gaze toward me. "You didn't send Dean to help her. You sent him to execute her!"

Her words and her expression drain my lungs of air. When she launches herself at me, and Chase holds her back, I freeze.

"Let go of me!" she screams.

"No," my brother says.

"Let go of me right now or so help me God—"

He still doesn't.

"Chase, please," she begs, her voice breaking.

"Did your sister take the diamonds, Ivy?" Clancy asks.

"I don't know," she says.

I start laughing, a nervous, uncontrollable laughter, the sort of laughter that possesses mourners during funerals. I try to stop it, but everything inside and outside of me has become uncontrollable. Tears drip from the corners of my eyes. I shut them to push them out. When I crack my lids open, Ivy's expression has morphed into pure hatred.

Clancy turns to her partner. "Take him away," she says, at the same time as Chase whispers, "He's not worth it," in Ivy's ear.

Those words shatter what's left of me.

PART 3
AFTER

THIRTY

3 WEEKS LATER

JOSH

Today is the fourth week of Aster's coma. The doctors aren't pessimistic about her remission, but they don't offer guarantees. One of the nurses tells me she's even noticed spikes in her pulse. The EEG waves in her brain are faster, and apparently that's a good sign.

I've spent so little time with Heidi in the past few weeks, I decide to make it up to her tonight by taking her to a fancy restaurant. I don't really feel like it, but it'll probably be good for me. Talk about something other than Aster's coma, with someone other than Ivy.

Although, am I even able to talk of anything else?

I've barely asked Ivy about the show and about Chase. Our conversations somehow always revolve around Aster. Plus, I don't especially enjoy talking about Chase. I've met him, and I don't trust him. Maybe I'm biased, but he's the brother of a convict...that's bad news. When I mentioned it to Ivy, she reminded me she was the sister of a convict. I told her the parallel wasn't amusing.

As I iron my shirt for my date, Ivy phones me.

"I've just spent thirty-five minutes pressing a shirt," I say, lifting the iron. I've created a huge crease along the front of the shirt. "I suck at this."

"Can you come over?" she asks, her voice a mere whisper.

The hot iron slides out of my hand and falls on my foot. Thankfully, I have a sock on so it doesn't burn my skin, but it still hurts.

"Is everything all right?" I ask, as I unplug the damn thing.

"I...I got a package today."

A sour taste spreads from the back of my throat to my palate. This cannot be starting again. "You got to be kidding me."

"I'm scared."

I remember her mentioning Chase was coming over for a visit. "Isn't your boyfriend there?"

"He is, but I need *you*," she whispers.

"Okay. I'll be there in fifteen."

I put the iron back on the board, yank on my shirt, and grab my dinner jacket, wallet, phone, and keys. On my way over to Ivy's, I phone Heidi to tell her I'll be thirty minutes late. "I have to stop by the office to grab something," I lie. I think she'll give up on me if I tell her the truth. "I'll be there at seven-thirty. I promise."

"Okay," she says unenthusiastically, and hangs up.

I drive like a madman over to Ivy's. When I get there, she's standing by the door, a flimsy shawl draped over her pointy shoulders. She's starting to look as skeletal as Aster. I jog up to her.

Shadows press across her pale face. "Come in."

I look for Chase, but don't see him. I hear the shower, so I imagine he's in the bathroom. Wordlessly, the shawl still pulled tight around her, Ivy extricates a small, lumpy envelope from one of the kitchen drawers and hands it to me. Her name is printed on it, along with the hospital address.

"A nurse gave it to Chase, who brought it up to me," she says.

I shake it, and a small, black velvet box tumbles out. I pop it open and my eyes widen. A gold pendant spells Ivy's name and a diamond as big as a blueberry dots the small *i*.

"Christ, is that one of the diamonds?"

She holds a finger to her lips. "It looks exactly like the one that was stolen from me in New York," she whispers.

I suck on my bottom lip and watch the stone wink at me maliciously. I click the box shut. "I'll bring it to the precinct. And I'll stop by the hospital to find out who dropped the package off."

"There's a stamp, Josh. It was mailed."

Right. I look around the living room. "Any new ideas where Aster could've hidden the rest of them?"

"I'm still convinced Brook has them."

"He swore the stones never got to New York."

"Like I would believe a word that comes out of that guy's mouth." Her voice is low and hard. "What else did he say?"

"That he was moving them for Dean Kane."

"Of course..." Ivy mutters. "Why would he ever take the blame? Putting it on someone else is way easier."

"I do believe he was moving them for Dean Kane."

"Are you taking his side?"

"I'm not taking sides," I say gruffly. "It's been a shitty month, Ivy. A real shitty month. Do you know that Heidi is barely speaking to me anymore? I'm supposed to take her out to the restaurant tonight, but now...now I need to deal with this."

"I'm sorry."

The shower stops.

Looking remorseful, she takes the box from my fingers and

slips it inside my jacket pocket. "I meant to ask you something... I felt like sewing today, and when I went to pick out some fabric from Mom's special drawer, not only was it unlocked, but the latch was broken and the fabrics were in disarray. Do you know anything about that?"

I unbutton my jacket, then button it up again. "I didn't want to worry you..."

"But now you are."

"There was a break-in."

"A break-in?"

My face goes hot.

"*What* break-in?"

"While you were in New York, someone searched your apartment."

Her eyes have become as round as those translucent psychic balls her mother adored. "What?"

Footsteps resound. I glance at her to see if she wants to continue talking about this, or if she wants me to leave before Chase makes an appearance.

"Whoever broke in probably found the rest of them, then." There's a bitter edge to her voice.

I don't like it, but I deserve it. "I doubt it. A few days later, we caught Angela Discoli rifling through the motel room she'd used with Troy Mann, so my guess is that they're still missing."

I spot Chase in the entrance of the hallway, a towel knotted around his waist. His brown hair drips water along his chest. He's not as scrawny as he looked on TV, but he's far less muscular than me. For some reason, I find satisfaction in that.

"You know those diamonds Special Agent Clancy told us about—the ones Troy Mann hid in my quilt? Apparently they're still missing," she tells him.

I scowl at her. I don't think she should be sharing so much information. What if Chase is working with Brook? After all, he brought the package to Ivy. "It's just a theory."

"Someone broke into my place to search for them," she adds.

Chase strides toward her and wraps an arm around her. He's getting her clothes wet. "You're not safe here, Ivy. You should come back to New York with me."

"Because New York is safe?" I snort. "Give me a break."

"I can't leave Aster anyway, Chase," she says, tilting her face toward him. "I'll walk Josh out. I'll be right back." She breaks away from her boyfriend and steps out ahead of me in the darkness. Once the door shuts, she asks, "Can you go see Brook? Tell him I will press charges if he makes another threat?"

"I'll phone the Feds. Maybe they can send someone—"

"You mean those detectives who interrogated me?" She snorts. "No. I want *you* to go. You're still the only person I trust."

"I'll try to get a flight out in the morning."

One of her neighbors drives down the street. He glares at Ivy as he unloads his sleepy kid from the backseat. "Everyone hates me around here. Maybe it would be safer, at least for everyone else, if I left."

"Don't you dare go anywhere. And especially not with Chase." I don't tell her about my suspicions, but from the way she winches her eyebrows, I think she gets it.

"I won't."

After a quick hug, she goes back inside and shuts the door. I get in my car, but don't drive off. I call the chief.

"She got a diamond in the mail today," I tell him.

"A real one?"

"I...I hadn't even considered it could be fake."

"Bring it to Fred. His wife did some gemology course if I'm not mistaken."

"Okay. And, Chief, I'd like to go to New York tomorrow to pay Brook a visit. You think I can go?"

"I think you *should* go." I'm hoping he says the precinct will fund the trip. He doesn't. "And tell Fred to phone me after his wife's done looking at the stone," he adds before hanging up.

I stare at my dark dashboard. I knew that until we caught Dean Kane and retrieved those diamonds, life wouldn't go back to normal, but the fact that Brook is targeting Ivy with scare tactics bothers me. I get back out of the car and knock on Mr. Mancini's door.

The lights are on and the TV is painfully loud, so I know he's awake, yet he takes a mighty long time opening up.

"Sorry. I got the runs," he explains as he tucks his plaid shirt into his high-waisted pants. "Everything okay?"

"You haven't seen anyone lurking recently, have you?"

He farts, long and loud. I grimace as the terrible smell reaches me. "Besides your pretty cop? Naw. I'm keeping watch."

"My pretty cop?"

"Yeah."

There was only one woman in the precinct who was remotely pretty. A Puerto Rican girl—

"Long red hair, yay tall." He taps his chest.

"We don't have a redhead at the station."

"I asked to see her badge, and she showed it to me."

"When did she stop by?" I ask, scanning the street for movement.

"'Bout ten days ago."

"And you're sure she had red hair?"

"I might be old, but I'm not blind. And her badge was real. I inspected it."

"Did she give you a name?"

"Officer Carella."

Goose bumps crawl over me. There is no Officer Carella. "Can you call me if she stops by again?"

"Yeah."

As I turn to leave, I scan his porch. A tiny red dot catches my attention. I stride over to it. "Did you put this camera up?" I ask him.

"Your guys installed it. For Ivy's security. They did a shitty job if you ask me."

"What guys?"

"I don't know, Josh. You sent them over a couple days after Ivy got home. Even though I didn't feel like piercing holes in my beams, I let them. I thought I was doing you and the twins a favor."

"What did they look like?"

"They looked like your usual security guys. One had a beard, I think."

"Did they mention what company they worked for?"

"Securitox."

I type it into an Internet search page on my phone. "Doesn't exist." I gape up at him, sweat beading behind my ears.

"Well, don't just stand there. Rip it out," he yells.

I raise my arm and tug on it, but it's screwed in tight. Mr. Mancini storms back into his house, then back out, rifle in hand. I'm about to tell him not to shoot it down when he starts hitting the camera with the stock of his gun. After four blows, it falls down.

I was wrong. Ivy isn't safe here.

After asking Mancini to call me if anyone else approaches him, I return to my car and drive over to Fred's with the camera and the diamond. While his wife gets a loupe and a pair of tiny tongs to inspect it, I tell him about the fake cop and show him the camera.

"The stone's fake," she says.

Like the cop, but not like the camera.

THIRTY-ONE

Brook

"Inmate Jackson, you got a visitor." I rise from my seat on a bench in the outside pen they take us into for some fresh air every day, come rain or shine.

As I follow the guard, the other inmates stop lifting weights or tossing a ball to stare at me. Since I was booked almost a month ago, only one guy tried to mess with me, but I beat him to a pulp, bruising my knuckles badly in the process. It served its purpose: the others left me alone.

I half-expected to cross paths with Diego Discoli, but he was moved to another prison upon my arrival. A higher security one. I'd been hoping to run into him since he's one of the reasons I'm stuck inside this shithole, but a meet-and-greet never happened.

Not much has happened at all in the past weeks.

Dad came to visit a few times. Mom comes nearly every day. She's been staying at a hotel nearby. I told her not to spend her money on a hotel for my sake, and she told me to shut up. Carmelina and Diana have also visited me religiously. Chase is the only person who hasn't made the trip. Even Diana's father came up once.

He's been trying to counter the no-bail rule since I'm not innocent of the crimes I was charged with, but no judge is willing to discuss it until my "associate" Dean Kane is brought in.

A few days ago, I took matters into my own hands, and sure enough, when I see who's come to pay me a visit through the bulletproof glass, my plan worked.

I sit down and pick up the phone. The young officer on the other side of the glass has his phone already pressed against his ear.

"Joshua Cooper, right?" I ask.

He nods. "How do you know my name?"

"You investigated me so I investigated you. Only fair."

"Did you send Ivy a package containing a necklace?"

"Yes."

His eyes narrow. "Did you also send a fake cop and have a camera installed?"

"What? No."

"You admit you threatened her with a necklace, but didn't—"

"It wasn't a threat."

"Was it a gift?" he asks sarcastically.

"No."

"Then why the hell did you send her a necklace?" he yells, but then, he glances around him and drops his voice. "Are you some sort of sicko?"

"It was a message." I lean my elbows on the table and stare straight into Josh's pulsing green irises. "I'm done playing games, and I'm done playing nice. I want out of here, Josh…Can I call you Josh?"

"You've been convicted of a federal offense. What makes you think you can get out of here?"

"What if I told you I can get Dean Kane to come straight to you?"

"If you say *you* aren't the one monitoring Ivy, then my guess is, he's already around."

"Have the diamonds been found?"

"That's none of your business."

I grind my teeth. "It's become my business."

"Look, I made the trip out here with money from my own pocket, money I earned the hard way, the lawful way. And the only reason I came is to tell you to strop threatening my friend."

The young cop makes to hang up the phone, but I knuckle the glass to stop him. Reluctantly, he brings it back to his ear.

"I can help you nail Dean Kane for murder."

"Murder?" Of course that gets Josh's attention. "Aster didn't die."

"I wasn't talking about Aster Redd."

"Who were you talking about then?"

"Get me out, and I'll talk. But I'll only talk to you and to Ivy, no federal agent."

"What makes you think I have that authority?"

"*You* don't, but I'm sure you can make contact with someone who does."

"I can't get you out just because you're asking me to."

I close my eyes. "What if I told you where you can find one of the missing stones?"

Josh blinks. He's hooked, sinker and all. "Where?"

I lean forward. "I want an official release paper signed by a judge."

"That could take me days to get."

"Then it'll take you days to find out the whereabouts of the diamond."

TWENTY-FOUR HOURS GO BY.

And then twenty-four more.

Joshua Cooper either didn't bite or didn't have the political pull.

When my mother stops by to see how I'm doing and notices my glummer-than-usual mood, she assumes something appalling has happened to my ass. It takes a while to convince her I wasn't raped.

An hour after she leaves, Joshua Cooper returns with a signed, supervised release form. The paper is my first tiny victory. That very day, I walk out of jail with leg irons, hand-cuffs, and hope.

He's leaning against the prisoner transport van that's been prepped for my twelve-hour trip to Kokomo. "You better not make a run for it, Jackson, because my chief and I are risking a lot taking you out of here."

"I have nowhere to go, Josh," I tell him as I climb into the empty minibus. "So I'm not running. But my mother needs to be informed. She's the only one who visits me every day. She'll ask questions if I'm not there."

"We're not broadcasting your release," Josh says, climbing in the back with me.

"I wouldn't want you to. Have the prison guards tell my mother I was moved to a restricted area."

He grumbles something, but makes the call. Once he hangs up, he asks, "So where's that diamond?"

"You know the D.A. on the Discoli case?"

Josh's jaw slackens.

"*That diamond* is around his wife's neck. Type Hope Gala

and her name in Google's search bar and you'll find several pictures of her wearing it. Ask the D.A. for the stone's certificate. He won't be able to produce any. And then, he'll either tell you it's a family heirloom, or he'll tell you it was a gift. Whatever lie he chooses to go with, you'll have one of your missing jewels."

Joshua stares at me long and hard before calling his chief. He stays on the line a while, probably to verify my information. Finally, he disconnects. "The chief saw the picture. He's calling New York to have someone pick it up." He bites his lip. "So the Discolis sent the diamonds to New York to pay off the D.A.?"

I nod.

"And you only got one to him?"

"*Dean* only got one to him."

"What about the others?"

"They never arrived in New York."

Josh keeps chewing on his lip. "How'd you get the necklace to Ivy?"

"I asked a friend to have it made and shipped to the hospital."

"What friend?"

"There are enough people involved, don't you think?" I ask. "Plus, she wasn't aware of what she was doing. She was just doing me a favor."

"Like someone else I know…"

His comment doesn't rile me up like it would've done a few days back when my future was as bleak and forbidding as that blue hole I dove into during a long-ago boat trip in the Bahamas. Besides, he's right. I *was* stupid. But I'm done being stupid.

"How's Ivy?" I ask after another long bout of silence.

"Like you care."

"I do care."

He shoots me a sideways glance. "She's not doing too well."

"Mom told me Chase was visiting her. Is he still there?"

"No. He left last night."

Frustration at the fact that he *was* there, doing God knows what to Ivy, stings my heart. "So she's alone?"

"I put a security detail on her."

An hour slides by in thick silence. Josh plinks around on his phone. It buzzes repeatedly, and repeatedly he types back messages.

"What happened between the two of you?" Josh asks, and it takes me a minute to understand that we're speaking about my brother again.

"We were both after the same thing."

Josh runs a hand through his short brown hair. "You mean, the art school?"

I nod, even though the Masterpiecers was just the igniting incident. "He wanted the family business, and I would've gladly given it to him if there was anything left of it. But you must be aware by now that my family's bankrupt. It's been all over the news. If I remember correctly, the day after the show closed, the *Times* published an article titled, *The Jacksons: Win Some, Lose Some.*"

Josh doesn't respond. After a long while, he says, "I didn't tell Ivy about the fake cop or the camera. I don't want to fuel her stress, so don't mention it when you see her."

"I won't breathe a word of it tonight."

"Tonight? It'll be late. You can see her tomor—"

"Tonight, or I stop talking."

Josh turns away from the window. "How do I know you're not planning on hurting her?"

"I suppose you don't. You'll just have to trust me."

"Trust you?" Josh pounds his fist against the headrest of the seat in front of him. "How am I supposed to trust a felon?"

The bus driver glances into the rearview mirror but doesn't slow down.

"Josh, who has more to lose? You or me?" I ask.

He leans his forehead against the seat in front and shuts his eyes. "You swear you're not playing me?" His eyes are still closed.

"I tried to save my family. That's how I found myself in this mess." Mess sounds too insignificant for what it truly is. "I'm not a bad person, Josh. I'm just a person who did bad things."

He opens his eyes and glares at me.

"I admit I was looking for easy money, regardless of whether it was clean or not. But unlike Dean, I didn't murder anyone to preserve that money."

"*Who* did he murder?"

"How do you think Kevin died?" I say, slipping one of my aces out of my prison-issue jumpsuit sleeve.

Pressing himself upright again, Josh blinks. "I knew it!"

The driver's gaze skirts the rearview mirror again.

"And you have proof?" he asks excitedly.

"I know where to get proof; however, and—this is non-negotiable—the person who possesses the proof cannot be charged with anything. If you don't promise me this in writing, I will not obtain it for you. As I said before, there are enough people involved already."

"Why now, Jackson? Why wait three weeks?"

"I was giving Dean and his father one last chance to save me."

"His father?" Josh says. "You mean mother..."

"No, I mean father."

"Who's his father?"

I don't tell Josh because Ivy deserves to be the first to find out.

THIRTY-TWO

JOSH

When we get to the safe house, it's late. After signing discharge papers for the transport guard, I take hold of Brook's arm and lead him inside the small apartment where Claire is waiting. Guarda ordered one of us to remain with the prisoner at all times, so we're doing eight-hour shifts. Claire starts tonight, Fred comes in tomorrow morning, and then it's my turn.

I help Brook out of the leg irons and the handcuffs, but leave the ankle monitor in place.

"This is for you," Claire tells him, shoving a brown paper bag filled with clothes and some toiletries into his arms. Her gaze lingers on him, and I swear she wets her lips.

As he takes everything inside the bathroom, I turn to Claire. "Are you going to jump him or guard him?"

"Funny, Coop," she says, pursing her lips.

"I'm going to go collect Ivy. I'll be back in a bit. Don't screw this up."

I phone Ivy on my way over to her place and tell her to get ready.

"For what?" she asks.

"Can't tell you over the phone. Just get dressed."

I should probably have specified what she should wear because when I arrive, she's put on this little black dress, sheer tights, and ankle boots. "You have no idea how much I've been wanting to get out of the house," she says, locking her door the minute I pull up in front.

I let her think we're going to dinner during the entire drive. It's way better than telling her about Brook.

"How's everything with Heidi?" she asks, combing her fingers through her long hair. It sparkles each time a streetlight hits it.

"We're taking a break."

"What?" she exclaims. "When did that happen?"

"After I took your necklace to have the diamond inspected, I lost track of time. She assumed I'd stood her up—which wasn't honestly too far from the truth." My fingers clench around the steering wheel. "I'm a lousy boyfriend."

Ivy touches my arm. "No. You're an amazing boyfriend, but you're also an amazing friend, which has made your dating life hell. Do you want me to talk to her?"

I cock an eyebrow at her suggestion. I even raise a small smile.

"I'm the last person she'd want to talk with right now, huh?"

"Not the last. But yeah, somewhere down there."

She makes a face. "I ruined your love life."

"You owe me."

She nods. "How can I make it up to you?"

I slide the car in front of the safe house.

Ivy looks around. "Where are we?"

"You asked how you can make it up to me? Come inside."

"What's inside?"

I don't answer.

"Josh, you're scaring me. What's inside?"

I get out of the car and walk over to her side. After I pull her door open, I extend my hand. "Do you trust me?"

"Of course."

"Then trust me."

She latches on to my hand, because a decade and a half together inspires trust in people. Making her face Brook without warning could harm our bond, but it's a risk I'm willing to take to have this be over.

THIRTY-THREE

Brook

I jerk upright as the door opens. When I hear Ivy's voice, I pull my shoulders back and sit up straighter, attempting to salvage some of the pride prison stole from me.

"Is this a joke?" Her head veers so wildly from me to Josh that her long curls whip her face. She picks the gold strands out of her eyes. "What is *he* doing here?"

Josh looks down at the floor, clearly uncomfortable. "Brook is cooperating with the police to help us apprehend Dean Kane."

"But they're both as evil," Ivy screams. "He laughed at me the day he was arrested! He laughed when he heard Aster had been attacked!"

"I wasn't laughing at you, Ivy, or at your sister," I tell her.

She swings back toward me. "I heard you!"

"When I'm nervous, I laugh. I can't control it. I laughed at my grandfather's funeral. Ask Chase."

The mention of my brother makes her stick out her chin. "Does he know you're here?"

"No one knows except you, and Josh, and his *squad*," I say, gesturing toward the blonde cop who's been ogling me like a tourist in front of a gelato display.

"The name's Claire," she says, twirling the tip of her ponytail around a fat finger.

"Well, I'm thrilled you have some inside help, Josh." Ivy does not sound thrilled at all. "But there's no way in hell I'm talking to him."

"Ivy..." Josh's Adam's apple bobs. "Please."

"Why me? Have I not been through enough?"

I stand up and take a step toward her, but stop when she steps back. She folds her arms over her chest.

"You're one of his reasons for cooperating," Josh says. "Hate me for this later, but help us catch Dean. Please. I worry so much about you and Aster. I don't want to worry anymore."

Ivy's beautiful lips press tight.

"I beg you, Ives."

I keep my gaze on her mouth until the firm line becomes pliable. Then I dare look up into her eyes. They still glow with hatred, but also with reluctance.

"Will you sit?" I ask her.

"I'm fine standing." Her chest heaves, rising and falling underneath her pretty black dress.

I sink down on the cheap, foam couch and explain how I ended up running errands for Dean Kane. As I talk, her arms loosen. She doesn't walk up to me and lay a comforting hand on my shoulder, but at least, when she looks at me after I'm finished explaining, all that's left in those vivid blue eyes of hers is pity. I'm not sure I like the pity, but I like it better than the fierce loathing.

"So where is Dean Kane hiding?" she asks.

"My bet is on Dominic's yacht."

Josh starts at the information. "Dominic...as in Dominic Bacci?"

"Dominic is protecting him?" Ivy's voice is shrill.

My fingers overlap and my palms squash together as I stare up into Ivy's face. Her eyes have grown so wide with trepidation I don't feel the thrill I thought I would at the big reveal. Instead, an ache blooms in my chest at having to tell her that yet another person she trusted deceived her.

"Dominic is Dean's father."

JOSH

"No way," I whisper, at the same time as Ivy rocks back on her heels, face incredibly pale.

"Dominic"—her voice cracks—"Dominic and Dean..."

Brook gives a heavy nod, but doesn't gloat. I have to give him that: he doesn't seem proud about all the information he's feeding us. He seems sad. For a brief moment, I take pity on the guy, but then I remember he had a choice, and he made the wrong one. Whatever his reasons.

I'm expecting Ivy to ask me to drive her home, but instead she sits down.

"It's enough for one night," I tell her. "Let's go home."

"I just want to understand—"

"Tomorrow, Ives. Tomorrow, you can spend all afternoon babysitting Brook with me, but tonight, you and I are going home."

Brook glances up at me, his dark eyes shiny. I suppose he's

happy at the prospect of spending all day with Ivy, which leads me to wonder if anything happened between them in New York.

"Now," I say when I don't see her move.

She springs off the couch.

Brook stares at her and she stares at him. Those Jackson brothers are bad news. Both of them. She still hasn't moved, so I grab her arm and tow her out, yelling at Claire to stay alert. She gives me the finger, and I'm so riled up against Brook that I growl. Inside the car, I give Ivy a large chunk of my mind.

"Geez," she says, "you sound like your mother." She plops her elbow on the armrest and cradles her head with her fingers. "I can't believe Dominic has a son. I can't believe I didn't realize they were related. How did I not see the resemblance?"

"Stop tormenting yourself."

She sighs.

I stare ahead at the broken white lines that rhythmically vanish and appear around my lane.

"Josh?"

"Yes?"

"If Aster—I mean *when* Aster wakes up, what's going to happen to her?"

"There'll be a trial, which she won't need to attend if we use the power of attorney you made her sign."

"You know about that?"

"Yeah."

She bites her lip. "I did it to protect her...in case...in case prison made her...made her..." She carves her hand through her hair. Her fingers tremble. "Made her worse."

I catch her hand in mine and squeeze it. "Ivy, you thought you were doing the right thing. Turns out, you did, even though you should've discussed it with her."

"She would never have agreed."

"Probably not." I stop at a traffic light. "I'll call Kelley tomorrow. Ask him if he can help out."

"Kevin's lawyer?"

I nod.

"You think he would help us?"

"He's friends with my chief."

"Is he expensive?"

The light turns green. "Don't worry about that."

"How can I not worry about that?"

"Because I'm asking you not to worry about it." I make a left turn into her street. "Maybe he'll do it for free."

"Dean wanted to make her plead insanity. You think that's what he'll suggest?"

"I think that might be her only option."

I park. My fingers latch onto the handle but don't pump it open. "Just because Brook's cooperating doesn't mean he's a nice guy."

"I know, but what he told me tonight...it clears so much up."

"Did anything happen between the two of you back on the show?"

"No." Even though it's dark inside the car, I see color splashing her cheeks.

"Then why are you blushing?"

"I don't know." She throws her hands up in the air. "I always blush. Plus, I'm dating his brother. That would be wrong in too many ways."

"About his brother...are you being safe?"

"Oh my God, Josh! I'm not discussing my sex life with you."

"So you *are* having sex," I say.

"No, I'm not."

"Why not?"

"Because I'm stressed out... He's stressed out. It's never the right time." A weighty sigh escapes her. "And he keeps asking me if I'm sure."

"Well? Are you?"

"I'm nineteen. Even Aster—" She stops talking because she knows who took Aster's virginity.

Me.

"Are you sure you want to have sex with *him?*" I clarify.

"He's my boyfriend. Who else am I supposed to have sex with? And don't suggest you. Yuck."

"Yuck?" I say, right before I burst out laughing. Then she cracks up. Tears stream out of my eyes. After a while, our laughter is replaced by large smiles, and then by weaker ones.

"We needed that," she says, pressing her head back against the headrest.

"We seriously needed that. But really"—I stick out my bottom lip—"yuck?"

"I adore you, Joshy, but you're the brother I never had."

"I love you too, Ives. And agreed; I would never do you either. Even if you begged me."

She opens her car door and steps out. Before shutting it, she asks, "Can you stay with me? Until I fall asleep? I know it's juvenile, but I don't like being home alone."

Never able to say no to Ivy, I go inside and sit at the foot of her bed, and discuss Brook and Dean until I'm the only one talking. Once she's sound asleep, I head over to the hospital to check up on Aster.

It's the middle of the night, yet several cars are parked in front. As I walk toward the dimly lit entrance, I do a double take in front of a powder blue bumper. Running my hand against the pointed tailfins, I circle Troy's Cadillac and peer inside. A lady purse and a discarded blouse lay on the backseat. I assume both are Stephanie's. She mustn't have found a buyer, which leads me to wonder how much she's asking for it. Probably a bunch. Troy kept his ride in pristine condition.

I startle out of my price-assessment. Stephanie hates Aster. If her car is here that means— I sprint through the sliding glass doors toward the welcome desk, point to my badge, and ask if a Stephanie Britton has checked in. The nurse shakes her head no. I describe her. Again, I'm met with a headshake. I take the stairs two-by-two and hold my breath until I reach the guard stationed in front of Aster's room. I ask him about visitors. Like the nurse, he says there weren't any.

She must've sold the Cadillac then. I long to ask Heidi, but how can I call her in the middle of the night to ask about Troy's car when I haven't had the courage to talk to her about us yet?

Breathing deeply, I enter the small room and listen to the rhythmic beeping of the electrocardiograph machine until my pulse evens out. Then I pull up a seat next to Aster's bed and latch on to her hand, and I tell her about Brook, about New York, about Dean and Dominic. If it weren't for the oxygen mask covering her mouth, Aster would simply look as though she were sleeping.

Her hair has been chopped so short it looks fuzzy. I caress it, then stroke her cheek. It's warm and pulsates from the air that's being pushed into her lungs. I rest my forehead against the side of her face.

"I'm going to make your world safe again, Aster. I promise."

I press a gentle kiss onto each of her eyelids. I want her to feel I'm here. Her heart spikes on the EKG. I suck in a breath and watch her face, hoping to see her lids flutter, but they don't.

I take her hand and squeeze it. "I'm going to go home and try to get some sleep. I'll be back in the morning."

As I stand up, her fingers tighten around mine. I shoot my gaze down to her hand. It's definitely curled around mine. The pressure happens again. It's light but it's there.

I jerk my gaze up to her face. Her lids are open.

"Aster?" I whisper, not wanting to spook her.

Her eyes don't meet mine. Instead, she stares up at the ceiling. It's a little freaky. Without letting go of her hand, I move my face into her line of sight.

"Aster," I whisper again. She blinks but her eyes remain focused on nothing. "Hey, you." When her fingers begin slipping out of my hand, I crush them. "Blink twice if you can hear me?" I stare at her eyes. They're lighter than Ivy's, almost translucent, with steel-blue circles around the iris. I've missed those eyes.

They close. I will them to open again, but they remain sealed tight. I don't move for a long time. It's the door of her room swinging open that jolts me. A nurse trundles in and frowns at me.

I think she might ask me what I'm doing visiting at this hour, but instead, she says, "You should go home and rest, honey. You look terrible."

"I'm going," I say with a sigh.

Delicately, I place Aster's fingers back on the bed sheets and rise. I head to the door, but instead of walking out, I stay inside and close it, then I turn back toward the nurse. She's inspecting the EKG machine and jotting something down in Aster's chart.

"She opened her eyes," I tell her.

The nurse looks up. She has all these lines on her face even though she doesn't look old enough to have that many. "When?"

"Fifteen minutes ago...a half hour. I'm not sure. She even squeezed my fingers."

Her lips slope up. "I thought I detected an elevation of the ST segments."

"Does that mean she's out of her coma?"

"It means her chances of recovery have just improved. But, Joshua, she's reaching the minimally conscious state. She could stay in that state a long time before making a full recovery. Your mom told me not to get your hopes up too high."

"You spoke to my mother?"

"She's stopped by a few times to check on Aster. We talked.

She's worried about you and the twins. I hear their mother's no longer alive, and the father's not around."

I find myself smiling a little. Even though it's late, I text my mother to thank her for taking care of the girls.

"Can you call me...if she wakes up again?" I ask the nurse. "And don't leak this to the press," I add. "It's really important."

"Deal. But get some sleep. You're going to run yourself into a hospital bed."

"Tell the other nurses, too."

"Okay, Officer. Now, go."

As I take the elevator back down to the lobby, I brace myself against the wall to keep my knees from buckling. The doors open, but I don't get out. And then they close, like Aster's lids. And I just stand there, watching them.

When the elevator goes dark, I tap the back of my head against the wall and let the relief of the day burn away the fear and worry that's been gnawing at me since Aster discovered Troy Mann's file on my desk.

Brook

"You want us to do what?" Josh exclaims the following afternoon. He's flushed beet-red and beads of sweat track down the sides of his face.

"I want you to put out a news brief that Aster woke up. If he thinks there's a way to get his hands on those diamonds, he'll be on the first flight back from Cuba," I tell Josh, his boss, Fred, and Claire. "Ivy can give an interview from Aster's hospital room, posing as Aster."

"No way." Josh shakes his head.

"You have to admit, it's a sound idea, Coop," the chief says, rolling the ends of his mustache.

"I'll do it," Ivy says.

"Absolutely not! The guy killed someone in cold blood. Do you think he would hesitate for a second to do the same to you when you can't tell him where the diamonds are?" His forehead is so shiny it reflects the ceiling light dangling over the wooden coffee table.

"She'll have increased protection," the chief says. "They'll both have increased protection."

"It would be *crazy*," Josh yells.

"It really isn't that crazy," Ivy says calmly, glancing at me. I wouldn't go so far as to say she's excited, but she's definitely animated by the idea.

"You don't even have the same hairdo," Josh says. He's nitpicking now.

"I'll crop mine short like hers," Ivy suggests.

This time, I say no at the same time as Josh, because one, I love her hair, and two, no pictures of Aster have been leaked since she was wheeled out of the prison and transported to the hospital.

"I didn't even know her hair had been cut. So Dean probably doesn't either," I say.

"Why don't we just arrest Dominic and force him to bring his boat out of Cuban waters?" Claire suggests.

Josh blinks at her.

"All that would do is spook Dean. The only thing Dean wants is to set things right with the Discolis before they off him. Trust me. We let him think Aster woke up with no memory loss, and he's going to come straight to us."

"How do we know this is not some ploy to get *your* paws on those diamonds?" Claire asks. I almost laugh at the word paws, as she has quite the pair.

Ivy sits up straighter and frowns.

"What exactly would those diamonds do for me, Claire?" I ask in a brittle voice. "I wouldn't be able to sell them. I wouldn't be able to trade them with the bank to cover our debts. They belong to the Discolis, so then I would become a target for the mob family. And let's not forget the FBI...they'd lock me up forever. The only real thing those diamonds would win me is a one-way trip to the graveyard, and I don't care for dying. I still have things I want to do."

"Like returning to the Masterpiecers?" Fred asks.

"I don't plan on returning to that school, or to New York."

"Where are you going to go then?" Ivy asks.

"I want to move to a small town, maybe work with horses on a ranch."

Her lips part in surprise.

"I can picture you in a pair of cowhide slacks and a cowboy hat, chewing on some long grass," Claire says.

I don't enjoy her picturing me in her head.

Ivy snorts a laugh. She claps her hand against her mouth. "A ranch?"

I smile. "What?"

"Can we please get back to the matter at hand?" the chief says.

I nod. We all nod. Even Josh, who's glaring at me.

"When do we do it?" Guarda asks.

"Next week," Ivy says.

"Why wait so long?" Fred asks.

"We are not doing it," Josh says. "I'm going to come up with a better plan. Ivy and I will brainstorm this weekend."

"I can't this weekend," she says, a blush slinking over her nose.

"Why not?" Josh asks her.

"I'm, uh..." She stares down at her Stan Smiths. "There's a party. Remember Maxine? She's throwing a party at her house in the Hamptons for everyone from the show."

The smile snaps off my lips.

"You shouldn't be going anywhere until we catch Dean," Josh says.

"I agree with Josh," I say.

"I need to go. I promised—"

I interrupt her. "How are you even getting there?"

"Um...uh...by plane."

"What plane?" Josh asks.

"Someone's," she says cryptically.

"Ivy, just get it out already. What plane?" he all but growls.

Has my brother chartered a private aircraft with the hundred grand he won? If he has, he's an idiot. Mom and Dad—

She sighs. "An art dealer wants to meet with me. He wants me to bring over some of my quilts. So he's sending his jet over to pick me up." She lifts her eyes to mine. "Brook knows him."

I suck in a furious breath. "Paul? You're going on Paul Willows's jet?"

A blush floods Ivy's face.

"I told you not to sell anything to him. He's as sleazy as they come."

"You should talk," she says, and I recoil, my body, like my ego, taking a hit.

I don't raise my eyes to hers once while the rest of them discuss the safety of leaving Indiana. When the chief stands up, the others accompany him to the door. I stare sullenly at a sticky stain on the coffee table. Specks of lint are trapped on the surface. They shiver in the cool, musty air blowing from the AC vent above my head.

"It came out wrong," Ivy says.

My jaw clenches like a steel trap.

"I know you're not sleazy."

Still I don't say anything.

"I'm sorry."

I pump my jaw to loosen it, and ask, "Is Chase going with you?"

"He's meeting me there."

"Good." I never thought I'd be glad my brother was with Ivy, but I despise Paul that much.

"By the way, what do you mean, he's sleazy?" she asks, picking at bits of flaking turquoise nail polish.

"He has a reputation for sleeping with most of the artists he represents."

She wrinkles her nose.

"Does Chase know you're going on his plane?"

"Yes."

"And he's not worried?" I'd be going out of my mind if my girlfriend were locked in a compartment several thousand feet above ground with a scumbag.

"Paul is already in the Hamptons. Chase has a meeting with him the afternoon of the party."

"Josh," I say, and the cop whirls toward me.

I wave him over. "Can you accompany her?"

"He has better things to do than play chaperone, Brook."

"Dean is out there," I say. "He might've heard about the party. If he corners you there—"

"Why do you even care?"

"Because"—I stare down at the floor—"I just do." When I raise my eyes back to hers, she's contemplating me as though I were some curio in a shop window.

"Brook's right, Ivy," Josh says. "Either I go with you or you don't go at all. Your choice."

Ivy's face goes through several emotions before settling on resignation. "Fine," she sighs.

Even though I would've liked to have been the one to accompany her, Josh cares about her so deeply I know he will do everything in his power to protect her, be it from Dean or from Paul.

THIRTY-SIX

JOSH

As we drive to the private airstrip, Ivy casts a long sideways glance at me.

"What?" I ask.

"Nothing."

She whisks her gaze away, propelling it on the gleaming silver jet beyond the security gate.

"What?" I ask her again.

"Did you have to wear a Hawaiian shirt?"

I peer down at my floral, short-sleeved shirt. "We're going to a beach party."

"In New York, not in Key West."

"You're wearing leggings and a T-shirt."

"I'm going to change on the plane."

"What *was* I supposed to wear?"

"A plain shirt...with long sleeves."

"Well, I didn't have a clean one," I say, feeling as annoyed as when I was bullied back in middle school. I jab my thumb against the window switch to lower it, then punch the call button. When did Ivy become so hoity-toity about dress codes anyway?

Once the gate opens, I raise my window and drive over to the parking area. Still reeling from Ivy's comment, I pop the trunk and grab my duffel bag and Ivy's suitcase. Aster would never have made me feel bad about what I was wearing. We walk up to the plane, and to the pilot standing beside it. He's wearing a plain white shirt. If I'd cared to fit in, I would've asked him to trade.

He ushers us onto the sleek aircraft that smells of new leather and warm coffee, and seals the hatch. As he takes his seat up front, we settle on two squashy beige leather seats that face each other and click on our lap belts for takeoff. The stewardess introduces herself and asks us what we would like to drink. Ivy asks for coffee while I ask for nothing. I don't want to take anything from these people. I fold my arms together and stare out the small, round window as we shoot upward through a thick layer of clouds. The plane shakes. Ivy grips the armrests while I just squeeze my arms tighter against my chest.

Suddenly my phone rings. I'm so stunned it works at this altitude that it takes me a second to fish it out of my khakis' pocket.

"Can I take the call?" I ask the stewardess.

She nods, so I press it against my ear.

"Cooper," I say.

"Joshua, this is Sabrina, the nurse from the hospital. You told me to call you if there were any changes."

"And? Have there been?"

"Aster started to obey some commands. When I asked her to pinch her nose, she touched it. It's a good sign. Will you be able to stop by to see her today?"

"Not today, but I'll be there first thing tomorrow."

"Good, I think it's important for her to have her loved ones around. It speeds up recovery."

My pulse bleats inside my ears. "Thank you for the news."

"Of course."

After I hang up, I stare at my phone for a long time.

"Who was that?" Ivy asks.

"Claire."

"What did she want?"

"To update me on Angela Discoli's movements," I say, burrowing deeper in my shameful pit of lies. I should tell her the truth, but I don't want to raise her hopes. What if Aster's recovery stops? Or worse, what if the coma returns?

Can a coma return?

"And?" she says.

"Huh?"

"Angela Discoli...has she been on the move?"

"She's, uh...been seen around the motel again."

"They really want their stones back, don't they?"

"The one we seized from the D.A. was estimated to be worth close to five-hundred thousand dollars, so if there are seven more like it, you do the math."

Ivy gasps. "Five-hundred thousand dollars?"

I nod.

"I had half a million dollars sewed into my bag," she murmurs. "If I'd sold it—"

"If you'd sold it, you'd be in jail."

Her cheek dimples; she must be biting it.

"How many quilts did you bring with you?" I ask, to change the subject of jail and diamonds, which is all I've talked about in the past month.

"Four."

"Which ones?"

Her eyes shine with excitement as she tells me about them. Sewing her magnificent quilts is what keeps her sane and happy, even as the world disintegrates around her. A half hour into the flight, she takes out the quilt she's working on and stitches more pieces to it.

"What is that?"

"A sunflower."

I stand up and grip the side draped against her legging-clad leg to see the larger picture.

"You can't see it from this close," she says. "Stand back."

She hangs the quilt over the chair, then pushes me as far back as possible.

"Wow, that's gorgeous," the stewardess says. "The one you did for that show, that one was exceptional, but this is something else."

Ivy's eyes cloud at the memory of her ruined quilt.

"So tell me about this one," I ask.

"It's supposed to represent pieces of my life. The brown petal is for Mom." She points to an oblong pointy shape made of chocolate-colored silks and velvets. "I'm using only the fabrics my father gave her."

I loop one arm around Ivy's shoulder. "A sunflower, huh?"

She turns toward me. "My happiest memories were of the weekends we spent at your grandparents' house. I don't think I've thanked your mother enough for making them happen."

"You don't need to thank her for anything."

"Are you kidding, Josh? Your family saved Aster and me. You were so kind, taking us away from Mom when she had to work...or when she'd *check out*. Most people don't open their doors to strangers, yet your family did. Your parents got us into a better school, helped us with our homework, fed us when times were rough. Whenever I ask your mom why, she tells me it was the normal thing to do. But it isn't the normal thing to do."

"She cares about you girls."

"But why?"

"Because that day in McDonald's, when she found out your mom had left you by yourselves so she could go run errands—and you told her it wasn't the first time—she was outraged. She wanted to call child services."

"But she didn't."

"If she'd called them, Ivy, they would've placed you in foster care. They might even have separated you and Aster. It would've been worse. Plus you'd become my friends by then. I never had any friends before you."

"Stop...you're going to make me cry," she says.

"I'm serious. No one wanted to be friends with the Hamster."

She rolls her eyes.

I squeeze her against me, then shoot my chin to the quilt before us. "What's with the black petal? Does it symbolize your trip to New York?"

She snorts. "Funny. And no. It's supposed to symbolize our swing."

"Ah, our tire swing." The one Dad had hung from the branch of a grand old tree before my grandparents' field was bought back by some multinational and razed, replaced by an ugly gray factory. "Am I going to get a petal?"

"More than one." She glances up at me, then at my Hawaiian shirt. "Maybe I'll even create one from the fabric of your shirt."

I snort a chuckle. "What do you have against my poor shirt? Grandpa gave it to me."

"Was it one of his?"

"Ha-ha."

"Only senior citizens in Florida wear them."

"And me."

"And you." She pecks my cheek. "I'm happy you came. I *am* a little nervous about this trip."

"Don't be. I'm here."

"What if I don't sell anything? I filed a tort claim for Aster's medical bills, but I still have so many of Mom's to pay—"

"Maybe my parents can lend you some money."

"No way am I asking your parents for anything, Josh. I owe both of them too much already."

"You owe them nothing." I squeeze her hand to drive my point home.

As she collects the fabric sunflower from the seat, she asks, "What happened to my quilt?"

"The one on the show?"

She nods.

I sit back down and reattach the lap belt. "Brook told me Dean shredded it."

"Asshole," she mumbles.

I wonder if she means Brook or Dean. "In other news, I called Kelley. He said he would defend Aster. For free. And he said that, considering her current condition, he could represent her without either of you present."

"Wow. That's amazing."

I dip my chin toward my neck. "It's not that amazing, Ivy. He said the best case scenario would be institutionalization."

She takes a sharp breath. "What about a suspended prison sentence?"

"It was premeditated," I remind her softly. "Premeditation cancels any chance of parole."

Tears moisten her eyes. She grinds the heels of her palms against them, but can't stop their fall. When her cheeks are as wet as her hands, she picks up her handbag and disappears into the small bathroom. She emerges minutes before touchdown, looking as though she hadn't cried, and also, as though she were auditioning for a cabaret act.

"You're not wearing that," I say, pointing to her short, backless red dress.

"Then you're not wearing your Hawaiian shirt."

"I didn't bring anything else. You did. Put your leggings back on at least."

"I can't wear leggings with this dress."

I grouse about her outfit until we land, while she just grins. As we're released onto the tarmac, she grabs my arm. At least she's added a jean jacket to her red dress, but it does nothing to cover her long legs.

A sedan is waiting for us. I see two people in the backseat and stall, trying to make out if either of them is Dean, but Ivy keeps striding toward them, a huge smile stretching over her lipstick reddened mouth, so I assume he's not there.

When we get closer, I recognize Chase. And I imagine the other one is the notorious scumbag Brook warned us about. Their driver holds the door open.

Chase's dark eyes narrow as they set on me. "You came with *him*." Being referred to as *him* is downright demeaning. I have a name, which he knows well.

"Ivy's under police protection," I tell them. As I let go of Ivy, I curl my fingers into fists, then stretch them out before I punch something...or someone.

"Why? Did Brook break out of prison?" Chase asks.

Ivy's posture stiffens.

"We're worried about Dean," I reply.

"Party starts in thirty. We should get going. Hop in." Paul pats the space between Chase and him.

As she climbs inside, I see her underwear, and it incenses me, because if I can see it, others can too.

"Nice shirt," Paul says with a smirk right before he shuts the door.

The driver takes Ivy's suitcase from me.

As I settle in up front, next to the driver, Paul asks her about the quilts.

"I brought four."

"You'll show them to me at the Specter property," he tells her. "They have many rooms we can use for private viewings."

I gag. *Dirtball.*

"Okay," Ivy says, in a small voice. The guy probably thinks she's trying to sound cute, but I know the airiness in her voice has nothing to do with appealing to him and everything to do with being frightened of him.

I lower my sun visor so I can have a view of the backseat in my vanity mirror. While Paul chats on his cell, Chase asks Ivy about her week, and she lies quite superbly when she tells him it was uneventful. He has one hand on her bare knee and the other playing with her fingers.

I snap the visor shut and stare out at the flat greenness from which rise ridiculous mansions. The Discoli house would fit right in here. Between the houses, I spy the navy ocean lapping at stretches of white sand and wild grass.

The car finally pulls into a horseshoe-shaped driveway covered in small white pebbles that make a crunching sound under the tires. Round, rectangular, and accordion-shaped, white paper lanterns are strung up across the house's façade. Waiters, all in white, perhaps to resemble the lanterns, wait by the open front door with platters of drinks. I grab a glass of water and down it, then plop it back down on the platter.

As we infiltrate the monstrous front hall, people stare—mostly at Ivy, but my Hawaiian shirt garners a few glances.

"Ivy!" The girl with the buzz cut from the show struts toward my friend in a pair of strappy silver heels that make the long muscles in her calves pulse. She's way hotter in person than on TV, even though she was pretty hot on TV. "You made it!" she says, hugging Ivy, who tenses at the contact. Even her fingers, which are still wrapped around Chase's, whiten.

Maxine kisses Chase's cheek, then Paul's, then starts to lean in toward me, but rocks back on her heels. "I don't believe we've met."

"I'm Joshua Cooper." I'm tempted to add my title, but don't want to alarm anyone. I settle on, "Ivy's friend from home."

"Well then, welcome, Joshua." Her eyes skim my shirt before settling on my face. She smiles. "The others are on the patio," she says, before going to greet some other guests.

"I would go topless, but I don't want to shame all these rich bastards," I murmur into Ivy's ear.

She giggles. "Yes, keep those abs hidden or you'll cause a riot."

The patio is decked out in candelabras and plush couches that don't look suited for the outdoors. I scan the perimeter for Dean. It's probably pointless, but one can never be too careful.

Ivy leans toward me. "Look at that. Another person in a floral shirt."

My gaze bounces to where Ivy is looking. It's the gay dude from the show with the big poufy hair. His shirt is black with miniature purple and red flowers, and it's tucked into his narrow black pants. Maybe I should tuck mine, but I get a vision of my grandpa—he always tucks his in—so I leave it hanging out. I'm not trying to fit in, I remind myself.

"Mine is way cooler," I say over the loud music that streams through the evening air from a live DJ.

After a lengthy round of introductions, where I meet everyone from the show, Paul reappears and takes Ivy by the elbow. "I had the driver set your quilts out in one of the bedrooms upstairs. Shall we take a look at them?"

Ivy gulps. Lincoln, who's standing in the circle sipping a shaded orange and yellow drink, studies Paul and Ivy.

"What did you bring back from Indiana this time?" she asks.

Ivy stiffens, whereas I vibrate with animosity.

"What?" Lincoln says, when she realizes everyone is gaping at her. She sucks on her straw.

"*Wow*...I definitely didn't miss you," Ivy tells her, and I want to pump her hand in the air for her brazen retort.

"Totally reciprocal," Lincoln says, with a smile that makes her large green eyes gleam.

"Can you guys keep the claws in for tonight?" Herrick says. "For Maxine's sake. She's thrown us such a fabulous party. Show a little respect."

Lincoln rolls her eyes and walks away.

"Josh," Ivy says, holding out her hand toward me, even though I would never have let her go alone with Paul, or anyone else at this party.

"I'll go with you," Chase offers.

"No, stay here. Enjoy the party," she tells him. Gloom explodes over his face, darkening his already broody expression. "Josh?"

"I'm right behind you, Ives."

As I trail them upstairs, I sense waves of hatred rippling off Chase. He keeps sulking until this girl sporting a pair of teeny black shorts and a lacy white blouse comes up to him. As she runs her fingers through her long, strawberry-blonde hair, he squares his shoulders and narrows his eyes, which gives me the feeling he knows her.

We've reached the landing, so I can't see him anymore, but my curiosity is piqued. We walk past one door and stop at the next one. Her quilts have been draped over the furniture. One over the bed, one over what I imagine is a desk and chair, one on the floor, and the last is draped over a velvet armchair.

I'm about to step inside, but Paul holds me back. "I have to talk shop with my future artist. I cannot have anyone around. It's not conducive to good negotiations."

Ivy's alarmed eyes find mine.

"I go where Ivy goes."

"Fine. But I don't like doing business like this."

Like I care.

We go inside and he inspects her works, asks her for details and stories, examines the stitching and the fabrics from up close before stepping back. "They are *very* nice." He scratches his chin. "If I remember correctly, you sold the one on the show for seventy-five hundred dollars, right?"

She nods. "But I sold my web—you know, the piece I made on the beach—for thirty thou—"

"Did you ever get paid?"

She frowns. "Brook didn't have time to pay me."

"Because you think crooks pay? Sorry, sweetie, but I have no respect for the guy. I didn't have any before the scandal, but I have even less now. He's a lowlife who belongs behind bars. Even Chase agrees."

Ivy's skin darkens with anger, and tendons pinch in her throat. I rush to her side to prevent her from saying something that could compromise our operation.

"Don't you see he still upsets her?" I blurt out.

"I want fifteen thousand per quilt. Paid immediately," Ivy says, voice as tight as a mooring rope during a storm. "I believe that is not only reasonable, but also a bargain, considering my fame."

Paul smiles. "I'm going to like working with you," he says in a syrupy voice. I expect him to bargain her down, but instead he tells her he wants exclusivity, and then he asks her to sign a three-year contract.

"I need to read it first," she says.

"Of course. When you return it signed, I'll deposit the money in your bank account. Now we should get back to the party before Maxine notices we're gone. Oh, and, Ivy, you can no longer sell your quilts privately or you'll be in breach of contract. Have you ever sold any besides the one from the show that I should be aware of? Just in case they surface on the market...I don't want to think you ignored my demands."

Ivy gulps. "Josh has one."

"Are you planning on selling yours, Josh?"

"No."

"If you ever do, you sell it to me, okay?"

"I'm never going to sell it."

Paul turns to Ivy again. "Anyone else owns one?"

"Just one other person."

"Can you send me his or her name? I'd like to buy it back. If the person isn't too unreasonable, that is," he adds with a smile.

She nods. As we leave him to study his purchases, I ask Ivy about the buyer. A blush streaks her cheeks and nose.

"Is it Chase?" I ask.

"No. It's uh...it's no one important."

"Ivy..."

She fidgets with the bangle around her wrist. "Fine. It's Aster's warden. I gave him one so he would take care of Aster. I can't tell Paul about him. It'll be seen as a bribe. And if Aster ever returns to jail, and he's still the warden, and—"

I squeeze her arm. "First off, she won't go back to jail."

Her eyebrows furrow.

"Second off, I'm pretty sure you can give presents to prison personnel, as long as they're not monetary." I'm not sure at all, but if I want Ivy to relax, I need to act like I am. "Now let's go back down to the *fabulous* party," I say with a smile that makes hers reappear.

"You hate it," she says, as we clamber down the sleek wooden staircase.

"I'm hanging out with you, so no, I don't hate it." I almost bump into Ivy, who halted a few steps from the landing. I follow the direction of her gaze.

In a corner of the living room, Chase is leaning against the wall, talking to the girl with the tiny black shorts and the long hair while stroking her back. Instead of cowering in the opposite direction, Ivy strides over to them. I trot to keep up with her. When he spots her, Chase yanks his hand away from the girl.

"Chase?" His name is the only word Ivy utters, yet I can hear a thousand others in the silence that ensues.

"This is Diana."

The girl's face is stained with tears.

"My ex."

Ivy sizes up Diana, and Diana sizes up Ivy.

"She was just telling me that she tried to go visit Brook today, but apparently he's locked in some high-security cell where he isn't allowed visitors."

Ivy's hands, which were planted on her hips, slip down.

"She suspects it's because of the necklace he sent you," he says.

Ivy rubs her palms against her red dress. "The necklace?"

Chase narrows his eyes. "You know, the one the nurse gave me in the hospital? The one you told me Kevin stole from your room."

Ivy gulps.

"He asked me to have it made for you," Diana says. "I thought it was to make up for what he'd done. I didn't think it was an intimidation technique."

"Why did you lie to me?" Chase asks Ivy.

Her posture shifts from guilty to infuriated. "Because I was freaked out. And you're his brother, and I wondered if maybe *you* had anything to do with it."

He shakes his head. "How little you know me, Ivy...I understand I share the same blood as the guy who ruined your sister's life, but I'm nothing like him. Nothing." He pushes away from the wall and winds his way through the room.

"Did he just break up with me?" Ivy asks.

I'm not sure if she's asking me or Diana.

Diana bobs her head, and her long hair brushes my bare forearm. It's soft, like Heidi's. "A word of advice. Chase holds grudges. If you want him back, you need to go over there and talk it out."

Ivy's shaking. I put my hand on her shoulder to soothe her, but it doesn't work. "Why did *you* come to this party?" she suddenly asks Diana. "Are you an artist? A dealer?"

"No. Chase told me about it when we were driving up to the Hamptons yesterday."

"You guys talk?"

"Not much, but we live in the same house, so we're bound to exchange a few words."

"Rewind. You live in the same house?" Ivy has gone so still that I nearly wish she'd go back to trembling. I don't want her to flip out.

"He didn't tell you?" Diana asks.

She looks at Chase who's chatting with Herrick. "Must've slipped his mind," Ivy says between gritted teeth.

"Chase and his father moved in with us. It's a temporary solution to their...money problems. He's supposed to get a room on campus this week." Diana touches my friend's arm. "Nothing happened between us."

Ivy pins her down with a frigid stare. "I'm ready to go, Josh."

"Then let's go."

"Ivy," Diana calls out. "I don't think Brook was trying to scare you. He felt terrible for what happened."

Slowly, with a neck as stiff as the rest of her body, Ivy nods. "I know."

My eyes bulge.

Diana frowns. "You *know*?"

Ivy shuts her eyes for a second, then she looks to me to save her.

"I went to visit him to understand the meaning of the necklace," I say.

"Is the necklace the reason they locked him in a higher-security cell?" Diana asks.

"Uh. Yeah. Probably. I mean, I'm no expert on the prison world, even though, considering my line of work and my acquaintances, I should be."

"What do you do?" she asks.

"I'm a cop. But I came here as Ivy's friend," I add quickly, hoping it sounds believable.

"Do you have a phone, Josh?"

I cock an eyebrow up. "Yeah. Why?"

"I want to give you my number. In case you need any information I can provide from New York."

"That's kind of you, Diana," I say, handing over my phone.

"It's not kindness; it's revenge. I want Dean locked up and Brook released," she says.

"You're the ex who slept with Brook, aren't you?" Ivy suddenly asks.

Diana's eyes slant toward her perfectly straight nose. "I never slept with Brook."

"Chase caught you," Ivy says.

"Chase did find me at his brother's place. But we didn't sleep together. Brook's the person I run to when my life goes to shit. That's why I was with him. Because Chase had turned my life into a pile of shit."

A muscle ticks in Ivy's jaw. She looks at Chase again, but he doesn't look back at her.

"Thanks for your help, Diana," I say, grabbing Ivy's hand to drag her out before her heart explodes with jealousy...or with sadness.

THIRTY-SEVEN

Brook

I lean against the tiny pantry's wall. "How was last night?"

Ivy stares at the coffeemaker without blinking. "Paul asked for exclusivity. He gave me a contract."

"You want me to look it over for you?"

She peeks at me through the disheveled curtain of hair she's been sporting around her face since she's walked in. She's barely glanced my way—or at anyone, for that matter. Something's up. "Would you?"

"Of course. I'm good at catching the pesky clauses. It was one of the things we learned back in school."

Ivy returns her gaze to the coffeemaker. She presses some buttons. "When you offered me Dean's services, did you know he would attack my sister?" The tone of her voice has changed.

Did I? I think back on that day in the elevator with Ivy. "I didn't want him to show up at your sister's jail without your knowledge of it."

She turns to face me. "That's not what I asked."

"I didn't think he would attack her."

She fiddles with the buttons again, but no coffee drips out. "Why isn't this thing working?"

"Because you've pressed this button too many times."

She lets out an annoyed breath.

I point to the largest button. "Just push once and wait."

She does. After a few seconds, the machine beeps. As she waits for the coffee to trickle out, she turns around to face me. "Were you ever going to pay me for the web?"

This interrogation is worse than any I had to endure back in jail. "I wanted to. Dominic allots a budget to buying art for the school."

Her eyes darken. "When he picked me to replace Kevin, was it based on my talent or because he wanted access to my quilts for his son?"

"Both," I admit, tracing the yellow tiles underneath Ivy's Stan Smiths with my eyes. I'm afraid to look up...afraid she'll see I didn't think much of her quilts back then. Now—and not because of my feelings—I see what Dominic saw.

"God. This is so screwed up," she says, raking back her hair.

"Tell me about it."

I hitch my gaze back on to hers. She doesn't blink as she stares at me. I don't either.

"You told me the other day that Kevin was a PI. Is that why he was eliminated before the show started?"

"Yes."

"Dean paid the wife to doctor those photos?"

"He paid her to take the blame. He and I doctored the pictures." I rub the back of my neck. "Look, I'm not proud of what I did, but I can't change the past. I can only change myself. So that's what I'm doing. I'm changing myself into the person I'd like to be."

She tips her head to one side, observing me in a way she never dared to before. It almost makes me uncomfortable. "Did you help kill Kevin?"

"No!" I gasp. "No. Dean did that all by himself."

"Kevin was a private investigator. Didn't he know about Dean?"

"Josephine hired him to investigate the Masterpiecers. He wasn't aware of the connection between Dominic and Dean. No one was aware of it."

"How did Dean do it?"

"He gave him…" I weigh the pros and cons of confessing it was her sister's medication. The truth will set me free, right? "He gave him some of Aster's anti-psychotic medication."

"How—" She freezes. "*He's* the one who broke into my place?" she exclaims, which wins us a few cocked eyebrows and a stopover from Josh.

"What happened now?" he asks.

"It wasn't the Discolis who broke into my place. It was Dean." I flatten my back against the wall as Josh gapes at me.

"He's been inside my house." She shivers.

"You have police protection around the clock now, Ivy."

"He knows where I live," she croaks.

"He can't get in."

"I don't want to stay there anymore," she whimpers.

"You can stay here with me. He doesn't know about this place. Plus there's a cop in here all the time," I add, to make my invitation sound less creepy.

Josh surprisingly doesn't say *no*. "It's not a bad idea, considering how often I have to leave you alone."

An incredulous look settles over Ivy. "You'd rather lock me up *in here* with *him?*"

"It would just be for a short while. Just until we catch Kane."

Ivy flinches, seemingly horrified by Josh's suggestion. I'm comforted by it, because it means Josh understands I'm not the enemy. I wish Ivy would feel this way too, but that's a lot to ask from someone I wronged so terribly.

"What if it takes you a long time to catch him?" she says.

"It won't."

She shakes her head. "I'll stay with Aster at the hospital."

Josh blanches. "That's not an option."

"But—"

"No." His eyes are wide, fearful even. He's hiding something.

I lift an eyebrow, which makes his eyes bulge further. Ivy's too busy brooding to notice.

"You can have the bed," I tell her.

She scowls. "Whatever."

"Ivy—" Josh starts.

She raises her hand. "I understand. I don't like it, but I understand."

"Good," he says, right before his chief calls him back to inspect the hospital blueprints. They must have a new plan.

"I met Diana last night," Ivy says.

I startle at the change of subject.

"She told me she's the one who sent the necklace, but she thought she was sending me a gift." She grunts. "Like you would ever send me a gift. You're calculating, not generous."

I narrow my eyes. "When I had money, I was generous."

"You don't have to have money to be generous." When I stay silent, she adds, "Did you know Chase was living at her house?"

I nod.

"Why didn't you tell me?"

"It wasn't my place to tell. Besides, I thought Chase would've told you about it."

"Well he didn't. I had to hear it from Diana."

I lay my palms flat against the pantry wall. "I'm sorry."

"You know what else she told me?"

I shake my head.

"She told me nothing ever happened between you and her."

I stay quiet, attempting to comprehend where she's going with this.

"Why didn't you contradict me in the elevator? Why didn't you contradict Chase?"

"Because Chase only believes what he wants to believe."

She snorts. "Yeah. I learned that about him last night."

I frown.

"We broke up," she explains.

"Why?"

"Because I dared voice my concern that he might be working with you. When I got the necklace, he's the one who brought it up to my room."

"Chase would never do anything for me."

"I realized that. But it made me wonder..." Her eyes redden, unlike her face that's as pale as the dawn that broke over Kokomo this morning. "Would he ever do anything for me? You're his brother. He's supposed to love you, but he never visited you in jail."

My heart twists at her words. "Do you love Aster because you're *supposed* to?"

She shakes her head.

"Unfortunately, I've learned that sometimes you'll love people who won't love you back, and there's nothing you can do about it."

Her eyes redden. Audacity—or perhaps folly—seizes me, and I move toward her and gather her in my arms. I can't erase the pain my brother caused her, but perhaps I can ease it...if she'll let me. I stroke her back and she leans into me, and I realize she's letting me.

"I'd do anything for you," I whisper into her hair, but she's crying, so I don't think she hears me. I sort of hope she didn't.

I press my cheek against her head and rock her until the tears subside.

And then I rock her still.

And still, she lets me.

JOSH

"Hey," I whisper, stroking Aster's icy hand.

"Josh," she whispers. My name sounds like a gush of steam. And feels like it too. It warms me up, straight to my core.

"How are you doing, Sleeping Beauty?" I ask, keeping my voice low. I don't want to overwhelm her senses.

A smile slowly climbs over her face. "Good." She no longer has a respirator taped to her cheeks, and her skin is no longer gray.

"How's the head? Does it still hurt? One of the nurses told me you were in pain this morning."

"A little." Her speech is slow and labored, but articulate. "How...is Ivy?"

"She's fine."

I don't tell her Ivy is now spending most of her days with Brook. Our newest plan was delayed due to an impromptu visit from two federal agents who worked the case in New York.

They came by because, after the D.A. was arrested for accepting gifts, they stopped by the prison and were told Brook had been checked out. They came straight to us. Brook has refused to meet with them, but he's aware we're joining forces.

"Mom...stopped by," she says. "I kept...eyes closed."

"Your mother? She's dead, Asty."

Slowly, she points her finger at me.

"Oh! *My* mom?"

She nods heavily, as though her neck were a spring holding up too hefty a load.

"Good girl," I say. I'm relieved that she remembered to appear sleeping. I don't want anyone to know about her recovery. Dean could come back before we're ready for him.

"When Ivy...come?"

"Soon. I promise. Now let's get you up a little."

"Tired, Josh." Her lids flutter close.

"You have to take a few steps every day." The nurses told me it was important to prevent bedsores and muscle atrophy. "Just lean on me, okay?"

Her eyes open again. I drape her arm around my shoulders and heave her up. Holding her around the waist, I guide her around the room. Her feet move as though there was no gravity to seal her soles to the ground. In her white robe, she looks like a fairy. Remembering that one time in prison when she told me I never paid her compliments, I tell her that. I think it's a nice thing to say. And sure enough, it makes her grin.

We turn and go the other way.

"Asty, do you remember those diamonds you told me about once when I came to see you in jail?"

Her eyes brim with tears.

I kick myself for not keeping my trap shut, but finding them could make a huge difference.

"Ivy. One."

I blink. She remembers. *She understands!* "Yes. Ivy had one. Where are the others?"

"I...I"—she starts jerking her head from left to right—"put them..."

"Where?"

"In quilt."

"No."

Sweat coats her deepening complexion, but at least she's stopped shaking her head. "Yes."

"No."

I can't tell if she's trying to keep her secret safe or if her memory is spotty.

"I...I...bed please," she whispers, lowering her eyes to the floor.

"It'll come back to you."

She starts shaking. Even her teeth rattle. Delicately, I help her back onto the bed. She's still trembling, and she's still sweating. I press on the call button, then climb in next to her and tuck her body against mine to soothe her.

Rubbing her arm with my hand, I whisper, "I'm right here, baby. Right here." Still she shivers. I can't seem to supply enough comfort to chase away the goose bumps.

Finally the door bursts open and the nurse called Sabrina strides in. After a glimpse at Aster, she plugs a tube into her catheter. I climb off the bed, but keep one hand wrapped around her wrist. Her trembling lessens, her arm goes limp, and then her lids slam shut.

Sabrina turns her lined face toward me. "What happened?"

I shift from the heels of my feet to the balls and back. "I asked her a question I needed an answer to."

"It upset her."

"But I needed an answer."

"Joshua, she just woke up. Give her some time."

"We don't have much time."

"What's so important?" she asks.

"It's about the case."

"Why don't you tell me, and I'll speak to her when she feels better?" She prods my friend's wrist to measure her pulse.

"It's okay. I'll come back tomorrow."

She sighs. "Well, whatever it is you need an answer to, I hope Aster will recover quickly to give it to you."

"Me too. I need to get to work now. Call me—"

"If there's any new development," she says. "I know the drill."

I kiss Aster's cheek and murmur a promise of returning soon. As I walk out of the hospital room, I check my phone and see seven missed calls from Claire.

I sprint down the stairs, phone pressed against my ear. "What's going on?" I shout.

"My kid's little league game starts in ten minutes and I'm stuck here. You were supposed to be here an hour ago!"

I slap my palm against my hammering heart. "This is about a baseball game? God, Claire, I thought Dean Kane had taken you hostage."

"Family's important to me, Coop. Are you on your way?"

"Yes. I'll be there in fifteen." High on adrenaline, I dash to my car and drive over to the safe house. Claire must have heard my car, because she's already opened the door, handbag swinging from her shoulder.

"I got tied up at the hospital," I tell her.

"Just get inside," she huffs.

I step past her.

"How's Aster?" Ivy asks as I close the door.

"Same old," I lie.

Ivy is sitting on the couch, stitching her quilt. She must be getting to the end because the sunflower almost looks like it has all of its petals.

"Where's Brook?"

"He's taking a nap. Apparently Claire talked to him all night. I suggested that he come and sleep in the room."

"You did not..."

"It's just to sleep."

"You can't invite a guy to share your bed, Ivy."

"You and I do it all the time."

"First off, we don't do it all the time," I say snippily, "and second off, he's going to take advantage of you. Haven't you seen the way he looks at you?"

Ivy blushes. "It's not like that between us." She shakes her head. "Not at all."

"Ives, you're a smart girl, the smartest one I know, but sometimes, you don't act very smart."

The redness recedes from her face. "That's not a very nice thing to say."

I squash my lips together, regretting my words. "It's because you're innocent."

"You're right. I am too innocent. Instead of sitting around here stitching quilts, I should become reckless, go to the Neon Cactus, dance and drink too much alcohol, pick up some guy, do things girls my age do instead of living in constant fear that my sister won't wake up, that I'll end up broke and homeless, that Dean will catch up to me and kill me."

I tread over to Ivy and drop next to her on the couch. "Hey. Slow down. Where is this coming from?"

"He killed Kevin, Josh. He almost killed Aster. How easy would it be for him to kill me?"

"No one's going to kill you, you hear me?"

Her lips twist.

"I promise," I whisper. "Promise, promise."

A door opens. She swipes her knuckles quickly under her glistening eyes and focuses her attention on her quilt.

"Hi," Brook says, stretching.

Muscles move underneath his skin. I think of Ivy sleeping

next to him, and how defenseless she'd be if he decided to have his way with her. If only I could be there to protect her all the time.

His arms drop alongside his body. "Everything all right?"

"Everything's fine," I mumble.

Brook cocks a thick eyebrow up at me, but doesn't say anything. Instead he goes into the kitchen to pour himself a cup of coffee, to which he adds his weight in cold, full-fat milk.

Sighing, I grab the remote control and turn on the news, convinced that watching other people's lives spiral out of control will beat the present situation. But boy am I wrong.

I try to click the TV off but the remote control slips out of my clammy hand. I bend over to grab it from the floor, but it's too late.

Ivy has lifted her gaze to the screen.

THIRTY-NINE

Brook

"My sister is awake?" Ivy shrieks.

Holding my mug of tepid coffee, I stride back into the living room and stare at the television, at the reporter gushing about the miraculous recovery of Aster Redd, the girl who was savagely attacked a month ago by another inmate.

Josh's face is as red as the shell of a boiled lobster.

Ivy tosses her quilt to the side and stands up so fast that she sways. "That's why you've been keeping me away from her? Not for my protection but because you didn't want me to find out she was awake? When were you going to tell me?"

"After we apprehended Dean. I didn't want to overwhelm her," he mumbles.

"Overwhelm her?" she shouts. "She's my twin!"

"I was trying to do the sensible thing. The right thing."

"You don't get to decide what the right thing is without discussing it with me!"

"You didn't discuss the power of attorney with me."

Ivy's eyes bulge. "How dare you!" She whirls away from him, dashes into the bedroom, and slams the door shut.

"Is Aster coherent?" I ask after a beat.

"She recognizes me."

"Has she asked for Ivy?"

"What do you think?" he hisses.

His phone rings. As he glances down at the screen, sweat forms on his upper lip. Sponging it away with the hem of his polo shirt, he picks up. From the way he squints throughout the call, I take it his chief isn't tremendously pleased with the news. When he hangs up, he cradles his forehead with his hands before inhaling a long breath and pressing himself up. He paces the small living room, head bowed in thought.

"Why did you really keep it from her?" I ask, interrupting his manic marching.

"Because. I didn't want Ivy to get her hopes up in case Aster's progress stopped or reversed."

"She's a big girl, Josh."

"With a big heart that's gotten crushed over and over. She could do with fewer shattered hopes."

Some time later, there's a knock at the door. After checking the peephole, Josh pulls it open and his squad files in. Even Claire. She looks particularly unhappy to be back. I imagine it's because she's missing her kid's baseball game. She told me all about it while I was trying to sleep.

"I'll go check on Ivy," I say, but no one pays attention to me, too busy tearing Josh a new one. I knuckle the door. She doesn't tell me to come in, but I do anyway.

Sunlight streams around the edges of the flimsy drape that covers the small window, which is more of a porthole than a window. Shutting the door softly, I walk over to the bed where Ivy is lying in the fetal position and crouch down. A slender beam of light falls into her eyes, rendering them as luminescent as lagoons.

She looks at me, and her lower lip trembles. "I didn't think she would ever wake up."

I run my thumb over her mouth to iron away the tremors. She blinks, and then frowns a little, so I lower my hand.

After a long stretch of silence, she whispers, "I should've been there. The moment she woke up, I should've rushed to her side. I don't want her to think I abandoned her."

"I'm sure she doesn't think that."

A tear snakes down her cheek. I lift my hand to brush it away, but stop midway when I see her looking at my raised fingers. Again, her eyebrows tip toward her nose and her gaze connects with mine. When I was coming out of the bedroom, I heard Josh insinuating I'd take advantage of her if she shared my bed. From the way she contemplates me, I fear she believes him.

"I'm so mad at him," she says.

"He did it to protect you."

"Protect me from what?" Her voice is rough with emotion.

"From disappointment in case her progress was short-lived."

"She's awake, Brook! Even if it lasts only minutes, I want to see her, to hold her, to speak to her. Keeping it a secret was selfish." She sits up, flinging her legs over the side of the bed, and stands. "I have to get out of here."

I rise from my crouch. "Not in your state."

"I *need* to see her. It's visceral."

"I understand, but you have to absorb this first. You're in shock. You don't want her to feel your shock. Plus I bet the hospital is crawling with reporters. They'll pounce on you if they spot you. And Dean—" I stop myself from voicing my greatest fear. She's already terrified of him.

"Do you truly think Dean will come back?"

Thinking of my ex-best friend cleaves my heart open. "Yes."

"Do you regret working with the police?"

I shake my head. "Go to the hospital with Josh. Just in case."

Her gaze turns somber. "You didn't care about my safety back in New York, but now you're worried?"

"I did care. I just didn't think Dean was dangerous until... until he drowned Kevin."

"That was two days before the competition ended. Three, if you count the day off. Why didn't you warn me then?"

My lungs contract as though there is no oxygen in the small, dark bedroom. "Telling you would've put you in danger."

"Because not telling me worked out so well?" She backs away toward the door.

There is no fear in her eyes, but there is regret. When I was in prison, I used to think that if Aster made it out alive, Ivy would be able to forgive me once she knew my reasons for doing what I did, but that scenario played out, and the wariness remains. My only hope now is that capturing Dean will sway her.

But what if it doesn't?

What if I'm stuck loving someone who could never love me back?

FORTY

JOSH

Ivy interrupts our frenzied meeting with an insane request to go to the hospital.

"No way," I tell her.

"You don't get it, Josh. This isn't me asking; this is me telling you I'm going to see Aster. Now either one of you can take me, or I call a taxi."

"Claire, can you accompany her?" the chief says, sighing.

Claire grumbles but stands up.

"No, I'll go," I say.

Guarda glances at Ivy for her approval. What he doesn't get is, even if she puts up a fight about me coming, I'm not letting her out of my sight. Now that Aster's recovery is all over the news, I'm expecting Dean or a Discoli to crawl out of their shadowy dens.

In the car, Ivy doesn't talk to me. She doesn't even look at me.

"We're monitoring the airstrips, the state borders, the bus stations. And the hospital is swarming with federal agents. If he comes, he won't make it out."

"What about my house? Are you still monitoring it?"

Hearing her voice makes me giddy with relief. "Since you've been at the safe house, we've stopped the patrols, but Mr. Mancini is looking out."

"So are you just going to wait now?"

I nod.

"That's a shitty plan."

"You have a better one?"

"Yes."

"Let's hear it."

She releases her lip and turns to look at me. "Eyes on the road, Joshy. You're a guy; you cannot do two things at once."

"Is that right?"

"It's a fact."

"You do know that's never been scientifically proven, don't you?" I say.

She snorts.

"So what's your stellar idea, Miss Redd?"

"After I leave Aster's room, I can give an interview that her mind is clear and her memory is intact. Dean will think she told me where to find the diamonds."

"And he'll hunt you down."

"And you'll catch him. Or I can send him a private message to ask him for a meeting through Facebook?"

I smile, but shake my head.

"What?" she asks.

"Inviting him to dinner is cute, but I don't think he'll bite—even if he's hungry. He knows Aster's awake. He'll come. He's probably already here." I think of the camera, from which we didn't get anything. *Stupid digital contraption.*

The hospital comes up on my right. I put my blinker on and

wait for the light to turn green, tapping my fingers against my steering wheel to the beat of a P!nk song.

"Do you trust Brook?" Ivy suddenly asks.

"Yes." I glance at her. "Don't you?"

"I want to."

After I park, we walk up to Aster's room. I spot a handful of agents wandering through the hospital. They're conspicuous even though they're in plain clothes.

The guard on duty lets us through. Inside the room, Sabrina is sitting beside Aster. "I didn't speak to the press."

"It's all right."

Her eyes lock on Ivy, but my friend's attention is riveted to her sleeping sister.

"Could you leave us, Sabrina?"

"Of course."

Once the nurse is gone, Ivy strokes her sister's cheek. "Can I wake her?"

Aster's eyes flutter open. They grow wide and wet, and her lips part but no sound comes out.

"Hey," Ivy says gently.

She picks up her sister's hand and presses it into her own, and, as though Aster's palm were connected directly to her tear ducts, tears spring out and trail down her gaunt cheeks. Ivy wipes them off before they reach the small mole over her lip.

"Hey, baby sister," Ivy says.

Aster's lips wobble into a smile. They always bickered about who was the oldest one. Some people say it's the twin who's birthed last. Apparently that means she was created before the other. I never took sides. To me, Ivy and Aster are two parts of the same person. In the womb, a person's right arm doesn't grow sooner than the left.

"Really you?" Aster whispers.

"It's really me," Ivy says, sitting down on the mattress.

Aster's smile manages to stick to her pale lips. While Ivy

asks her how she feels, Aster reaches up and touches the ends of Ivy's curls. They're not as flat and shiny as usual. They're more like Aster's—when her hair was long.

"Yours will grow back, Asty," she reassures her.

Aster gives a minuscule nod. "In looong time."

"Time goes by so fast," Ivy says.

"For you."

Ivy fiddles with a slender gold band she wears around her thumb.

"Slow in prison," Aster says, letting her hand fall back against the thin sheet.

"You're not going back there."

Furrows groove Aster's forehead like the perfect rows of sunflowers we used to wander through as kids to reach the tire swing.

"I'm making you a quilt," she tells her sister.

"Really?"

"Yes."

"Can I see it?"

"I can bring it tomorrow."

Aster's lids droop a little, but she heaves them open. It looks difficult.

"She's going to feel groggy for a while," I tell Ivy, whose eyes flash to mine in worry. "It's normal."

Aster's lids collapse again, but she wrenches them back open.

"I was here a lot when you were sleeping," Ivy tells her. "I told you stories. Did you hear them?"

"I like stories," she murmurs. "Tell me...a story?" she breathes. "The faerie one."

"You mean the one I made up when we were eight?"

Her head dips at the same time as her lids. This time they don't come back up. Ivy nestles against her sister.

"Once upon a time," she begins, "there was a little faerie

with transparent wings and a translucent body. She was the only one of her kind who was see-through. All the other faeries were big and dark blue, with sharp talons and pointy teeth. She had no such attributes. Her teeth were rounded and her feet soft. The others would laugh at her and terrorize her with their barbed extremities. Some would fly right into her, pretending they hadn't seen her.

"Many times she tumbled onto the forest floor and injured herself. Once, she tore her wing on some brambles and couldn't fly back up into the tall tree they lived in. That day, she learned to walk. It hurt because her feet weren't used to it. She discovered that moss felt nicer than rocks, and that grass tickled. She walked until her wing healed. It took days, weeks.

"By the time it mended, she'd arrived in a big city with big cars and big people. No one saw her, because she was transparent and so small. She was almost stepped on and swatted so often that she took to flying again. And high. She would stare at everyone and everything with her wide, clear eyes. If she'd been navy blue, the humans would have captured her and studied her, but no one could see her, so no one could catch her. It was the first time in her life she felt thankful for being different.

"But after months, it turned lonely. Even though her people made fun of her, at least she existed in the forest. Here, no one knew she existed. So she started her journey home. Tired one evening, she landed on a big green shrub full of flowers that resembled Ping Pong balls. She suckled the flowers, and it was the most delicious nectar she'd ever drunk. It put her straight to sleep and she slumbered until she heard a little voice saying hello.

"She zipped off her leaf, heart beating as fast as her wings. It was silly, because no one could see her, so no one had said hello. But a small girl with wild, blonde corkscrew curls was staring straight at her. Not through her. *At her.*

"You can see me? she asked. The little girl nodded. How?

she asked. Because I'm looking, the little girl said, widening her eyes to prove her point. She poked her clear body with her chubby finger, which made the faerie look down. She'd turned a little blue during the night. Frowning, she gazed at the white ball-like flowers, then back down at her body. She checked her feet for talons and felt her teeth, but they had not sharpened...*yet*.

"All her life, she'd longed to be like her kind, but suddenly, she feared it. What if becoming blue turned her into someone mean? She refused to believe it. Looking like someone else didn't turn you into someone else. She decided that if she were to stay blue, she would also stay kind..." Ivy's voice trails off and I startle back into the room, blinking away the little see-through faerie.

She's fallen asleep right alongside Aster. They look so peaceful, so happy, so whole, that I don't dare wake them. I let them enjoy each other's company before they're uprooted and torn apart again.

I call my mother, I call my father, I call the chief. He sounds funny over the phone. Excited. "We have a new plan," he gushes.

When I ask him about it, he says he'll fill me in when I return. I toy with my phone a long while after that. I write a text message to Heidi, but delete it. I stand up and stretch my legs just as a nurse comes to check on Aster. I gently shake Ivy awake and tell her we should get going. She kisses her sister's cheek, then rises and follows me out.

"Aster always told me she hated that plant," I say as we reach the elevator. "The buttonbush," I add, in case sleep erased her memory of her faerie story.

"She did?"

"Yeah."

"That's weird. She's the one who bought it. With her allowance. She even planted it herself."

"Didn't your mother say that it would grow wild and block out all her light?"

Ivy sighs. "That does sound like something Mom would've said."

"Why do you think she was so hard on Aster, but more lenient with you?" I ask as we walk out into the dusk-covered parking lot. I never asked her this before, because I was afraid to bring it up...afraid it would create friction between the sisters, or between us.

"I used to believe Mom was trying to make her tougher, but now I think it's because she saw herself in Aster," she says, getting into my car. "When she acted out against her, she was acting out against the pathology they shared."

"Sorry I brought her up."

"Never be. It's good for me to talk about her sometimes. Even though she wasn't perfect, I don't want to forget her." She grabs a tissue from the car's backseat. After she blows her nose, she says, "Now you owe me a really good dinner and a really strong drink."

"You're underage."

"Josh, silence your inner cop. He's being rude to me."

I chuckle. "Fine. Shall we pick up some roast chicken and potatoes?"

"What about going to a restaurant?"

"When Dean is caught, I'll take you and Aster out, on my measly little salary, to the best damn restaurant in all of Indiana, but until then, we're laying low."

As I drive away from the hospital, my phone rings. I pick up. "Hi, Mr. Kelley," I say. "You're on speakerphone, and Ivy Redd is next to me."

Ivy's eyes grow wide and eager.

"Here's the deal from the courthouse. Your sister was found not guilty by reason of mental disorder. So now she has two options, either she is transferred to an institution for an indefinite amount of time, or she is returned to prison. Considering she was found *not guilty*, if she returns to prison, she could probably get out in a couple of years, once the system deems she's no longer a threat to society."

"So you're saying she's better off returning to prison?" Ivy exclaims, horrified.

"I'm suggesting it might be the better of two evils," Kelley says.

"She almost died in prison!"

Kelley lets out a heavy sigh. "I have two days to inform the judge what we are going to go with."

A tear glides down my cheek. I haven't cried since the first time I was nicknamed Hamster. I sniffle. "We'll call you tomorrow. Thank you, Mr. Kelley."

Ivy is dry-eyed, but her jawline quivers. She's as racked by emotion as I am, but doing a better job at holding it in. "We can't send her back," she whispers.

I nod my agreement.

FORTY-ONE

Brook

"I can't believe I got stuck taking care of the two of you," Josh says, tossing a piece of pretzel at Ivy, who ducks out of the way, but it still lands in her hair, and since her hair is so springy, it gets stuck.

As I pick it out, I say, "You did take Claire away from her son's little league game."

"I did no such thing. That was the chief. He should be here instead of me," Josh says.

"That would be way less fun. He'd probably make us stop drinking," Ivy says, tipping her glass of wine to her lips.

"I should make you stop drinking," Josh says, even though he's downed a couple beers himself.

"Don't even," she says. "After that phone call, I'm allowed as much wine as I want."

I eye them, not privy to the phone call they're referring to.

Ivy spots my curiosity, gulps down more wine, then says, "My sister can choose between going back to jail or getting stuck in an institution for an"—she hiccups—"*indefinite* amount of time." She replaces her glass on the table next to her neat stack of quarters. "Will you also have to go back to jail after this...*job?*"

"It's not a job," I say in a low voice.

She shoots me a wry smile.

"And no. I got a commutation of sentence for meritorious service."

"In English?"

"I won't go back to jail because I'm cooperating with government authority, but I also won't regain my civil rights." I spin a quarter between my index and middle fingers. "If they catch me gambling, though, they might overturn their ruling. I don't think it's too well regarded as a pastime for a reformed conman. I bet gardening would be way better viewed."

Ivy smirks. "Gardening? First a ranch, and now tilling soil? You're so down-to-earth, Brook. A true peasant."

I crack a smile. "Yeah, yeah. Make fun now. When you visit my ranch someday, you won't be laughing."

Although her eyes are bright, the mirth has vanished from her face. "Crap," she whispers, tossing her two cards face up on the table. She stands up so abruptly that both Josh and I frown.

"What?"

"I think I know where Aster put the diamonds."

"What?" Josh and I say at the same time.

"I mean, I have an idea. *Crap.*" She looks for her shoes. Once she locates them, she slips them on. "You have to drive me to my house."

"Right now? I'm a bit tip—"

"Right now," she says.

Josh jumps up, slips his loafers on, and grabs his car keys. I get up too, but I don't have shoes to put on. They didn't think I was going anywhere.

"I'd like to come," I say.

Ivy glances at me, but her eyes are glassy, focused inwards, on her breakthrough.

"It's not like I can leave you here all by yourself." Josh rubs his short hair. "Crap. I shouldn't be driving in my state."

"You had three beers and a lot of chicken," I say. "I think you'll be fine."

He glowers, rubs his eyes, and unlocks the front door. "You're sure, Ivy?"

"No. But it's worth a look," she says.

She's out the door quicker than Josh.

"Will this beep?" I point to my ankle monitor.

"Nah. It will just send your GPS coordinates to the transmission unit."

"Could you maybe phone in that I'm not trying to escape? So that I don't get shot down or anything."

As he locks the door, he calls the precinct and informs them that we're heading over to the Redd place. I scan the dusky street. Any moment, I expect Dean's silver Ferrari with its blinding lights to rev right up, but the cars parked along the sidewalk are as humble as the shadowy buildings next to them. Only one car sticks out from the lot, and thankfully, it's not a Ferrari but a vintage, light blue Cadillac. For some reason, I feel like I've already seen this car, but I can't put my finger on where.

Ivy climbs into the backseat, so I sit next to Josh, who rubs his eyes at least twenty times during our drive. I've never seen where Ivy lives. I'm imagining something minuscule and rundown, but in fact, it's much nicer. At least from the outside.

Josh moves toward her front door, digging inside his windbreaker for keys, but Ivy touches his arm and shakes her head. She leads us to the side of her apartment where a veranda curves out into a tiny yard. She drops to her knees and starts digging under a plant.

Josh crouches down next to her. "She wouldn't—"

"She had dirt under her nails, Josh. Don't you remember?"

"Shit..." he whispers, mouth gaping. He kneels down next to her and digs also.

Minutes go by and the only thing they turn up is wet soil.

"A little help, Earth Boy," Josh says.

A car drives by. I peer into the darkness for it, but all that remains by the time I locate it are burning taillights.

"I didn't think you'd want my help," I say, lowering myself to the ground on the other side of the enormous shrub. I feel hard filaments, which I imagine are roots, and slippery soft bodies, which I suspect are worms, but no diamonds. We dig so long and so deep I worry the plant won't survive our foraging.

As I start to press the dirt back against the spindly roots, Josh gasps.

"Did you find something?" I ask, springing up and rounding the bush.

Ivy rocks back on her heels and extends her shaky hands toward me. In her palm rests a tiny square of yellowish-brown paper that crinkles as Josh plucks it from her. He unfolds the sealed edges with his dirt-coated fingers. Under the moonlight, seven diamonds, the size of the one Dean found in Ivy's room during the show, sparkle.

Josh stares at Ivy, who hasn't moved or said a single word since her discovery. "We found them," he whispers.

He smiles at her. When she doesn't reciprocate, he smiles up at me. I'm too stunned to smile.

At the sound of approaching footsteps, he folds the makeshift envelope back up and stuffs it inside the pocket of his windbreaker. An old man shouldering a shotgun creeps up to us. I stick my hands up because he has it aimed at me.

"You're that guy from TV. The mobster," he says.

"I'm not a mobster."

"But you're that guy from TV, aren't you?"

I nod, swallowing hard as the nozzle gleams in the night, too close to my stomach for comfort.

"Mr. Mancini, lower your weapon. He's with us," Ivy says.

"But he's that guy. The one—"

"I know who he is. Put your gun away," Ivy says, standing up. She steps in front of me, her chest almost pressed against the rifle. "Please."

The old man's lined forehead smushes up, but at least he draws his gun back down. "What are you three doing, digging up a garden in the middle of the night?"

"I lost a lucky penny," Josh says.

"Under the buttonbush?" The old guy narrows his eyes. "Joshua, you promise this guy hasn't taken you hostage?"

"I promise, Mr. Mancini. Thank you for coming to check. I truly appreciate it."

He harrumphs, steals a few shadowy glances at us, and finally treks off. "If I read about your bodies being found buried in some ditch, don't expect my pity," he throws over his shoulder.

Josh's smile widens. I don't know what Ivy's feeling as she still has her back to me. Her hair blows against my neck. I place my hand over her shoulder. She shivers. I raise it but let it hover over her cold skin as I walk around her.

"Thank you," I tell her.

She bites her lip. Her eyes, which sparkle like the diamonds in Josh's pocket, turn up toward me. "This can be over now, right?"

Josh clears his throat. "There's still the small detail of his crazy friend."

"He's right, Ivy. Dean's still out there."

Josh dials his chief. Although he keeps his voice quiet, it's animated. Ivy wraps her arms around herself, as though finally realizing that all she has on is a tank top and leggings. I peel off my long-sleeved gray Henley and drape it over her shoulders. Ivy's eyes travel over my bare chest before climbing back up to my face. She tries to press the shirt back, but I shake my head.

"You don't even have shoes," she says.

"I'm getting ready for my life as a peasant."

She smiles. When her teeth clatter, I drape an arm around her shoulders and walk her back to Josh's car. He beeps it open. I press her into the backseat and sit next to her, keeping my arm around her shoulders. She leans into me, and my heart gallops. I close my eyes and tuck her in closer. Josh is speaking quickly, dizzy with the delight of our nocturnal treasure hunt.

He pumps up the music until the car is filled with a hectic beat that mirrors the thumping inside my head.

"This is incredible. Incredible," he exclaims, whirling around to look at us. The traffic light above the car tinges his hair red.

"That was a clever hiding spot," Ivy says.

Another car is stopped at the sleepy intersection, the vintage Cadillac I saw earlier. Instead of advancing through the green light, it waits.

"Josh, that car was parked next to the safe house," I say, just as the light turns green for us.

Slowly, too slowly, Josh spins back around. The other car crawls over the pedestrian pathway, or perhaps I'm imagining it moving in slow motion. If Josh reverses, the car will miss ours. But he doesn't go backward. He doesn't go forward either. He just stares at the Cadillac as though it were a ghost.

Keeping one arm around Ivy, I lunge forward and latch on to his headrest. "Go, go go!" I yell into his ear.

Ivy's body hardens in the crook of my arm.

He hits the gas. But so does the other car. I spring back and curl my body around Ivy's. And then I wait, bracing myself for impact.

FORTY-TWO

JOSH

A scream reverberates inside my skull. Is it mine? The scream turns into a bizarre, brassy symphony. Metal, glass, air, and light explode around me.

Inside of me.

Shrieks and shouts and sobs sound softly in my ears. An ache blooms in my jaw, in my legs, in my waist. Something cuts into my chest, cracks my left arm, yanks on my neck.

I flip.

I land on a multicolored sea of plastic balls beside the tire swing, and Aster and Ivy laugh, long blonde curls flapping in the sunflower-scented breeze. I reach behind me to push up, but there's no ground beneath the balls.

And soon, there are no balls.

And there is no Aster, and no Ivy.

I fly.

Granddad and Grandma wave as I soar above them, while

Mom and Dad blow me kisses out of their palms. Mom's lips are cherry-red, her favorite color, and Granddad has his special flower shirt on. The one he gave me.

The one I never gave back.

I float.

Heidi skips and twirls, and her metallic hair and freckles glint in the bright, pale light. She smiles and whispers my name.

And then I see Jackie again. The flash of her warm, sad smile, of her badge that warded off evil.

She grows smaller and dimmer as I drift higher. Farther.

There is no more sound.

No more gravity.

No more pain.

Only bright...white...light.

FORTY-THREE

Brook

I tuck my chin into my chest and squeeze my eyes shut as the car flips in the air. With no seatbelt to hold me down, my body, still entangled with Ivy's, levitates. Glass shatters and embeds itself inside my bare back like miniature daggers, and metal slices through my thigh. My muscles tauten and my limbs harden as we roll again and again. With every thump, fresh pain stirs inside my wounds; with every scream, my pulse thunders and my heart swells. I sweat, I bleed, I shiver.

When the tires of the car slam back into the ground, I pry my eyes open. Josh's body is bent at an unnatural angle, and his eyes, although open, are veined with blood. Vomit shoots up my throat and burns my mouth. I bounce away from Ivy and lean as far away as possible in our crumpled metal box. Although I grind my teeth closed, the vomit sprays out of me. My ears ring, yet I hear someone cry. *Ivy*. She's alive. I swipe my arm over my mouth, before turning back toward her. Her cheeks are streaked with blood and tears, but there are no cuts on her face, at least none that I can see. It must be my blood.

She shrieks and propels her upper body over the central armrest. "Josh!" Her hands prod and stroke Josh's lifeless body. "He has no pulse," she screams.

I knew that before she touched him. He has the same look Kevin had when he was fished out of the ocean.

His body moves.

Could he still—

Large hands, not Ivy's, run over Josh's windbreaker. I want to think that someone has come to save us, but a gold ring glints on the person's pinkie.

"Dean," I croak. It's not a plea for help; it's a warning for Ivy.

She looks at him, body immobile, face impassive. Unable to predict what his next move will be, I latch on to her waist and yank her back. I kick at the door until it grinds open, and then I shove my entire body against it. Cradling her, I crawl out.

"Josh," she whimpers. "Josh." Pink tears course down the side of her face.

Gravel scratches my knees through my ripped jeans, yet I push forward, taking us as far away from the car as possible. Setting her down gently, I press both my hands into the ground and rise, grinding my teeth to avoid screaming in pain as I straighten my spine.

"What have you done?" My voice sounds unfamiliar to my humming ears.

"Recuperating what is mine." In Dean's hand rests the rumpled, yellow paper filled with diamonds. "I heard you were planning some elaborate scheme to trap me, but a mastermind stays one step ahead. Always one step ahead." He rounds the smoking front bumper. "You disappointed me, brother." He taps the left side of his chest with the butt of a gun. "But I expected it the day you stopped wearing your ring."

I curl the fingers of my right hand into a fist. "That ring tied me to someone I no longer recognized."

"Speaking of recognition...Dominic is terribly upset with you after all he's done for your family. Fabricating and feeding stories to the FBI"—he gestures toward Josh—"that's low of you." He shakes his head from side to side, his silver eyes reflecting the cold gleam of the headlights. "You almost ruined everything when you chose her over me. *Oh*...and you can forget about your commission."

An almost feral sound shoots out of me. I lunge toward Dean, but hands close around my chest and hold me back. A flashback from our boating trip catapults into my mind. "I saved your life once, Dean! Troy and I pulled you out of the water. If I could've predicted any of this—"

"You wouldn't have saved me?" Pain flashes in Dean's eyes.

I gulp as more memories flood me. Toasts to undying friendship and great success.

Our friendship is dead, and so is our futile attempt at success.

"Just leave us," Ivy says, her breath warming my bare back.

Dean laughs. "After what you've done to me, what your sister has done to me, you're deluding yourself if you think I'll let you live."

"Ivy's done nothing to you."

"She stole what wasn't hers to steal," Dean says.

"She had no idea! Her sister gave her that diamond. Besides...it wasn't even yours."

"Oh come on, Brook!" He slaps the hood of the car with the gun, which makes Ivy jump. "Have you seen where she fucking lives? It's a dump. People who live in dumps can't afford diamonds. She knew her sister stole it. Didn't you, sweetheart?"

Her hands tremble and glide down my skin, wet, slippery, and cold.

"Put the gun away, Dean," I say, my voice as cool and hard as the ground beneath my feet.

"When Mom gets here, I'll put it away." His eyes dart to the empty intersection.

"Is she late? Maybe she's busy getting naked with some guy. Isn't that how she makes money these days? Screw anyone with a big wallet and hope for another kid?"

"Fuck you," he says. After a beat, he adds, "She's coming."

"She's not, Dean."

"She's already here." A manic smile curls over his mouth. "She's been in this goddamn town from day one, monitoring the girls' house, speaking to their neighbors. She even stopped by the hospital for some updates."

Ivy springs out from behind my back. "No way. The police would've known—"

"The police *did* know. At least your little cop friend knew. It took him a while to figure it out, but he did."

"That's impossible..." Ivy says. "Josh tells me everything."

"You're sick, Dean," I tell him. "You need help."

His eyes dart to the still-empty road.

"The only ones coming will be cops. They're tracking my ankle bracelet." I want him to feel as alone as I felt the day the Feds burst into the Temple room to arrest me. Alone, and helpless, and petrified. "You better start walking, because I don't think Troy's car is in any shape to be driven." It finally came back to me where I'd seen the Cadi...in a picture Troy sent me after he'd fixed it up. He'd been so proud.

Doubt crosses Dean's face. He takes a step back, then another, but then stops. There's movement somewhere behind him. It's not a car though. It's a person. I squint to see if it's his mother, but my eyesight is blurry, and all I can make out is a shape.

"On second thought"—he grins, resembling the Joker I was so terrified of as a child—"I have no desire to spend my life looking over my shoulder." He points the gun at Ivy.

I leap in front of her, hoping my body will be strong enough to shield hers. The shot rings out, echoing inside my eardrums along with the rest of the quiet world around us.

My jaw cracks as my cheek knocks into the gravel, but nowhere else hurts. Dean must've missed...or I wasn't quick enough and the bullet hit Ivy first.

I open my mouth to call out her name when pain, worse than the one in my face, erupts inside my waist. I can't see anything. There's too much blood, and dirt, and sweat in my eyes to see anything, but I can feel everything. Warm blood oozes out of my mouth, trickles down my lips. Cold hands press against my skin.

Ivy yells, but her words don't make sense.

A second explosion rips through the night.

"Ivy?" I murmur, attempting to stand, but the ground sucks me in, and the world spins.

Something falls...a long, dark shape...a body.

"Ivy?" I croak.

The burning sensation in my waist starts to fade. I can't feel her hands anymore. He must have shot her... A cry rips out of me, and I flatten my palms against the ground and press as hard as I can to turn over so I can see, but something, someone holds me back, cradles my jaw, a gentle voice murmurs my name. I think it's an angel, but I realize that it's Ivy with her backlit halo of curls and her beautiful face.

"He's gone," she says.

"Gone?"

"Dead," she murmurs, then adds, "Mancheenee." I frown, yet in some distant recess of my mind, the word calls back the face of an old man.

Sirens wail. Footfalls echo. I lock my gaze on Ivy's because I don't want to fall asleep. I'm frightened that if I do, I'll never wake up.

Ivy

I've left the hospital twice since Brook was wheeled in, bleeding and unconscious: once to pack a small suitcase of clothes, and once to visit Josh's mother.

I still can't believe he's gone. Every time someone calls me, I expect to see his name flash on my phone; every time I close my eyes, I see his face. I thought after ten days, the tears would subside, but I seem to have a bottomless stock of them.

"He was so handsome, wasn't he?" I tell Aster, scrolling through picture after picture of Josh on my phone. I pause on the one I took the day he made trooper. Just a year ago. "He was so proud of his badge."

I'm not sure showing Aster reminders of Josh is the right thing, but I want her to react. I want her to speak. Ever since he died, she's shut down. Losing Josh destroyed my sister. He meant everything to her. She's stopped talking, stopped smiling, stopped feeding herself, yet she keeps breathing...so I keep hoping that one day, someday, a small smile will bloom on her face like the white flowers of her buttonbush.

I stroke her dry cheek. "Margaret told me she had a beautiful story all picked out for you."

Margaret is Aster's private nurse. Even though my twin is no longer in harm's way—Alaina Kane was apprehended on her way to rescue her son and Dominic was arrested—I don't allow anyone beside Margaret and me by her side. That is...until I have to send Aster away, to the dreaded institution. I haven't told her yet. I don't know how to tell her.

As the cheery nurse seizes the book I laid on the overbed table, I squeeze Aster's hand. "I signed Paul Willows's contract."

Brook was furious about my decision, but I couldn't refuse the money. Besides, it's not forever.

Nothing lasts forever in this world.

"I can now buy you all the romance novels you can dream of," I tell her, hoping for a smile.

Her lips stay limp, like the rest of her. Only her eyes roll up toward me. I can read the wordless plea in them...to let her go... to help her go.

"I can't," I whisper. "Forgive me, but I can't."

A single tear drips out of her eye and travels down her cheek, tripping over her tiny mole before vanishing between her parted, chapped lips. Incapable of holding her gaze any longer, I slide her hand out of mine and flee her room, dashing down the hallway. I slow when I reach the cafeteria. Even though I have no appetite, I force myself to eat.

"Hey, Ivy," Chase says, waving from a table.

I buy a muffin, then wind my way toward him. "How's Brook?" I ask, taking large bites of my breakfast to get it down fast.

"Better. They're talking about releasing him today."

"Oh." My heart draws this strange arabesque against the walls of my chest. "Will he return to New York with you?"

"That's what my parents want."

"How are your parents?"

"Back together, so there's that."

I smile even though I don't feel much like smiling.

He rubs the back of his neck. "There was something I wanted to tell you before I left."

I frown.

"About Kevin."

"You want to talk about Kevin?"

He grimaces. "Remember that day I told you he'd hit on me?"

I nod. The memory of the private investigator feels distant, like he was part of some other lifetime, lived by some other girl.

"Well, he didn't. He questioned me about Brook. Told me about his suspicions. He asked me to help him keep an eye on him...and on you."

"What?" The word shoots out of me like the bullet from Mr. Mancini's rifle, the one that brought Dean down. "*Wow.*"

"I wanted to tell you for some time now, but it was never the right time."

"No kidding."

"Don't be mad, Ivy. Please." He gazes at me through brown eyes rimmed with terrible sadness.

"I'm not...mad. I'm just surprised. I thought the great Chase Jackson never lied."

"I'm an ass."

"Can I get that in writing?" Humor returns, because after all I've been through, his lie doesn't hurt much. Doesn't hurt at all, actually. "Is that why you dated me for all of ten seconds?"

He shakes his head, and his copper hair flaps wildly around his blushing ears. "No. I promise. That wasn't why."

"Relax. I was teasing you." I squeeze his arm that feels unfamiliar, even though, once upon a time, that arm kept me upright when life insisted on tipping me over.

"Brook's asking for you," Diana says, appearing next to our table. Chase's face is so uncharacteristically red that she frowns. "You okay, Chase?"

He coughs. "Fine."

"I wanted to go back to the hotel. Can you give me a ride?" she asks.

He nods. "So we're good?" he asks me as I start walking off.

I toss the rest of the muffin into a bin. "We're good." I quicken my pace to reach Brook.

When life finally tipped me over, it wasn't Chase's arms that caught me; it was his brother's.

From his sick bed, Brook shoots me a smile that makes my heart twist again. "Hey," he says as I approach. He's propped the backrest up.

"I heard the big news..." I try injecting some enthusiasm into my voice. "All fixed, huh?"

Dark eyebrows pinched together, he scoots to one side of the bed, then pats the empty space next to him. I climb up and rest my head against his bandaged shoulder. I want to act cheery, but nothing remotely cheerful comes to mind.

"My parents' former housekeeper came to visit me yesterday," he says. "I think she cried more than you."

"I doubt that's possible."

"She brought me tamales. Want one?"

"I'm not really hungry."

His thumb strokes my cheek. "I'm buying my ranch."

I press up to look at him. "What? How?"

His dark eyes turn down to the white sheets. "She kept something safe for me. Something very valuable." He lifts his eyes to mine. "I didn't want to take it back, but she didn't want to keep it."

"What was it?"

He swallows hard. "One of my mother's...one of her diamond necklaces."

I bristle. I hate diamonds. I even hate the word.

"I get to start over," he says.

I nod. "That's great." I avert my gaze. "So you're going straight to Montana, or wherever it is you buy ranches these days?"

"After I stop by Troy's grave, yes."

I close my eyes as Josh's headstone swims into my mind. Even though he was never my real brother, his mother had the words *Beloved Brother* carved next to the words *Beloved Son.* "Everyone keeps leaving me."

"Hey," he says, gathering me in a hug. Maybe our last one.

I inhale a shaky breath. "You'll call me, right?"

"Why would I call you?"

I press away from him, hurt. "Because we're friends, aren't we?"

"I took a bullet for you. So no, Ivy, we're not friends."

I think the bullet might have hurt less.

"We're more than that. And I'm not going to call you because"—he raises his hand to my jaw—"because I'm not leaving without you. I don't have much more to offer than my heart, but I was hoping it could be enough for now."

I stare at him.

Just stare at him.

"Please say something."

I can't unearth a single word as my wild heart has overpowered my brain. Even though I rue the day Dean shot Brook, it made me realize I wasn't ready to lose him. Not after I'd just found him.

His gaze turns uncertain. "Ivy?"

A breath whistles through my lips. It doesn't calm my pulse

but it brings oxygen into my faulty brain. "After everything... you still want me?"

"I've always wanted you. Even when you didn't choose me, I kept wanting you."

My chest clenches. "You weren't a choice back then, Brook."

He sits up straighter and tucks a long curl behind my ear. "Well, pick me now."

"I've already picked you." I gaze at the pale green wall, beyond which lies my sister. I can't see her, but I can feel her.

My other half.

My sweeter half.

My shattered half.

I nestle my cheek into his open hand, then slide my mouth against his warm skin and kiss it. "But I can't leave." His hand stiffens. "I can't leave Aster."

"You can't move into the institution with her. You'll visit. Often. After I sell the necklace, I'll put some money aside for your trips."

"You don't have to do that," I start.

"Yes, I do. I don't want you using any of Paul Willows's money."

My lips quirk up at his jealousy.

He tips my chin up, then slowly runs his thumb across my mouth, before pulling me in close. He stops when the tip of my nose touches the tip of his. "I love you, Ivy Redd. I've loved you since the first night you walked into the Temple room in your blue dress, and I'm going to love you for a very long time. Forev—"

I kiss him before he can finish the word, hoping that if I seal the syllables between our lips, forever might happen...for once.

ACKNOWLEDGMENTS

All my thanks to my usual, wonderful crew: Vanessa, Theresea, Katie, Astrid, Marina. Your enthusiasm and keen eyes transformed yet another one of my tall tales into a story worthy of being printed and bound. I am so deeply grateful to have each one of you in my life, as beta readers, and as friends.

Jessica, thank you for cleaning up my writing and helping me kill my darlings.

Joshua and Brook owe their lives to all of you.

To my three lovely children, I'm sorry for the time I spend away from you immersed in my fictional world, but know that I adore you more than anything.

To my husband, you are my life.

CONTEMPORARY ROMANCE

GHOSTBOY, CHAMELEON & THE DUKE OF GRAFFITI

NOT ANOTHER LOVE SONG

ROMANTIC SUSPENSE

***Cold Little Games* series**

COLD LITTLE LIES

COLD LITTLE GAMES

COLD LITTLE HEARTS

ABOUT THE AUTHOR

Olivia Wildenstein grew up in New York City, the daughter of a French father and a Swedish mother. She chose Brown University to complete her undergraduate studies and earned a bachelor's in comparative literature. After designing jewelry for a few years, Wildenstein traded in her tools for a laptop computer.

When she's not writing, she's psychoanalyzing everyone she meets (*Yes. Everyone*), baking up a storm, and attempting not to be late at her children's school.

Wildenstein lives with her husband and three children in Geneva, Switzerland, where she's an active member of the writing community.

oliviawildenstein.com
press@oliviawildenstein.com

9 781948 463935